Colored Edges

I0612932

I've jumped off
   the Golden Gate Bridge
& lived.
It's no joke/to have died
   so many times.
        —Geoffrey Cook

Whatever colors you got in your mind,
I'll show 'em to you, and we'll make 'em shine . . .
        —Bob Dylan

The question isn't who is going to let me;
it's who is going to stop me.
        —Ayn Rand

Kindness and truth are met together.
Justice and peace have kissed.
        —David, Psalm 85:11, The *Torah*

Colored Edges

Sharon Skolnick-Bagnoli

Spaceframe Press

San Rafael
Marin County
California

COLORED EDGES

2nd Edition
Black & White

Published by Spaceframe Press
San Rafael
Marin County
California

010203

ISBN 978-0-9650530-5-1

Book and Cover Design: Visigraf Communications and Design
http://www.visigraf.com

Printed in the United States of America

Whether what follows is a flight of fiction
or a stream of fictionalized recollections
is a good question.
The truth is that I am not Iris Miller.
At the same time, many of the following scenes
are informed by experiences that have touched me,
some of them deeply and profoundly.
The reader is not asked
to unfurl the threads of memory
from imagination's yarn.
In reality, it doesn't matter.
While traveling with Iris and sharing her road,
parts of your own trajectory
will appear.

I hope you enjoy this many-hued journey.
And may you find your own
colored edges.

S.R.S.B.

Advance Praise

"Breathtakingly honest. Or as honest as a poet can be, anyway."

—**Bob Fass.** 50 year+ Host/Creator, *Radio Unnameable* (WBAI-fm NYC, additional stations, and the web); Progenitor of free-form radio and the 1960s counterculture

"*Colored Edges* is an entertaining journey of conflict and resolution through Native wisdom and inner peace, as only the author, with her personal style of writing, can touch our hearts."

—**Sacheen Littlefeather** (Apache/Yaqui). Contemporary Elder and Activist

"… each color somehow informs each chapter in a way that is refreshing and unique."

—**D. Jayne McPherson.** Poet; Teacher; Author, *Orphan at the Well*

"… I read *Colored Edges* as I read the *I Ching*: a natural attraction to colors of the day, the hour, the minute."

—**rose Pat Farrington.** Innovator; Visionary; Founder, New Games Foundation

"This is a penetrating story that effectively reflects a colorful blend of cultures and conflicts into a sensitive woman's search for truth, and, additionally, shares awareness of the power of the color spectrum. The goal is peace, and while the book is a personal journey that covers different worlds, it is totally satisfying and fulfilling as Iris seeks answers, balance, and healing."

—**Stevanne Auerbach, Ph.D.** Toy and Childcare Expert; Author. Books include *Choosing Childcare*, *The Contest*, and *My Butterfly Collection*

"What a unique visceral and visual treat!"

—**Gar Smith.** Editor; Investigative Reporter; Author, *Nuclear Roulette*

"Sharon is truly a woman for all seasons. What could possibly be next?"

—**Gerald Pearlman, M.A., JD.** former Editor, *MuirBeachcomber*

"*Colored Edges* is a sentient look into a woman's yearning for spiritual and political fulfillment. The author's florid yet edgy writing cuts deep into the Native American narrative, always interpreted by her ontological longing. The combination of these intimate and broad-brushed political perspectives is not only radical but acutely relevant."

—Marc Twang. Activist; Singer-Songwriter. Albums include *Raw Twang, World Where We Belong,* and *The Kidney Kid*

"… the debut novel *Colored Edges* invites the reader to experience a variety of moods in a sort of multi-sensory way. Reading at a leisurely pace enhances the passages, revealing an importance of color in our lives perhaps previously unnoticed."

—Helen Anderson. Educator and Activist

"I found myself totally engaged and compelled to continue reading, finding a surprisingly perceptive grasp of human nature and a delightful capturing of the human dilemmas we act out. There is a transparent, reflective quality. Well worth reading."

—Maxine Steingold. Presence Coach; Writer; Wisdom-seeker

"I love the treatment of all five senses. The visual descriptions of Marin County and Hawaii are particularly stunning. Iris, our heroine, is sexy and plucky, with a great sense of humor. I also like the attention drawn to Native Americans. I'm glad some of the focus is on California tribes, which are often overlooked."

—Rebecca LaFontaine Laravee. Therapist; Social Worker; Archeologist

"Extremely enjoyable to read. Adult content without crudeness. Strong creative element, with words that keep the reader's attention. Uses words as the creative tools of expression they should be."

—QUARTERFINALIST EXPERT REVIEWER. 2010 Amazon Breakthrough Novel Awards

"In *Colored Edges*, we follow Iris as she struggles to find herself and move beyond her doubts and insecurities. During the telling of the story, the author demonstrates her unique creative abilities as we become privy to Iris's believing in herself for the first time.

—Mark Susnow. Life Coach; Musician; Author, *The Soul of Uncertainty*

"The sound and color of the words themselves—writing in colors, a word picture. Delight in the words, the poetry of vocabulary. Made me replace words with emotive strings of descriptions: *golden fruit brass ring dream man.* The book's layout is like a sculpture, carved ..."

—Bobbi Cox. Arts Supporter; Director, Bobbi Cox Realty, Laguna Beach, California

"... this superb specimen should make anybody quite satisfied to possess it, to handle it, and to read it."

—Edward Barry Skolnick, M.S. Microbiology Researcher

"I enjoyed the adventures of Iris. I find *Colored Edges* very interesting. The author paints wonderful pictures in describing all of the emotional happenings. The way she combines the meaning of each color with the content of the particular chapter is unique. Congratulations to her on writing this 'colorful' book!"

—Salina Sherlock (Muskogee Creek/Cherokee). Basketmaker; Founder, Marin American Indian Alliance

"I am enjoying *Colored Edges* very much! I'm on 'Denim,' so almost at the end of this compelling opus."

—Lynn Arias Bornstein. Community Volunteer; Author, *Laura English*

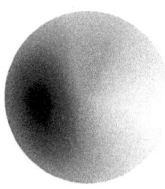

Infrared Heat — Dayglow

The shiny, deeply-tufted quilt glowed with every rainbow color, bathing the barren extended care room in subtle reflections of opalescent luxury. Its slick gloss quieted her nerves as she stood by the big picture window and scanned the room. Sometimes, especially in the mornings, her memory was knife-sharp. Other times, often after sunset, she waded through swamps of confusion just to remember her name: Iris.

Iris didn't know how she had landed in this narrow institutional bed. She had never been analytical, instead almost worshiping spontaneity, but now a sense of order had surfaced that pushed her to triangulate, echo-locate, and add things up. Her 2036 mind cartwheeled over the years and back again, dancing along the zippered seam between two centuries in a carnival caravan of highlights and lowlights. Memories careened around the hospital room and bounced through her eyes into the valley of her soul, which she wasn't sure she had managed to save after all.

Was this it, then? What difference does it make if this is it, she snickered to herself, if there's no heaven, no afterlife at all, and no Higher Power to call me to judgment?

She wasn't quite certain about that, however, and she thought she'd better hedge her bets, like that American Indian guy she'd heard of who joined 27 different Christian denominations just before he died, so he would be covered.

The urge was strong within her now to review her past and come to accounts. Had she been a good mother? Or her version of a mother at any rate. Had she changed the world toward the better? Was she leaving behind something that improved things, even slightly, for the planet and its living creatures? Would her art and writing endure throughout the generations? Had either her political acupressure or her intermittent teaching-of-teachers done anybody any good? *What was her actual legacy?* Her gaze gyroscoped across the hospital walls, looking for something or someone. And where were those exceptional men she had reached for and touched? She knew that some had passed away and that others still lived, now old men. Had they truly loved her, had they even known her? Would any of them love her now, with her curtains drawing to a close? What about the madness and the obsessions and the rage? Did her monsters still lurk in wait, hulking in the dark corners?

Iris squinted to see herself more clearly in the mirror and try to trace the edges of the driven woman she had been. She closed her eyes and softly swayed against the bed's metal bars. The nurses were off somewhere, and she was alone and free to trip. She gripped the rough mane of her past for one more windswept ride.

Red Threads

1 Coral

In the middle of the 20th century's final decade, on a
solo picnic in Marin County, a world of its own pasted
just above San Francisco's peninsular thumb, Aarona
Iris Miller sat heavily on a horizontal piece of concrete
rickrack. She bit into her turkey and Camembert wrap and
gazed past masses of tiny deep green acorns festooning a
pin-oak tree and out onto a liquid field of teal rivulets lined
up horizontally straight ahead, rolling in to splash on the
tiny beach. That was when she came to the conclusion that
this place did speak to her soul after all, and that it might
be worthwhile to stick around and hold onto her life here,
pitted with potholes as it was.

Iris knew Marin County brimmed with educated,
shapely, and unmarried women pretty much like herself.
She was also aware that their male counterparts were
amassed fifty miles to the south, in Silicon Valley's
technology haven, and couldn't be bothered to commute
north for a date. Thus, a reluctant celibacy often turned
out to be the price for single women to bask in the glorious

coastal nature located just north of the Golden Gate Bridge.

The way things were going, though, it looked like she would probably remain single, whether here or anywhere. That pesky extra twenty pounds kept her out of the running. Lose the pounds and men's heads would turn. Gain them back and the looking would abruptly stop, leaving her stranded in matronly invisibility. Only twenty pounds! It was so damn Pavlovian!

Recognizing that fact did little to cheer her up. She supposed she'd turned out way too feisty and direct in her midlife to ever snag a handsome and happening male. Most guys these days were blinded to all but the currency-groomed willowy blonds, with whom they would conjugate to spawn throngs of stick-thin children. This was the reality of America in the 1990s, so why didn't she just get used to it? Sighing, she stacked the remnants of her picnic lunch inside the fraying wicker basket, hoisted it to her shoulder, and trudged uphill to the State Park gate, and her car.

Without a plan, Iris wandered lackadaisically from day to day. But beneath her featureless flat surface, a psychodrama continued to roil. At its very center pulsed her secret ambition to achieve greatness by saving the world—an ambition that would lead her over some very sharp edges.

2 Scarlet

She wanted to deliver a mud pie ice cream cake to Jefferson Stetson's place. She recalled that when she'd brought one the year before to an open workshop at his farmhouse, he'd really liked it.

As for her, she really liked him. It had started with a dream where she and Jefferson stood on a rowboat, like Washington crossing the Delaware, and he slipped a twisted iridescent celluloid ring (the promise of movie-star fame and shared greatness?) onto her finger. She knew they would do great things together. After waking up, the remembered dream seemed a sure sign that Jefferson Stetson could be the one, her soulmate, her brass ring dream man. Her prince.

"Why *shouldn't* I bring him another mud pie?" Iris grumbled petulantly, her tense voice and wound-tight body language at odds with the astonishingly spacious vistas spread out beneath them: the aquamarine Pacific Ocean on one side, the smooth animal-haunch layering of lush green hills on the other, and, very far off, the two architectural model cities, San Francisco and Oakland, shooting their minuscule skyscrapers toward a layered sky.

Bettina Coates and Iris Miller had driven up the winding roads of Marin County's singular mountain, Mt. Tamalpais, passing through its paradoxical soils and flora and micro-climates that overshadowed the lowlands and foothills and patiently fended-off an ongoing onslaught of New Age fantasies and fake-indigenous fabrications.

The two friends sprawled in languid disarray in a sunny spot that warmed their blankets and their bodies. Behind them only a baseball diamond's-length away, wild winds whipped a stand of oak trees silhouetted on the summit and chilled the few hikers who had found this unmarked treasure.

"I don't see why you need to do that, take over another mud pie, I mean," said Bettina. "Just because you had this huge crush on Jeff last year. He's somewhere else now."

"Jefferson was crowned chief councilman of San Rafael, and he didn't invite me over. I know he thought that I was trying to do a seduction thing on him before he ran for office, before we started rubbing each other the wrong way."

"Were you? Rubbing?" Bettina sat up and reached for her ever present journal. She was an Impressionist painter's rosy-cheeked angel in the foreground of a pastel sweep of greens and blues, the San Francisco Bay Area at their feet.

"Not rubbing, not that way!" Iris cried. "I wasn't some teeny-bopper over there, out to hook the alpha male! At least I don't think so. Anyway, all we ever did is hug hello.

"But, oh my God, Bettina, the feelings! That guy can stir me up like I don't know what! Maybe it's not even him, maybe it's his fame that's the aphrodisiac. Or, maybe it was that dream I had before I went to find him, that told me to go out and meet him and get him. Not to *get* him, but— Hey, did I show you that poem I wrote about the charge I get from being around Jeff? I can hardly look at it, it's so intense. I know that poem might grab his attention, but I'm too chicken to show it to him. Besides, he never gives me any private time.

"Jefferson hides out. He's constantly among groups of people. But he does love those weekly pot lucks he throws."

"What does that mean, 'he hides out'? You mean he protects himself?" Bettina yawned, her *eeeyahhh!* ascending into the air like the call of a circling red-tail hawk.

"It means that Jeff doesn't do one-on-one's very well. He's really guarded. He always has this turtle armor on. He even collects little turtle sculptures, did you know that? I really tried to make a connection with him. It felt like a calling to me, spiritual and sensual at once, you know?"

Bettina snorted, "I think you saw your relationship with Jefferson as more than it was. He has a lot of people around him."

"Why don't you understand, Bettina? I had these very intense feelings for him. I thought he was my destined other, so I went over there to show him my portfolio, but—uh, there was sort of a seduction agenda tucked underneath."

"Well, no *wonder* he was guarded!" exclaimed Bettina, stretching out on the grass, her arms flung above her head.

"Yeah, I guess. I think I scared him, actually," Iris admitted. "I think he was afraid I would get myself upstairs, down the hall, and into his bed some night before he'd had a chance to bar the door and barricade his psyche."

"That must have hurt."

"What must have?"

"The way he wouldn't ever acknowledge you."

"What I really wanted was for him to totally fall in love with me, or at least to admit to me he saw the kindred spirits we are—our Shiva-Shakti link, you know, our male-female opposition. I did have that dream after all!" Iris's eyes welled up. She tossed her head and sniffled. "You're right, you're so right, Bettina. It did hurt, but I kept on going back for more. You know, you really are an empath, like that woman with the dark curly hair and skin-tight coveralls on *Star Trek*. You know, Counselor Deanna Troy?"

"I don't watch *Star Trek*," replied Bettina.

"Anyway, things got strange and weird with Jeff. I kept on hanging around there, going over to be around him, but he never let me in, not really, and he even got uptight that one time I invited him to leave the farmhouse with me and go into Bolinas for coffee. He has this way of protecting himself, and he makes other people come to him.

"Eventually I kind of gave up on him. I mean, I'm not really a hanger-on yes woman. I'm not, am I? When I seek out these mover and shaker guys, I sort of see myself as a guru-of-gurus, working to change the world by association."

Iris stood up and paced around. "Or maybe I'm lazy."

"Lazy?"

"Yeah, lazy, for not changing the world myself!

"Anyway, after a few months of feeling strung-out like that, I managed to stay away for a few weeks. Then, when I did show up for another pot luck at the farm, Jefferson complained! He said, 'I thought you'd abandoned us!' And I said, 'Oh, never! I couldn't do that—you're in my heart!'

"I think he'd missed me, I really do. But he hasn't been the same to me since then. I didn't know my presence there had made such a dent, but I guess it had."

"So he does care a little. That's something," Bettina commented, adding soft pencil shadows to her new drawing.

"But that Jefferson, he can kill you with a look! One time he gave me this withering look that said, '*Get out!*' and all I was doing was standing nearby waiting to talk to him after he had finished *schmoozing* with this Korean community organizer. Well, maybe I did interrupt them a tiny little bit by standing there—"

"How do you know Jefferson's look meant 'Get out!'?"

"If you'd seen how he looked at me, with absolute

brick-wall icy cold non-acknowledgment and animal rage, and then how he held that look until I had to look down and slink away, you wouldn't need to ask me that. If looks could kill, you'd be saying *kaddish* for me now!

"After that, I went to a gathering over there one more time, and I did one evening of phone-banking to help him with a county referendum issue, and that was that.

"The last two times there, I felt torn-up inside. It was like entering a minefield for me to open that farmhouse gate. I cannot begin to describe the weird twists of emotion I've been feeling about that guy since he sent me away. It's like, I see through him and his bullshit act, but I still want him!"

"Maybe he's a trigger for your childhood stuff or else some past-life stuff," reflected Bettina.

"Your New Age-isms are showing, Bettina! But maybe you're right," responded Iris. "Oh, screw him, anyway! But now I *really* want to take another mud pie over to his little pot luck circle!"

"Are you sure that wouldn't be stalking?" asked Bettina, her voice a cartoon's caption of stern authority.

"Stalking? Of course not, we're friends!" Iris sat down again and shifted her position so she could stare out at the Pacific Ocean's cobalt surface, skinny waves marching out to the horizon in thinner and thinner stripes. "You know," she mused, "if you threw one of those half-frozen mud pies into somebody's face, you could really hurt them."

"Are you still seeing your therapist?" inquired Bettina.

"No, why?" crowed Iris, and she and Bettina burst into howls of laughter, rolling around on the sun-warmed mountain grass.

"You deserve a lot better than Jefferson Stetson," decreed Bettina, giving Iris her final word. "You deserve someone who appreciates what you have to offer."

"Yeah, you're right," sighed Iris. "This Jefferson obsession is probably the last gasp of my tired old seduce-the-rabbi, move-the-mover, shake-the-shaker pattern. "When I was younger, my body and my female beauty, seemed to be tickets to somewhere. It all probably circles around my love goddess as female messiah thing.

"That started when I was ten years old and went downstairs to my Hebrew class, held then in our basement. I was in short-shorts on purpose, to get the young rabbi's attention. That was after I'd asked that same rabbi whether a woman could be the messiah, and his answer was, 'No!' Boy, was I mad! Job discrimination! I think I must have been the first feminist as well as the first hippie."

"But 'Mrs. Councilman of San Rafael'? Fund-raisers and boring meetings and hosting official dinners? Is that what you really want?

"Come on, Iris!"

"But that's not what this Jefferson thing is about! See, I figured that if a woman gets to be the power behind the throne, and that's it, that's our portion in life, then I was going to go out and find me the biggest throne in town and become some kind of super mega-power behind it!

"It's the ancient idea of the holy union, where the male and female energies dance and the energy they generate is amplified for the good of all. I've done it before. But it was easier then, when I was younger and looked more the part of the sensuous love goddess."

"With whom, may I ask, have you 'done it?'" Bettina's British accent lent a level of BBC news-reader dignity to her question, seeming to lift their conversation beyond girly gossip. Iris felt as if she were being interviewed on location.

"With a great man, a hero. I'll tell you sometime."

"And you were his groupie, too?"

"I was never a groupie! That is so *cold*, Bettina! There were no groups. It was an admiration thing, and I concede that in my mind, it was a nailing the alpha male thing, too. But it always had something more behind it, as though I'd been called by holy energies to merge with this person for the good of the tribe, and for changing the course of history.

"It was like mixing love with glory and dedication and the harnessing of Earth energies, all in a great big bowl for the purposes of heaven.

"It was such a heady mix! It was so high, like a cocktail from heaven! You couldn't get any higher than that feeling!"

"Only, Jefferson didn't want to play those high games, right?" asked Bettina.

"Not games! Well, maybe holy games. But Jeff did play with me for a while. It felt as though his higher self did pick up on mine, to some extent. I met with him about helping him write his book, things like that. But, hey, you'll keep all of this in confidence, won't you?"

"You mean about Councilman Jefferson Stetson of San Rafael, soon to be president of the world? Sure. Don't worry," Bettina soothed, "This mountain isn't bugged."

"OK, but just in case you ever do get a job at the *Enquirer* or the *Marin I. J.* or something, you swear you won't tell?"

"I swear, promise, and affirm. Unless you give me permission to speak about it later on."

"Thanks. Maybe this sounds like sour grapes and an obsessive disorder to you, but I did feel a rush of love for that guy, and sometimes it felt so profound. As though he were my muse, and I could change the world through him with my genius and his aligned together through man-woman chemistry in service to an evolution of reality!"

"Evolution of reality! Oh, wow." snorted Bettina.

"Only, he would never sit down with me and cop to it,

or even ever talk about it. That guy doesn't have a clue!"

"As to what?" Bettina asked, extending the interview.

"That it may be a divine connection to have me there. That I may have been sent to him. Guys like that can't easily experience genuine human connection. To them, it's more of an occupational hazard of their charisma.

"Did you know Jefferson was raised Catholic? He's never understood or tried to explore my Jewish intensity and straightforwardness, even though I obviously fascinate him. I think that for him, I've gotten to be some kind of loose cannon, and he's become meaner and meaner when around me, like a petulant five-year old on a playground."

"His loss, Iris. The grownup him, I mean."

"Yeah, maybe. Too bad he never lets his guard down. We could've had something so deep. And maybe then he would have learned how to relate better to other people. He really hurt my feelings that time he sent me away. I hope I've learned something from all of that *tsuris*."

"Do you feel like you've failed in your mission, on some level?" Bettina asked.

"Yes, and I feel like a fool on some level, too. But I still want to go to him and throw my arms around him and be there for him.

"And I still want to think that deep down, he misses me and wants me with him. I got to feel so useless around there: no function, no special close relationship. I couldn't make the transition into being just another member of the Jefferson Stetson club. He seemed to think I saw myself as above doing mundane tasks for the cause—really, his cause. But he was looking out from inside his own tunnel. Did I tell you he complimented me once? He said, 'You see the bigger picture.'"

"We all have our tunnels and our tunnel vision," Bettina sighed. "Iris, you've still got such a charge for this guy! It doesn't feel over to me, like you've let it go. I really think you should let it go."

"I do feel these intense feelings about him, but only sometimes. I don't know if it's love and destiny and a divine calling, or just wanting to smash a melting chocolate mud pie into that arrogant face!"

Bettina winced and sat up, smacking her journal closed. Iris stood, with her blanket gathered around her waist, and yelled down toward San Rafael, "Happy inauguration, Jefferson! I hope you enjoy running your little city!" Then she sat down near Bettina, who gazed at her silently.

"Could you read me your poem?" asked Iris. "Please?"

"No, you read it," Bettina lowered her eyes bashfully. "Here it is—" She handed over her journal. Iris focused. The page ruffled under her fingers. There in a few short words, was the entire panoramic setting for their fleeting afternoon. She was moved. "That's it, that's this place! You've captured it. Thank you!"

"You're welcome. I couldn't have done it without the mountain. Or without you. Thank *you*, Iris. And remember, you can't expect everyone to appreciate your gifts. All you can do is keep on giving them. Also, you should maintain an accounting, so you can give yourself some credit.

"If you want to, you can look at it like this: God works in mysterious ways. It's possible that Mr. Councilman Jeff wouldn't have made it onto the San Rafael City Council if you hadn't planted the seeds that you felt called to plant, or if you didn't love him enough to plant them. Without the work of Aarona Iris Miller, the world would be the poorer.

"See? Remember that, even if it's not printed up in a news article and even if it turns out you *are* delusional!"

"Maybe so," said Iris. "Looking at it that way definitely does feel better. But what price have I paid? I've spent years hanging around this kind of guy, and what good has it done me? I have no kids and nothing solid that's purely my own."

"You can't blame those men for that. They are who they are. They just gave you a place to be who you are."

"Yeah, I guess. And I am what I am, just another messiah without portfolio," concluded Iris glumly.

"You've *got* a portfolio!" concluded Bettina the empath.

"I do have a portfolio, yes," said Iris, wrapping up the exchange and the afternoon, "but that's not what's in it."

The next morning, Iris pasted two letters to Jeff into an email and sent it to Bettina so her friend could get a glimpse of the emotional tornadoes Jefferson spun inside her.

To Jefferson from Iris with love,
In order to speak to you at all in any rational way, rather than flinging myself into your arms the way I want to, I have to become more mundane than I really am, or feel.

You show me you will not tolerate my expressions of intimacy. It's your farm and it's your show, and I respect that.

I never told you this, but I still feel something for you, something strong. I wish we could go to a private place to find our union, and I think it's too bad you won't follow your bliss.

Sometimes the eye contact games we play at public events are so sweet. But other times, I tire of them. And I realize you want us to stop right there. But we do have a connection. I guess I have to let that link be enough. I guess I need to beat down my feelings for you with a stick.

You may be my final hero, or my first anti-hero. When we spoke last time, it was with such restraint. You played daddy, and you reminded me of aspects of my dad. Saying 'You've been looking a long time,' about my job-seeking, mirrored other things. I've been looking for a long time for a my great soulmate. But what can I do about it? What can I do but keep on looking when one I've found pushes me off and tells me to move along?

You cause the sap in me to rise and set my dreams free to fly! That's what you do to me. But the wild energy just under the surface is something you barricade against, Councilman. That you choose not to fly with me is a great sadness for me.

But I'll be strong and unburden you of my intensity.

I know you're here for all of us, not only for me. You're not the person people see, and you're different from your outer shell. But the idea that there could be somebody who actually needs the private you is obviously a world-shaker for you. I didn't come to you to shake your world, if you don't want it shaken.

I write these things because I don't know what else to do with this feeling you bring up in me. But I'll handle it. I will.

And I will never forget you. Because I love you.

I love your shining soul.

Iris

She never did send that letter to Jefferson Stetson. The note she actually did send to him contained something very different, as though she had written it to a different part of his brain.

Dear Jefferson,

Speaking of current spaces—with all that you're doing these days as the new San Rafael Councilman, you probably don't have too much space for amorphous projections. Me neither, and since I don't know when we'll get the chance to catch up, I hope this note brings us into the present.

I guess you know I'm still working as a journalist.

When I was around your farmhouse in Bolinas, when you were dancing the electoral dance, I remember feeling good there, like I belonged around you. There were even moments of joy.

But there were darker moments, too, when I sensed you felt invaded by me. That was never my intent. I was simply water seeking its own level, past all the seawalls and barricades.

What I wish for now is what I wanted before: to be a part of the scene—but with some space and time alone together, talking with you and enjoying one another. I want to be valuable to you and trusted by you, and I want to contribute whatever I can to the bigger picture.

Energizing the distance between us is an exciting way to enliven space, but ultimately it produces only verisimilitude. Which, as you know and I know, is not the same thing.

Warm regards,
Iris

3 Crimson

Iris entered Jefferson's office with a walking-on-eggs feeling. While in public Jeff faced the challenges of acting as San Rafael's council chair with gusto, his private self was another question. The turtle-man still sported his protective shell. Embarrassed, he shook hands.

At the same time the journalist in her took mental note of his spare, polished office, she felt her stomach clench, sure symptom of her addiction to this guy—an addiction making her vulnerable to his volatile emotional weather.

She saw him as so much like her father, filled with brash and headstrong Aries energy: a battering ram of tactlessness, uncensored reactivity that could demolish her with a glare and then go on about his business, utterly unaware of the destruction he had precipitated.

And so the game continues, Iris reflected, waiting to grab his attention. Even when you're off the board, there's still a game. She would have to keep her wits about her and not let her attachment to this man overwhelm her again.

Even after winning elective office, Jefferson maintained his open salons. These salons or pot lucks were an entrée for those wanting to get to know the person behind the public persona, to encounter the man inside the disguise.

Jefferson responded to her nervous query, saying yes, she could interview him for an environmental article, but later, at some future date. Then he turned away to answer a call. Her stomach roiled in its microcosmic thrill of fear.

It was late in the month. The fourth Thursday had rolled around, time for another Jefferson Stetson pot luck.

Iris duded herself up and slathered on some makeup. The makeup was barely there, but to her it felt like a slather, so overly-conscious was she of any attempts at duplicity.

Jefferson had called and personally invited her to his west Marin farmhouse.

She had assumed he would move closer to downtown San Rafael, somewhere more formal, now that he had won the election. Instead, he insisted on keeping the world he knew, traveling over the hill for official events and meetings. You didn't have to live in San Rafael in order to work there, and Jeff was taking full advantage of that.

Though Iris felt bloated and self-conscious, she knew she looked all right, and her drive over the mountain to

Bolinas was filled with song. She accompanied The Eagles'
New York Minute.

Any witness would have noticed only her heightened
color and the gloss of her chestnut curls. Nothing unusual.

She suddenly started to sob as the song *Desperado*
began, seeing too clearly the fences she sat on and patterns
of her own that were keeping her a prisoner.

> *Desperado, why don't you come to your senses?*
> *Climb down off your fences and open the gate.*
> *It may be raining, but there's a rainbow above you.*
> *Why don't you let somebody love you?*
> *Let somebody love you!*
> *You've got to let somebody love you*
> *before it's too late.*
>
> —The Eagles

Those were her lyrics the rest of the way to Bolinas.

"Maybe Jefferson will love me," she said out loud,
very tentatively. Then, speaking in a more accusatory tone,
"Oh, sure. The shiny new councilman of San Rafael is
going to make time for that, with you? Don't kid yourself.
You're only a shadow of the version of woman he thinks he
deserves, and anyway, in his eyes you're too fat. He's the
kind that goes for those skinny types."

The evening gathering was crowded but comfortable. It was a mostly white crowd with a smattering of blacks, Asians, Latinos, and a sole Native American wandering around, the A·I·A badge emblazoned on his vest.

She had heard Jefferson refer to himself as a moving target, one whom no paparazzi could track. When he ambled over to Iris and seemingly brushed up against her by accident, her stomach clenched and her skin tingled.

He said, "Hey, how're you doin'? Did you bring the gear I asked you to?"

"I'm fine. Yes, I did bring the gear," she murmured, "but I don't get it. You told me I might be able to interview you tonight. Did you want to do the interview outside or something? I brought my little video camera and a fresh battery, and the boots and warm jacket and blanket, like you said. What's going on?"

"Well, I could ask you why you wanted to interview me in the first place. I'm sure there are lots of better subjects for an alternative living piece for your ecological magazine."

"I just—I like the way you think, and I guess I wanted to find out if an article could come out of it. You do live kind of alternatively. But—I know you're really busy."

Her thoughts were shuffling fast.

"It's OK," he said softly, placing the warm butterfly of his hand on her arm for the briefest of moments. She felt the air electrifying between them—tiny invisible sparklers. Self-conscious, she smoothed her skirt. She was happy that her new chunky-heeled black boots had lent her a dose of self-confidence.

"These are my people," Jeff whispered to her gleefully, and then moved like a stalking cat into the human jungle. He merged into the crowd and worked the room, meting out compliments and comments.

Iris was mystified, unsure what Jefferson had in mind.

She spoke with Bill, the Lakota Indian guy, about an upcoming indigenous ceremony at *Kule Loklo,* the reconstructed Coast Miwok village, and about Daniel Firesmith's latest A·I·A protest action.

Feeling a tug on her purse strap, she whirled around, and there was Jefferson, grinning at her with two plastic goblets in one hand and a bottle of red wine under his arm.

"You ready? Get your stuff and let's go!"

"OK," Iris replied as Jefferson whispered instructions to his aides to make his excuses and keep the party going, and then ushered her out to the parking lot. They rode in his old red Jaguar to the Bolinas dock, where he pointed out a restroom where she could change.

Jefferson changed his outfit as well, shedding his dark olive brushed silk suit and Jerry Garcia tie for sweats and a baseball cap.

He waited for her on the silent dock. When Iris finally emerged in jeans and a windbreaker, Jeff led her to a small blue runabout, a survivor of the 50s—the type of vessel once called a 'pleasure boat.'

He handed her a life jacket and buckled his own. Then, asking Iris to loosen the lines, he held the main rope taut while they climbed onto the *Everyman*.

After they had joked about why the boat wasn't called the *Everyperson*, and how 'Everyman' could be construed as sexist, Jefferson pulled the motor's starter chord. The boat surged to life. They floated away from the dock, *Everyman* pushing forward in a smooth yet jerky motion like a water spider hopping across a pond.

They threaded their way between the channel marker poles. Good thing he knows what he's doing, thought Iris. The weather was overcast, with small patches of aqua sky hiding behind high gray bands of cloud. The shoreline was a tiny strip behind them. Iris noticed that *Everyman*'s motor was surprisingly quiet for 25-horsepower. Jefferson explained that this was a four-stroke, built more like a car engine and far less polluting than the usual two-stroke engine, since it wasn't spewing unburned oil into the bay.

"I've got to set a good example now that I'm an actual council member," he chuckled.

Just off a hidden cove on Bolinas Bay, Jefferson cut the motor, tossed out a small anchor, and then pointed out the stowed oars, his cellphone, and an air horn to an anxious Iris. He showed her three stars sparkling in the gradient sky and tugged at the anchor line to make sure they were stable.

The sun had left a calling card of golden streaks in what was now a dark rose memory of the dusk.

In the sudden quiet, Iris recorded her Jefferson Stetson interview, asking him a series of questions, some of them pointed and others quirky.

When the interview had finished, the two of them were growing zany with the wine and the soft rocking of the boat. By the time the wine bottle was drained, the bay had spread a midnight blue carpet all around them. All was silent and serene, like nothing found on land. Moonbeams from a full white moon wriggled on the water.

"Why are you doing this?" asked Iris.

"Tell me you don't want to do this," replied Jefferson, his gravelly voice a low, teasing challenge.

Iris's reply was smothered by Jefferson's lips as he bent to kiss her words away. They sank in a slow motion embrace to the sleeping bag and blanket on the floorboards.

Everything was warm, boozy confusion enveloped by

the chill of star-strewn air. Iris was frightened, thrilled, and disbelieving all at once, going with the flow in a wine-seeped blur and pushing down each red flag as it popped up.

Jefferson Stetson! Oh my God! On a boat off Bolinas with her, doing this! Could this be happening?

"I brought something," the councilman announced, waving a gold foil condom-coin in front of her.

"Do you always carry those on your maiden voyages?"

"Only on magic carpet rides with Jewish princesses," murmured Jefferson.

Iris winced. "Watch it, buddy! That's a stereotype!"

"Hey, I'm a politician. So there's no way I can be politically incorrect."

"Anyway, I'm not a Jewish princess, I'm true Hebrew royalty," Iris laughed sardonically, "with some American Indian thrown in by association."

"Your wish is my command, my Jewish American Indian princess," whispered Jefferson. Something in his husky tone tamped down the clichés and slowly lowered her remaining red flags.

While the party in his honor continued into the early morning without him, Jefferson drifted at anchor off Bolinas with Iris. Entangled, they slept.

The cawing of hungry seagulls accompanied their pre-dawn return to the dock.

Jefferson didn't call her after their night on his boat, and that hurt Iris—badly.

The next time she saw him, he was the featured person in a network documentary, with his agile blonde assistant appearing diplomatically busy in the background.

By now, Iris couldn't recall why she'd ever wanted him. Maybe it was nothing other than his trappings of power.

But who was she kidding? She wanted him. Jefferson Stetson, local councilman and dreamer of U.S. Senate chambers and White House halls.

Thoughts of Jeff often keep her up at night. It was a perverse longing for a man who had left only fading footprints of their occasional flirtation and the memory of one night rocking together on *Everyman* under the moon.

Eventually she sent him an email describing a recent dream where he invited her to write mood pieces about San Rafael and visit him in his secret office, rented so he could see San Rafael better.

She received no response.

Jefferson Stetson continued to dwell in a dusty cabin in one corner of her mind. She started to recognize that inside them both were adolescents in arrested development, each holding the key to the other. Inside that dusty cabin, explosive love and explosive rage in equal measure lay dormant. She thought that each of them knew it, and neither one wanted to go there. Except for the one small part of Iris that did, the part itching for a fight to the finish where the truth of everything would be revealed. Maybe they could become real friends after that. It was the same part of her still fighting the memories of her father. She wondered whether Jeff wrestled with such a scenario.

I should have been a therapist, Iris thought to herself. It probably would have paid better. Why was life so easy to analyze and so hard to live?

The months slid by, and Jefferson still had not made any effort to contact her. The initial deep shock of rejection eventually faded to an annoying twinge.

Despite that, however, her rebellious self continued to worship at his altar in an exquisite mix of pleasure and pain. What a drug he was for her! Jefferson was the blinding flame to Iris's flittering moth. Did ultimate ecstasy came only at the moment of extinguishment? She hoped not. If that was her subconscious script, there was obviously a serious need for revision.

When she heard that the councilman was sponsoring an upcoming art exhibit at San Rafael's City Hall, she found out that neither she nor her promising artwork was invited. Nonetheless, she figured that this might be a good time to re-enter his world. Even if he didn't make an appearance, maybe she could desensitize her feelings for him at the opening, and then maybe he would start to vacate her brain!

By now she knew Jefferson was no hero. She'd seen his clay feet, extending like wading boots up to his armpits.

Later in the week, Iris caught an afternoon community television show featuring Councilman Stetson. When the interviewer asked if he were dating anyone, Jefferson sarcastically replied that he had been with the same woman for five years, as though saying, "Up your game, reporter!"

Iris knew who Jeff referred to, and it was neither his touchy-feely blonde assistant nor herself, but a slender physician with a wild mane of dark, curly hair—a black leather bomber jacket and a tornado of hair.

Quiet and efficient—a nuclear warhead of a woman. They probably never said much, just jogged straight to the bone-jumping.

This was a woman who knew how to cover her tracks in a spare and spartan relationship. And wait.

While the tides of time dampened and faded Iris's wings, and despite what she now knew, she continued to feel herself flutter near the naked bulb of Jefferson Stetson, buzzing around the blinding light of a man who wasn't there for her. She convinced herself her devotion helped feed his far-sighted work. She lied to herself.

Trying to analyze her obsession with Jefferson gave Iris headaches. Why was she so fixated on this egomaniacal man-child with a knack for rising to the top of the political heap? Did she want his power for herself? Or did she want it inserted into her like a torpedo—the ultimate phallic penetration? Or was it really that she wanted his power down on its knees, desperately and adoringly begging for her attention? Was she nothing but an archetype-cast arrested teen acting out an internalized fiction? She insisted that her love meant more than that. It had to! Her life had to add up to more than shadowing a selected male genius. She herself wanted to make a difference in the world!

Time to wake up from this silly dream and energize her exhausted psyche for some new adventures. Stop ruminating, she sternly told herself, and put your secret dream of marrying President Jefferson Stetson and becoming the first Jewish First Lady, to bed!

4 Cerise

At the City Lights Bookstore outdoor street fair in San Francisco's North Beach district, Iris turned around and bumped into Jerry Brown, the mayor of Oakland. She recalled their animated conversation at his book signing the year before. He still remembered her. Mayors have the authority to marry people, so maybe he could officiate the marriage of Iris and Jefferson. Ha! Jefferson Stetson flitted across her mind-screen, so handsome in a muted fawn tuxedo, with his eyes filled with love for her and her alone.

And then there she was again, standing in front of Mayor Brown, his runner's body clad as usual in stark black minimalism, a costume diametrically opposed to Councilman Stetson's modified rancher outfits.

When Jerry asked her what she was doing these days, she could only blush and murmur, "I've been doing environmental magazine writing and design."

His offhand question, checking up on her from the Olympian heights of elected office, brought up for her a stream of shame that this downward economy had gripped her in a choke-hold and that no one was beating down her door to hire her for some great job. No one was recognizing her uniqueness and offering her a career position as a designer or editor, a job that would fill her with pride to report to someone distant and vaguely interested, someone like the mayor of Oakland. What was she doing to make this world better? What had she actually accomplished?

From inside her awkward pocket of embarrassment, Iris exchanged a few more words with Mayor Brown. Then he turned his aquiline profile away, and she watched him shrink as he crossed Columbus Avenue and headed toward Specs' Bar.

She turned back to peer over the heads of the crowd at the distant street fair speaker who waxed eloquent under City Lights Bookstore banners. The mood of this crowd was upbeat, happy.

Jerry Brown had seemed happy, nicely put-together and positive. Maybe it was the Aries in him, always racing toward the next challenge and not wasting time on regrets or any rehashing of the past.

He had his slings and arrows, everybody knew that, but who said the race was over for him? Nothing was over. He was always at the starting gate. Hadn't he just announced his interest in running for attorney general, once his mayoral term was ended? He was always in one race or another and always running to win. He wasn't a quitter.

"Now's the time!" Jerry would exclaim. For someone like him, the time was always now. If he wouldn't let things along the way pull him down, why should she let her own slings and arrows defeat her? Couldn't she be more like him, always seeing now as the time?

Her hands shook after this chance encounter with an American royal. What was it about the glitterati that got under her skin? Wasn't it their function to shine as beacons for us? Whoa, she thought, I sure must need that light!

A small bubble of ambition bobbed to her surface. Saving the world was the biggest task on her bucket list. What could she do now to make this world better?

Why can't *I* be a beacon? The question buzzed around her. Time was flitting by, and little lines on her face had appeared to mark the decades.

Spilling out onto the closed street, the crowd in front of the bookstore applauded the poetry they heard, cheered its readers, and continued cheerfully *schmoozing* as Iris trudged up Telegraph Hill into thick San Francisco fog.

The opaque air fostered meditation. Why had she left her east coast family, all her friends, and that entire world, behind, if not to accomplish something meaningful, something great, out here? Peace kept eluding the Middle East, while, closer to home, hostile neo-con cowboys disparaged and sabotaged the recently federally-recognized Coast Miwok Indian tribe's casino plans. And people all over were hurting and dying every day.

Was everything falling apart because she hadn't done right by her parents, or God? While her rational cerebral cortex knew the whole mess wasn't her fault, her hypothalamus reptile brain started to ache.

The tannins in red wine sometimes cured her headaches. She turned around and jogged toward North Beach to find an Italian coffee house and some *chianti*.

Safely home in Marin County, Iris paced aimlessly. Her head still ached with the beginnings of a familiar dull pain that bloomed behind her eyes and in her neck and then crept down her spinal cord like snake venom, a precursor to the toxic inner sludge the world called depression.

It was her signature brand of mind-body madness, somatizing inner punishment for failure and loss.

The witness in Iris picked up a clue: when she criticized herself too harshly, calling herself a failure, an also-ran, and a non-contributor to her time, that was the moment when the neck and shoulder pain could start, sending on a sick headache capable of dragging her down into a dark basement. Was it a result of those too frequent parental injunctions—those disappointed head shakes and furious invectives about what she hadn't done right? Had those acidic critiques burrowed into her head like trauma time bombs to await her next slip from grace? Involution, the psychiatrists call it. Chronic involution into a tyrannical, unforgiving superego.

It was not a ticket to success and not a winning card. Nothing like the easy self-confidence of a Jerry Brown.

When she arrived at work at the Jackson Street office of her magazine, *Eco Planet*, on a gray Tuesday morning, Iris was expecting another routine day of editing and art directing with a possible creative tilt into storyboarding before lunch, always her favorite part of any work day. That this publication utilized both her writing and her art direction skills was a fortunate twin gift, but even such diverse work could predictably sink into the mundane.

San Francisco showed her its best face that morning. The weather turned turquoise and sparkling, sharply-outlined ships floated in miniature on the distant bay, and the guy who sold coffee sang out a greeting from his sparkling aluminum cart. People at work smiled at her, and she smiled back. She settled in to open her email.

She looked up in surprise as the editor-in-chief entered her cubicle. This was a rare event.

"Here," he said, thrusting a sheet of paper at her, "We got this email. It mentions you, and I thought you might want to read it."

"OK. Thanks, John!" replied Iris. Her eyes widened at the identity of the sender: Councilman Stetson.

After a few diplomatic paragraphs about the work of *Eco Planet* and how its website was helping spread the word about Marin County's progress in going green, Jefferson mentioned an upcoming event he was spearheading, Marin County's Bio-Regional Symposium and Fair.

Two of your employees, Merrill Taylor and Aarona Iris Miller, have volunteered on my past campaigns. I'm sure they're tremendous assets to the Eco Planet *organization.*

If they had a little spare time, we could use their assistance in organizing our upcoming symposium. Janine Feldman is our events planner, and it's a daunting task. Your environmentally astute associates could be a big help. Not on Eco Planet's *clock, though, on their own time.*

Please ask each of them to contact Janine if interested. It's fine if they don't live in San Rafael. We're equal opportunity over here.

Iris could feel her heart beating hard. Jefferson must be sending her a message! Sneakily, to be sure, but politicians did things like that. He wanted her back in the fold! Maybe not to love, seduce, or adore, but back there anyway, in range of his vortex. He must miss her!

She'd have to think it over. Did she really want to enter that charged world again, to be under the thumb of assistant Janine as a volunteer? It had been difficult enough before to witness their flirtation at close range. But maybe it would be different now, after Iris had achieved some emotional distance from the aphrodisiac of his celebrity charisma.

That night, she dreamed about taking a subway into San Rafael and running through rough neighborhoods replete with sleazy characters leaning against every wall.

At home the next afternoon, she switched on her desktop boom-box radio and idly spun the dial between stations, hunting for something to capture her attention. She needed distractions to blur the latest barbs from work: the end of an assignment and the concurrent shrinkage of her paycheck.

The radio's AM dial twirled past infomercials on annuities, reportage on war and almost war, and various flavors of salvation. Suddenly there was San Rafael's Council Chairman presenting the annual State of the City speech, his gravelly tones worming their way into her heart.

Councilman Stetson quoted an ancient Roman pundit while aiming vibrations of triumph and certitude into his voters' ears. The speech trundled on until it went completely off the rails, Jefferson tripping himself up without knowing it.

Iris resented Jeff on general principles for having turned his back on her after their night in the moonlight. Her latest volunteer work helping out his symposium had once again embroiled her in a tense emotional game, still on the sidelines. While his assistant issued directives and critiques, Jefferson would wander by and semi-ignore Iris.

It felt like a divorce, but from what? Not a heart connection, certainly, and not the genuine meeting of minds and bodies she had so desperately yearned for.

She realized that their romantic encounter on his boat had been his deciding to fulfill a few of her obsessive yearnings. The way he was acting toward her these days, it was obvious that for him that night had been just another level of flirtation. He hadn't ever completely trusted her, and when he recognized she could see through his masks, he had behaved like he wanted her gone.

Over the airwaves now, Jefferson was painting word

pictures of the entity called California and how it had begun with priests from Spain constructing Catholic missions up and down the coast. How the state had started with the pioneers: first the Mexicans, then the English, and after that, the Americans. And how, along the way, the mission system had displaced and devastated the native population.

He did manage to mention that devastation, but tossed it in like an obligatory afterthought. Iris knew that for the American Indians and Latinos listening, his tone must sting.

She brewed herself a cup of strong coffee, cut its bitterness with milk and stevia, and sipped it while absorbing the rest of the speech. Although she had noted a few good points, after it ended she felt deflated.

A woman who called in during the radio program's post-speech analysis expressed her concern that Congressman Stetson had glossed-over the native cultures that had lived in California for so many centuries, from before the European and American invasions until today.

"I was surprised," she said, "Any schoolchild knows about the California Indian cultures." That disillusioned caller's reaction strikingly echoed Iris's own response. Each had expected big-picture insights to pour forth from the charismatic councilman, and each had noticed a surprisingly narrow viewpoint emerge instead.

Iris liked to believe that her serial liaisons with selected cultural alpha males were really teaching encounters with genuine heroes, and saw pursuing them as her calling. She wasn't just hanging out with a guy, she was teaching a teacher. She believed it to be a worthy use of her time.

But with Jefferson Stetson, there was a gap between his actual mindset and the visionary persona he offered his constituents as a takeaway.

I could have made him more, mused Iris, flinging her flip-flops into a corner, pulling on her running shoes and tying the laces.

She slipped out of the house for a walk to the neighborhood discount store, where her scavenger side sought solace scanning objects of current interest and reveling in the savings between retail, wholesale, and today's special low price.

A flowing black jersey dress in her size that retailed at $60 and usually sold here for $30 had come down to $13. And, now that the store was clearing out its women's clothing inventory, the dress was 40% lower! Eight dollars for a sixty-dollar dress!

A rush of good feeling flooded Iris, followed by her

sardonic chuckle. No longer was she the prisoner of her lust for great men: today that lust could be satiated by a phenomenal bargain!

Although her cougar inclination to pursue the dashing alpha male had remained intact, these days only paunchy men with questionable eyesight or loose-limbed Latino guys in large groups were giving her the wandering eye once-over. Otherwise it appeared that she was becoming increasingly invisible to the male of the species.

Iris asked herself why she continued to yearn for Jefferson Stetson, a fickle political animal and her current unreachable man, after she already knew him too well to believe his hype.

Not a question worth the price of therapy, but well worth the price of a flowing black jersey dress.

5 Rose

Iris once heard a radio interview in which a famous writer predicted that the content of the next great American novel would need to deal with race and the transcending of racial differences.

Upon hearing this, her literary ambition surged within her, and race became her chosen subject.

She intended *All Colors Wide* to be her first shot at long fiction. It would explore the idea that the way to become a truly multi-dimensional American was to embed yourself in the cultures of all the varied ethnic groups living from sea to shining sea, and internalize them—'embed' as in "in-bed."

By the time she was 46, Leah had slept with a man from every race in America. It had started thirty years before with Rocky, in the blanketed bed of a pickup truck outside the Chew 'n Chat on a humid night in West Virginia.

"Let's meet at the lake at midnight," Rocky had suggested. "You watch the sky and step high, so you don't trip on the lake path." He was half Italian and half Cherokee, and talked with a slooow draaawl.

Leah tiptoed out of her camp cabin just before midnight and sneaked through the dark woods to meet Rocky. She was 16 and a cabin counselor. Her campers at the isolated western Maryland summer camp were five sleeping 14-year old girls, one of them the daughter of a U.S. senator.

She and Rocky hadn't actually "done it." As a frequently dating teenage girl, she was more than expert at pushing away a groping boy—and at saying "No!

But this rendezvous carried her to another level. When she crossed the border from Maryland into West Virginia that night, she also crossed the border into her own womanhood.

—Aarona Iris Miller
All Colors Wide

Iris started to notice that the great American novel wasn't exactly flowing from her fingertips. Her frustration boiling over, she flung her translucent teal portable keyboard with the 4-line digital read-out across the bed.

"Don't be so damn journalistic!" she scolded herself out loud. And then she laughed, "Get *un*real!"

She had hoped that Leah, her protagonist, would lead readers down her path less followed, to the truth. But Leah was only words flashing by in LED light. How real could Leah ever be when she was only some character Iris had dreamed up? You could do anything in dreams.

6 Cinnabar

Tumbling edgewise through Jello waves
that beach in pie-crust rivulets,
you pour yourself between projections
onto the gentle land.

Sweet with inside fruit,
you spread out stickily
waiting for paradise.

But ancient Hawaiian dreams
are thorny vines
that wind around
the waterfalls

Careening over moonlit brinks
and just the beginning

So here it is, the Big Island whose actual name is Hawaii, its air so thick and pungent that you deepen your mainland breathing to receive it, and plants so lush and prolific that you do double-takes. Bird cries overlap the continuous rasps of thousands and thousands of tiny Coakie frogs, an infestation whose emigrating ancestors recently dropped from an Asian ship.

Chunky lava cliffs rim the southern edges of Hawaii Island in curves of viscous *pa hoe hoe* or sharp shards of *anh anh*, the remains of red-hot lava flows that once buried roads and incinerated an entire evacuated village to expand the Big Island's perimeter.

Scrawny yellow-green plants sprout from rocky cracks, improvising their own dirt. Sharp casts of lava-trapped tree trunks stand sentinel, guarding their charcoal rock-scape.

Nature scowls and continues on, and so do the people, but not the people you would expect to see. A pop-up culture of pale mainland hippie expats has replaced the duskier indigenous Hawaiians without a backward glance.

On the Big Island's edge, endless parades of ocean breakers crash and suck with frothy edges, beckoning ragged lines of surfers. And soft and sad slack key music fills the air in constant streams from malls and parks and moving cars.

For Iris, Nathan Paniolo was everywhere. She learned he now captained a merchant ship and had married a brilliant blonde University of Hawaii student who hailed from New England. They'd had two sons. It was what he had told her he wanted: a *wahine* and a family of his own. The entire package had been accomplished without Iris, left behind years before to her monstrous ambivalence.

While visiting the Big Island, Iris found herself consuming pint after pint of tuna *poki*: cubes of marinated tuna a-swim in tiny branches of red seaweed—chomping it down as though her cells starved for the tangy nourishment.

Her emotional numbness had not lifted. Hiking solo up the gentle slope of a dormant volcano, she prayed for her heart to thaw. This was why she was vacationing on the Big Island. It was a place left unexplored after the Nathan affair, during her graduate school years in Honolulu. She hoped daring to explore her magical "if-only" island now would provide the medicine to swap her current flat affect for her dimly-remembered full emotional range.

But with no Nathan beside her to guide an insider's tour, the magnificent vistas shrank down to sugar eggs holding tropical scenes too tiny and far away to reach. She explored area after area, photographing the stunningly multi-faceted island of Hawaii that Nathan had secretly promised her. She knew he lived somewhere nearby, the real, here and now Nathan, but it was by his own choice that he was no longer in her world, and she made herself stop short of tracking him down and invading his space.

Iris would often declare that "the gays don't own the rainbow!" She could claim the rainbow, too. Her personal hetero-rainbow overdose began when her friend, a woman strangely also named Iris Miller, introduced Nathan to her at a party. At first she saw a guy in a neat short-sleeved shirt: slight, slim, and Mexican-looking. He turned out to be Hawaiian-Chinese, mysterious and sad, social and witty. He was the son of a college professor and the great-grandson of an *ali'i*, member of traditional Hawaiian royalty and the spiritual advisor to Lunalilo, the last king of Hawaii.

Iris's sense of self was such a brittle thing that the idea of someone else named Iris Miller felt threatening. She had struggled to become herself, artist and bohemian, after fleeing her sticky suburban psychodrama. The stage was set for Nathan to appear as her life-changer. It was Nathan who painted the opalescent bubble of Hawaii into her head—and then burst it. Nathan was the *tsunami* who swept her away.

The island's-width away from Kailua-Kona, a high-end tourist mecca on Hawaii's western coast, the residents of the economically-depressed southeast island near the town of Hilo improvised with weekly outdoor markets piled high with recycled goods, New Age wares, and island-adapted crafts. Mainland expats converged each weekend to buy, sell, and barter, decked out in their new aloha shirts or skimpy *muumuus* and laden with natural or artificial *leis*.

At the edge of the market, local guys barbecued meat for the shoppers. They didn't say much to these *haoles*, trading insider wisecracks in Pidgin instead, along the lines of, "Keep a cool head, bruddah, dat's da main 'ting. You know, da kine!" Pidgin English, according to a study published in *Scientific American*, is an actual language.

More than a few mainlanders now living on the islands profess a belief in island magic, about which they actually know very little. They spend their days leaping like water insects over the still surfaces of deep pools hiding *huna*, the true medicine of Hawaii, along with the remaining generous *aloha* spirit, signature of native Hawaiian culture. That culture, exploited, betrayed, and trivialized, has nearly disappeared. Mesmerized into a European-style kingdom by a convoluted American missionary con job, the sweet-natured original residents now were only a memory—except for full-Hawaiian residents of the *kapu* island of Niihau and the part-Hawaiian activists working to keep their culture and diluted line alive. Some of those with Hawaiian ancestry are granted homestead rights by the State of Hawaii on parcels far from the Kailua-Kona tourists and hordes of new residents, who are called local *haoles*.

Ha-aole: *One one who does not inspire, does not breathe in spirit.*

Tiny bubbles. Little grass shacks. Lovely hula hands.

High in the hills above Sausalito, Nathan's small cohort
of merchant marines circled around him. Brimming with
gruff aloha, they danced their brotherhood dance. It was
like nothing Iris had ever known, a spectacular rainbow
captured inside a smoky bubble on a foggy ridge top.

Nathan was the only one there with Hawaiian blood.
She was his *wahine*, his woman, treasured and included.
It was the 60s, and her extended encounter with this
transplanted island culture was generously laced with
mind-altering substances. Nathan was the gleaming sea
floor revealed. Transfixed by scattered shiny objects and
bewitched by tales of the mystical and tragically ripped-off
Hawaii and his pain at its loss, she found herself exploring
the treasures they shared very far from the safety of shore.

Whoever said there is a price to pay for paradise certainly
got that right. When Iris couldn't—or wouldn't—let herself
commit to him, Nathan's eyes wandered, and Iris fell really

hard from the floating carpet of their dual fantasy. After an interminable fall that landed her in a mental hospital, her tropical dream was flattened. It would be years before she let herself recognize her own willful ambivalence as a significant contributor to her crash.

Gossamer crystals shatter. Best keep your wits about you on day-hikes into paradise. Best tread lightly, keep your head screwed on straight, and bring along reliable bug spray and a two-way radio. What cannot be seen with the naked eye can bite deeply. The *pa hou hou* lava you walk upon, that curving frozen licorice icing, can suddenly turn to *anh anh* with sharp shards that cut into every step. Dance lightly and fast between your effusive dreams and taking in too much candy for your shrinking reality. Dance for your life.

Meandering through lush, sunny meadows punctuated with *Kapu!* (Keep Out) signs, she kept pushing forward into forbidden zones, only to find herself flung headlong down to the shadowy underbelly. Or maybe it was the pine-smelling bathroom at Disneyland, tile hard, where colors turn gray. But she had never even been to Hawaii!

Nathan Paniolo's projected vision of the two of them raising an island family together became a palm-painted mural. Except for one thing: Hawaii, the place itself, was real, and his detailed stories about the culture of the islands had been true. That gave her a glimmer of light that lasted.

With their relationship *au pau* (over) and her shattered heart healing, Iris moved to Oahu for graduate school at the University of Hawaii, to continue building her own life.

She would sometimes spot Nathan biking across the Manoa Valley campus, his new wife cycling behind.

Although for years and years she kept missing the presence and promise of Nathan Paniolo in her life, Iris had brought herself to Hawaii on her own. In time she beat down new strips of mulberry bark and tapa-stamped upon them a different version of these incomparable islands, one not owned entirely by the measured approval in a lover's eyes. One that was hers.

7 Catlinite

It was another decade. Iris felt her stomach clenching like a fist. It was the remembered feeling from her childhood when she felt overwhelmed by fear or fearsome thrills. Seated in a *taqueria* across the street from the cultural center in San Francisco's Mission district, Iris munched on the sprig of cilantro pulled from her *carne asada* taco.

She could not believe how long it had been, nearly ten years, since she had first heard Daniel Firesmith speak. After meeting the A·I·A (American Indian Alliance) leader, her initial admiration had morphed into what she, at least, experienced as a deep emotional bond.

She saw Daniel as both brave and vulnerable, a naïve yet worldly traditional American Indian man who carried genius, and she glimpsed the outline of a contemporary cultural leader, possibly even a liberator.

He was massively handsome and charismatic, and a mix of witty and demanding. Firesmith's craggy face could command respect or dissolve into laughter. On seeing a child, his penetrating gaze would sparkle and melt.

This man looked familiar to Iris, that is, as though he were family. She felt a strong connection, empathy grazing the edges of love. He started to appear in her dreams. They moved in tandem as activist and journalist. He called her "Miller" and teased her all the time. The pounding of the giant drum and the haunting echoes of traditional drum songs filled an emptiness inside her, seeming to sound the ancient heartbeat of this Turtle Island most people now called North America. In the presence of Daniel Firesmith, these sounds would coalesce for Iris into a heady brew of truth and love.

As he brought her into the Indian world, he mentored Iris, and she felt safe around him. Paradoxically, she sensed that somehow her being around him was protecting him. It was romance novel stuff: Daniel Firesmith was Iris's outlaw king with a movable kingdom—an indigenous Robin Hood.

He put up with her constant presence, occasionally letting her tag along with his merry band of braves. Not that they were so merry, caught up as they were in constant strategizing to counter all kinds of anti-Indian injustice. But the Native American brand of humor, a dry and deadpan wit, would often erupt and lighten the gravity.

Despite Iris's daydreams about their bodies meeting at last, Daniel remained at arm's length. She thought the sensual energy coursing between them was harnessed for other purposes, or she kept telling herself that. And, after all, he was married.

During the evening presentation, one Indian speaker talked about children and how they were a gift from the Creator. Sadly, Iris recalled her own childlessness and the several foiled attempts to adopt. But then she remembered the decade in Indian country and felt a surge of gratitude.

Central to that emotional bounty was the man now entering the room. As Firesmith strode past her aisle seat, Iris pushed a small painting into his hand. He stopped, looked at it and at her, and then swooped down.

"How've you been?" he murmured, pulling her into his arms in a strong embrace. Without resistance, she flowed up to meet him, hugging his rock-solid body. "Fine," she whispered, "really fine!" Ending their hug, he moved up to the stage.

As usual, she left the event alone. Was it enough to have reached this moment? It had to be. Here they each were, long past their initial inter-ethnic blunders, a woman and man from two different worlds who had bridged their differences to find friendship and culturally cross-pollinate.

She knew that this was romance novel stuff, and a fine unrequited read at that. Were they a pair of archetypes on a sacred mission or just a Jew and an Indian? That sounded like the beginnings of a "walked into a bar" joke. But it was a good joke after all, she smiled to herself, a glorious joke!

It was OK.

Orange Ices

8 Coffee

Even the most ordinary scene could turn surreal. Cabs were like sharks cruising the streets, with their chrome grills like open mouths.

On the day the power went out in San Francisco, very little ended up normal. That day was an epiphany for Iris. She realized that the city that had intimidated her for decades was actually no more than a toy on a leash, an electronic toy plugged in to one enormous outlet.

On that winter's day, four human beings committed simple human error by neglecting to unhook their copper grounding rod before switching the power back on.

So all of the juice destined to keep the computers and lights going in San Francisco instead poured into the ground with a giant *whooossh*.

Somewhere else on our sensitive planet, at a faraway geothermal acupressure point, a giant *owweee* occurred that resulted in an earthquake or a volcano. Only no one was out there to connect the dots.

The cafe was crowded and overly warm. Its frosty windows sweated tears all the way down their panes. Aarona Iris Miller and Ephraim Kiever bent their heads close together to edit his psychology paper.

Then Iris sat up. "Before we go much more deeply into your paper, can I run a few mind movies by you?"

"You mean, about yourself for a change?"

"Yes. A *cinema verité* doc starring me, myself, and I."

"Featuring what part of you?"

"Emotional underpinnings, I suppose. Highlighted by sketches of some guys I've known in the past."

"Why do you talk about your old boyfriends so much?"

"I guess I do, don't I? I think it's because they stand out in my memory's ocean like lighthouses. I see my journey better by using the beams from their lights to move through the dark. Or something like that."

"OK, all right, go!" Ephraim leaned back in his chair.

Iris thought a chunk of her life story could prove a beneficial diversion for Ephraim, up to his eyeballs in psychology theory for class and obviously nervous about this paper. A handsome, dark blonde young man with intense green eyes and a curious mind, he had asked her recently how she came to be herself, and it sounded like he really wanted to know. In answer, she had pulled a few fragments of her collected audio diary entries into a time line that highlighted by boys and men she had dated.

"I pulled this together, and I brought the tape and player and a splitter and two earphone sets. It's in third person, like, 'She did this and she did that.' Here it is."

Ephraim took the audio kit, assembled it, and listened.

○○ ○○○○

Leaving behind her bat mitzvah *reception to escape with cute 16 year-old Brian Bloom, her best friend Rosy, and his best friend Jack, she felt a twinge of regret for giving her parents such a hard time. Brian had crashed the party. Iris was 13.*

○○ ○○○○

On a snowy night, kissing Howie Best at her relatives' doorstep on Park Heights Terrace in Baltimore, Maryland. The pressure from his warm lips mixed with the snowflakes. Howie was as short as she was, and very sweet and strong, with a thick neck. He played la crosse. *She was still 13. Howie later became a lawyer, then Maryland's attorney general, and he married a girl named Shelly. While on a visit home to see her parents decades afterward, she called his old number and asked to speak with him. His mother would not give her his number.*

In college, feeling so connected to Jim Pal, a Korean-American
sculptor and her teacher and first lover. The despair she felt
months later when her mother refused to let her bring him home
for Thanksgiving because he was an Oriental. 'What would the
neighbors think?' Jimmy and Iris remained together for years,
enjoying two leisurely summer vacations on Block Island, just
off the north coast of Long Island, where they rode rented bikes
along winding trails overgrown with wild blackberry vines.

I'm going back to New York City,
I do believe I've had enough.

—Bob Dylan

During and after college, a deeply sensual affair with radio
personality Robb Mast, the (married) holy man of nighttime
radio and her first Jewish lover. She was his hidden mistress,
aching for him on weekends and holidays and remaining his
delectable side dish through a series of marriages. Why did
he not marry her? *She finally concluded that she had always*
been a 'cheap date' for him—undemanding, satisfied with too
little. She ran to see him every time her edgy San Francisco
adventures flung her back to Manhattan.

Scenarios spiraling into his open ears and questioning brain, Ephraim envisioned the audio sketches merging into a full-body portrait of a nude reclining Iris, strewn with headshots of men and boys overlapping her nakedness like fish-scales.

Hearing her memoirs again reminded Iris that each boyfriend had been a college course in sociology and culture.

"I think their worldviews permeated my psyche and built the woman who sits before you today."

"Yeah, and you let that happen!"

"Oh, Eph! It's a good thing! And yes, I did. I invited them in to make soul children together for the good of the world, maybe."

"Of course you did," responded Ephraim, his voice a knife-edge of irony.

"I did that with them," echoed Iris. "And now you're here with me, my dear good friend."

"I don't know if I'm exactly ready to let my worldview permeate your psyche," responded Ephraim.

"Oh, don't worry about it," Iris said, leaning across her *latté* to hug him with one arm and whispering seductively, "Most of them weren't, either."

"OK, so now I know more about who you are. Thanks for the micro-course. Now back to my psych paper, OK? You know you're the only one I trust to read this," said Ephraim.

Sitting on the hard wooden chair, Iris's knees ached. She wanted to be back home at her desk, free to dream up and then capture her own ideas.

Instead, here she was supporting yet another brilliant, innovative man, helping him manifest his own personal expression. So what else was new?

"I know it's good, Eph. But why do you need me to read it? I'm no psych scholar."

"Because you have an ear for the flow, and you don't bullshit. And, besides, you're so darn cute." His hand slipped under the table and a little way up her skirt. "Not now, Eph, please—I try not to mix pleasure with *latté*."

"Ah, so you admit—"

"I admit nothing. A deal is still a deal, right? Platonic is the best way for us. We're such a great brother and sister act, why ruin it? We know way too much about each other. I can see right through you."

"Sure, OK, enough of that shit. In two hours, fearless and transparent me has got to hand this in, and I can still run home and change stuff if you find anything—"

She scanned a page, then flipped through the remaining pages and looked up.

"So far, I like it. *The Four Pillars*. It sounds stable, like a table. Not exactly the underground mystical sort of stuff you usually write."

"Well, ultimately it all gets mushed together by the great blender," Ephraim made a spiral at his forehead, "before sinking downward to feed the worms."

"*Ewwww,* that's disgusting!" Iris exclaimed.

"Hey, would you just read some of it to me out loud? Then I can tell whether it works or not."

"You mean out loud in front of all these coffee-sucking adolescents? What if somebody hears it and actually ends up learning something?"

"We'll have to take that chance. Read it to me?"

"OK, just a little."

"Here's a short chunk." Ephraim shoved the sheets in front of her.

"And then I'll surrender you to your steamed milk and *espresso* and the *Chronicle*. Unless—you don't have a sore throat or anything, do you?"

"No, I'm fine!" Iris felt an odd rush of comfort hearing Ephraim's concern.

She began to read in a pseudo-serious tone,

"*The Four Pillars: An Eclectic Psychological Theory of Personality.*"

But then, swept into it, she switched to a normal voice:

Belonging is the first pillar.
Empowerment is the second pillar.
Meaningfulness is the third pillar.
Self-esteem is the fourth pillar.

If I had all those pillars, I'd be set. And a lot less ambivalence, thank you very much, she thought.

As she continued reading Ephraim's paper aloud, an old image formed behind her eyes: herself in a Hawaiian muumuu, pregnant yet again, with five laughing children pulling at her skirt and an adoring mate walking toward her on the beach. Versus herself at a podium giving a talk on how to achieve world peace, with an adoring audience applauding and one special man in the front row sending her infinite waves of support. And then, as it had before, one image overlaid the other, their outlines blurring. But they never did manage to align.

"*Align*? What did you just say?" exclaimed Ephraim. "Where is it you go when you read?"

"I don't know! Sorry." Her mind raced to catch up and fill in. "I guess I'm wondering if you think one pillar is more important than another or necessarily precedes it, like 'belonging' coming before 'self-esteem.' Do they all align?"

"You don't need to impose a hierarchy on the four pillars," Ephraim answered, "That would be like favoring one table leg over another, and you'd end up all rickety. Each pillar counts.

"It's like this: where you sit at the table affects your viewpoint. It depends on where you're sitting."

"You're right, you're so right! That *is* the way it is! Now you should take your work and head over to your class. This paper flies! It's really good, Eph!"

Ephraim rose, pulled on his tan leather gloves, and shoved a wine-colored watch cap over the bright, tousled hair that Iris often imagined running her hands through.

After he left, sipping her coffee drink put her in a reverie. She felt distant as she walked to her car and then rolled home across the Golden Gate Bridge to Marin County. Crossing the iconic orange span, she stayed alert, catching glimpses of the landscape and waterscape of ocean and green cliffs, and against a distant horizon, a tiny city's toothpick skyscrapers. Past all of that, she saw an under-painting of a desert with rising sand-blown hills and a piercing violet/magenta sunset. Brush strokes moved through her mind as she set the scene to canvas. It was silent music—the familiar urging to make art.

Peeling off her scarf, hat, and gloves at home, Iris felt a rare contentment and decided to let herself off the hook and take a vacation from constantly pushing to do something, prove something, or mean something, that incessant internal pressure that could be driving her crazy.

I'm going out to hippie Bolinas tomorrow, she promised herself. West Marin is a healing place, and taking a walk on Agate Beach to look for sea glass is a healing thing. My part in saving the world can wait until next week.

The following weekend found Iris strolling higher, along a ridge in the Marin Headlands. This was just above the Golden Gate Bridge, where the view downward could be dizzying. Iris gazed out at the span, then quickly kneeled, sat on the ground, and hugged a big, safe-looking rock.

Today the visiting rabbi at the Tiburon temple she sometimes attended had told the congregation, "You cannot have peace until you can confront your own fears."

Yes, Iris thought, that's exactly what I need to hear.

Approaching the rabbi over the *kiddish* refreshments, she described her own wrestling with a personal writing project about the search for peace.

"Well, that's the big issue," he responded. "Give me a call when you've got it figured out." There was zero hint of sarcasm in his voice, only the respect due a fellow seeker.

Now *that's* a rabbi! she thought, driving away from the temple. Her mind mirrored the misty afternoon. If the weather is this way here in Tiburon, what is it like in the headlands? Deciding to find out, she drove southward toward the Golden Gate National Recreation Area.

After parking in the GGNRA lot, Iris climbed a nearby hill to a vista point where, just below, the massive, surreal bridge towers appeared and disappeared in the fog bank.

She thought, this is *so* not the East Coast, remembering the Indian tribe from here, the Coast Miwok, who would describe a fog bank billowing in from the Sundown Sea and slithering across the hills as "Coyote Man smoking tobacco."

Tobacco gets such a bad rap, she reflected, because of addictive smoking and hazards to health and all. It's understandable.

But tobacco is a power plant, calming and centering, and medicine in Native American ceremonies, a consecrated power substance that's never inhaled.

Now the entire north tower of the bridge had vanished behind opaque white fog until it was completely gone.

Thinking about tobacco reminded her of sweet red wine, a part of the Hebrew blessing called the *kiddish*. Each substance—tobacco, wine—was a sacred aid to prayer at one end of the spectrum, and addictive at the other end.

She walked further on up the hill, along the misty roadside at the top of a cliff on the edge of the world, and stopped to watch a huge black bumblebee flying nearby, buzzing between two star thistle blossoms against the background of solid whiteness that painted out the sprawling blue ocean and aqua sky. Now everything out there was nothing.

Trudging along the ridge road, musing inside the blank white field, Iris remembered cigarettes that led to wine and then vodka, and then Burton McCall, the craggy-faced, silver-haired improvisational actor who had fallen into alcoholism during the decades between her exuberant crush on him, or his stage persona, and their accidental reunion.

Only after they had become involved did she learn first-hand that there were two Burtons: the sane Dr. Jekyll and the drunken Mr. Hyde. She had then researched alcoholism, diving into the subject to help him. Or to save him? One helpful clue—he told her he used the sauce to drown the pain, explaining that it was 'quick.'

Searching through the literature, she read about the unbearable emotional suffering one's tyrannical superego can inflict on the psyche, and how the tortured soul might somatize that relentless mind pain into sickening headaches. Its victim ran to self-medicate, to blur the memories and douse the head pain in alcohol.

When she presented Burton with her findings, excited to discover a key to his healing, unrepentant Burton, who lived with a giant bottle of vodka the only item in his freezer, didn't want to hear a word about it, rejecting the thought of Alcoholics Anonymous and denying he had a problem, though he often referred to himself as 'pickled.'

One night Iris experienced a sick headache alone at home and got herself drunk on vodka—both to mute the pain and to feel where it was the drunken Burton would go.

The next day she wrote to him, "Now I know what it feels like and why you do it." But she couldn't live with his addiction and declined his invitation to move in with him unless he promised to quit drinking. That he refused to do, and they soon parted.

Iris released Burton from her mind and meandered further along the road, humming a New Age song into the chill wisps that swirled around her:

> *Let there be peace on Earth,*
> *and let it begin with me.*

If peace on Earth needed to begin with her, then the planet was in deeper doo-doo than she had thought. Her incessant inner war often made her shoulders ache, and there was never even the hint of a truce.

Why does this war rage inside of me? She had no idea.

Peace of mind would be such a relief, such a blessing! The visiting rabbi had said that to find peace, you first need to confront your fears. What were her fears?

Today, Iris was unafraid. Reaching her own precipitous sitting-rock that usually offered her incredible ocean views, she could see only whiteness everywhere.

Yet this place on the edge of space felt safe. You could see nothing. It was a total whiteout, as though this hill were the only hill in existence and she the only person.

Merchant Marine Nathan Paniolo, now a sea captain, had once spoken to her about fog. "When the world ends at the bow of your freighter in a solid sheet of white, you can't see a thing. So what is there to be afraid of?"

When she asked herself what her fears were, Iris could hear no answer, so what was she afraid of? She decided she would start keeping a notebook by her bed to capture her dreams. Her dreams might hold some answers.

An eagle banking and swooping above could gaze down and see a serene green ridge top encircled in white nothingness, on which a small multicolored collage of a woman was standing very still.

Iris was a tiny, solitary figure in a swirl of disappearing froth on the edge of a vanished sea.

9 Tangerine

White wine was served here to preserve Leon McLeod's white wool carpets.

The bartender spun a pile of napkins under a glass to make them spiral out on the counter. Italian delicacies could be found at the head of the wide hardwood staircase, while Japanese and Chinese specialties like *tempura* and duck or shrimp in soft white buns awaited guests in the back room.

Iris entered hesitantly.

After several compliments from fellow editors on her magazine work and a brief talk with a tall photographer who gazed down, laughed at her jokes, and declared her passionate, she felt more at ease.

Her long stay on the murky edges of poverty appeared to be ending, and things were starting to go better. There was nothing like the heady mix of flirtation, gourmet food, and sincere pats on the back from colleagues and strangers to bolster your self-esteem.

But this was Leon's world, and Iris was an uncertain guest. She headed upstairs for the shrimp buns.

It was later that evening.

"Leon, that feels so good. You know I'm still attracted to you. But I need some time alone right now."

"That's fine, I understand, but you've had some wine."

Leon drove her home. He had imbibed a bit as well, but his driving was rock-steady.

"OK, I'm going now. See you soon?" asked Leon.

"Sure. Thanks for the very cool party and for the ride." Iris walked him to the door.

But he ended up staying over. She had to admit that he was a beautiful man, tall and slender and ripply, and in his mildly buzzed haze, approachable and tender.

After her cat stalked his hand and then curled up on his chest, Iris knelt next to them both and snuggled in without a word.

Leon started to touch her.

Dreamily, she asked him, "Do you think what we're doing is an impeachable offense?"

"No." He murmured.

Her head burrowed into his warm shoulder and she felt great comfort.

But it was only Leon.

It had ended between Iris and Leon a while before, but his sharp wit still amused her. He was a non-practicing Catholic and the hetero mascot of a small cohort of gay men. Beneath his inviting exterior, she had found him opaque.

But they continued to dance in the same circles, spinning around for months now while going nowhere.

They could still find things to laugh about together, though, and neither of them wanted to say goodbye.

Iris had spent so many years pushing away the someones from now because they didn't measure up to her ideal someone from someday that she chose to give this now person another chance.

But time was tightening for her, and it really wasn't funny anymore.

Yellow Streaks

10 Lemon

Spring started with the birds. In her California world, Iris heard the season begin with the singing of birds. Busy with food-gathering and nest-building and territory-claiming and mate-attracting, they squabbled and trilled outside her windows in the early morning.

For the first time in decades, she let them sing for her.

She realized that she had been denying herself their company for a long time. She had believed she couldn't enjoy them because they weren't singing for her pleasure, and that the brilliant, sparkling beauty of the green rolling hills was not meant for her either, since she had left behind the east coast (the right coast?), her family of origin, her old friends, and that entire world for this west coast/left coast, with its often overly-perfect weather and its sky not the exactly correct color blue.

Tentatively, Iris let the springtime in, allowing the bird songs and blossoming plum trees to speak to her. One Sunday morning, she took a bicycle ride along the overgrown walkway near San Quentin. With an exterior that looked like a fairytale castle, San Quentin State Prison was a city in itself, set on San Francisco Bay's edge in its hulking vanilla deception.

Happy to be outdoors amidst the tall fennel weeds with groups of egrets pacing the shallow water like stick-figure dinosaurs, Iris pushed the peddles in an explosion of energy.

When she spotted a hummingbird perched at the top of a delicate fennel skeleton, she pulled the brake and silently stopped her bike.

She stood perfectly still.

Unbelievably, the hummingbird was singing! For the first time in her life, Iris heard the song of a hummingbird.

Chii chiii chii chii, chiii chii chii—chee chee,
Chii chii chii chii, chee chee chee—cheee chee.

It finished its song and flew off the fennel stalk in a vibratory blur.

Continuing down the path on her magenta mountain bike, Iris felt a surge of bliss. American Indian people had heard the hummingbird sing.

Now she had, too.

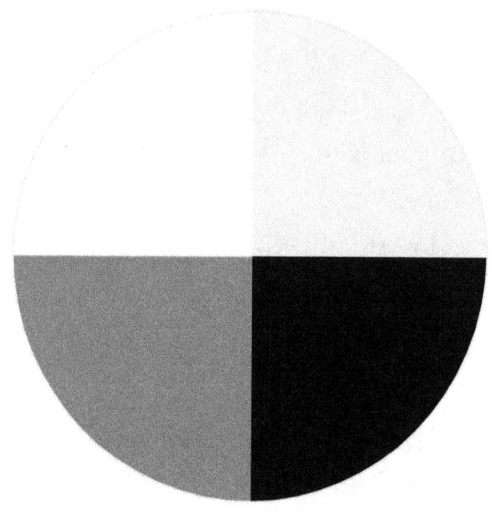

11 Sunflower

ris had kept a journal in longhand, pen on paper. At the dawn of the 21st century's digital age, she preferred a disembodied keyboard with a tiny screen. It acted like a word processor and felt as non-serious as a toy.

She could lie in bed and poke it with two thumbnails, and her thoughts would materialize on the screen, one ASCII letter at a time. It was a trick of light and hidden batteries. Later she would dump the accumulated contents into her desk computer's serious word processing program.

She lay back in a big chair one warm summer evening, her cat a deeply-relaxed ball on her belly, and committed to digital memory her recent visit to Indian country, pointing out in parentheses that Indian country was not a physical area but a map of festivals and ceremonies across the entire United States that brought American Indians together.

Her focus was the Big Time Ceremony celebrated by Coast Miwok tribal members, the neighboring Southern Pomo Indian band, their guests, and the public.

Non-Indians didn't seem to understand that Indian people often opened their powwows and other festivals to the general public. Iris wondered if a weight of subconscious guilt shackled today's white Americans, keeping them from even *seeing* Indian people because of what had been done by their own ancestors or other European, EuroAmerican, or American invaders to minimize and erase native peoples and their cultures from the continent the indigenous ones called Turtle Island.

While she wrestled her musings into words, Iris would sometimes wonder who would read them. Maybe no one, or a few friends. Even so, she wrote. She needed to, she had to. Basically, she couldn't help it. According to some, such as science fiction master Ray Bradbury, that was what made someone like her a real writer.

She polished and pruned and pushed her sentences out into the world like many women birthed their babies.

It is afternoon on a Saturday, and I'm heading out toward the Indian world on my little motorcycle, leaving behind my whine-fest about work and money and Bettina's torn edges.

Slipping back in time, I roll through the undulating ochre hills and hulking redwood forest, with an enormous grass-roofed Coast Miwok roundhouse as my destination. With every curve of empty road and pink streak of sunset cloud through the cerulean sky, the city and its chaos fade into irrelevance.

The ghosts of bears hunted to extinction inform the names
and signs and hulk in the shadowed memories of trees. A
treetop in the distance mimics the bent strut of a Miwok dancer.
Felix Moss will be at the roundhouse dance tonight.

On the phone this afternoon, he had chided me about
coming in late and interrupting the prayer circle, warning
me not to claim the group's attention by circumnavigating
the entire roundhouse all by myself, twirling counterclockwise
two times in place at each point of the four directions while the
rest of those assembled watched, already having done this in a
group as they entered.

"The Jewish princess has arrived," quipped Felix, in his
prophecy of what might be whispered if I didn't take care to
show up at the beginning.

To be respectful, I've packed a long skirt and shawl. When
I reach Kule Loklo under the full moon, I park a distance away,
slip into my skirt, wrap the shawl around my shoulders and
walk in to the camp, savoring the silence—until sharp bursts
of young laughter coming from the fire pit-preparers punch
through. They have buried a deer, killed for this festival, in the
now oversee its all night cooking on hot stones beneath the soil
for the dancers' feast the next day.

From a door in a hill mound that is the camouflaged
subterranean roundhouse, Felix emerges along with a friend
into the deepening dusk. Felix's hair is long and gray-streaked.

We hug. When I report that a tree seen on the way here was shaped like a Miwok dancer, the man with Felix says, "Sounds like you've had yourself a vision."

"Maybe," I reply, blushing to even speak about it.

Light from a round-faced moon shines through the roof's center smoke hole.

The sister of this ceremony's leader speaks about divine energy and how it is always with us. With praises and tears, the leader then honors the memory of their mother's spirit. I think about my own mother and weep inside, feeling surges of love and loss, regret and love again. I can feel the presence of Miragold, my mother, here.

In essence, this gathering feels very familiar. Some of the dances remind me of a slow-motion hora. And this ceremony is held after sunset, on the same circadian cycle of my people's Jewish observances.

I meet a woman in the roundhouse who is also Jewish, and during a pause in the prayers and dancing, we speak of orthodox versus progressive Jewish observances. We both feel at ease in this ceremonial roundhouse of the Coast Miwok.

A Persian (Iranian) man stands up and speaks about his Baha'i faith. His edges are blurry in the smoky roundhouse. He says his faith believes the world is going to unite, and that American Indians will be its spiritual leaders because they are *so close to nature and the Earth. He says the world needs the Indians. And then he says that what Indians need to do first is to unite into one nation and to forgive the white man for what he did to them.*

My mind bounces to horrific concentration camp images and rejects the idea that anyone could show up to tell me I can spiritually lead the world, and that all I have to do to get there is to forgive the Nazis for the Holocaust!

Forgiveness for that? *Forgiveness is unthinkable!*

After the Big Time ceremony, Iris resumed her journal entries with renewed energy.

Sometimes I yoke them together, the Hebrew and the American Indian supplications. For me, they do flow together.

Baruch Ha Shem   *Blessed be The Name*
Mitaque Oyasin   *For all my relations*

My time is compressing, and I swear I will no longer let fear of other people's judgments muddy my waters.

*American Indians have their own path to carve from a
trackless desert of hurt. And here we all are, still living our
parallel lives in our separate worlds on the glorious broad shell
of Turtle Island.*

Learning about Indian people is a whole different matter
when you spend time among them and with them, different
from absorbing data from books or websites or film.

Iris could feel the hurt they had suffered and were
still suffering from living in the middle of a foreign culture
that both devoured them and cast them off, and that now
expected them to live like any other American.

So much was unresolved, confusing, and denied.

America's damaged soul can be healed only after our
apologizing to the Indian people for what has been done
to them by the invaders. Iris believed with her whole heart
that her country had whitewashed genocide and buried it.

Her colleagues at work would sometimes ask if she
were Indian. She really didn't know, but it was a possibility.
Her father's Jewish grandfather had been a fur trader
in the far northern part of California and had married a

local woman rumored to be a Yurok Indian. Iris's family had never directly spoken about it. But then, Jews rarely admitted to any Russian *cossack* blood either. In the past, Jewish families had kept silent about rapes befalling family members and romantic trysts that occurred with non-Jews.

Spending time around American Indian activists, Iris found herself the brunt of resentments as well as good-natured ribbing. She would flirt with the guys, words singing back and forth in the air, and the women near them would lower their eyes when she glanced over. They would pretend disinterest in her antics. Iris stood out, got attention, and at times, made a positive impact in the Indian world. But she grew more self-aware as the months wore on and started to hold back on letting her emotions call all the shots. She recognized the outlines of still another obsession, but she kept on telling herself that they needed her there to hold up a mirror and show them their own beauty. Even if nobody would ever give her credit, she believed her energy and loyalty were making a positive difference at a key moment when the A·I·A was helping American Indians create their cultural renaissance. She believed her presence in Indian country must mean something.

The Indians truly had their own holocaust, just as real as the hideous *shoah* of the European Jews. That might explain some of what linked Iris's soul to these people.

New Age people were always talking about daring to risk forgiveness. But how could an American Indian person or a Jewish person ever forgive genocide?

Barricaded in her bed, Iris drifted between thoughts of fear and thoughts of forgiveness. What was meant by forgiveness? Wiping out all memory of hurt and murder? Excusing the inexcusable? Trivializing the horrifying end of beautiful, innocent people, some of them your own relatives?

Had her mother ever forgiven the murderers?

No, she had not. In Miragold's mind, the mass grave was always fresh. Even as generation grew up to replace generation and the gruesome details of the hideous massacres dimmed into time's filmy distance, how could such slaughter ever be forgiven?

Was this whole forgiveness thing a saccharine New Age whitewash? Even if hatred does harden the heart, it may be that it is the only honest response to sworn enemies who dehumanize you and then embark on orgies of systematized eradication the rest of the world does little or nothing, or less than nothing, to prevent!

Iris itched for revenge. But then, could doing the same thing back to them make anything better? No. *I can hate the Germans collectively from here to forever and never buy a Volkswagen or German brown bread, and what does that do but close me off from goodhearted people who happen to be from Germany or are of German descent, or happen to buy Volkswagens, or all of the above.*

Then it came to her that maybe it isn't forgiveness after all. *Maybe it's about letting in an awareness of the other's motivations instead, and climbing to a more farsighted level of awareness through discharging your own mad hunger for revenge. So you can make some space for peace.* In the end it isn't forgiveness after all but that classic Buddhist concept, compassion. *It isn't about forgiving an enemy's evil acts at all. It's the acknowledgment of our too easily-twisted human nature that can fertilize such destructive seeds, potentially in anyone!*

Each of us could find ourselves captured at some time or other by short-sighted impulses and immoral obsessions. Given compelling enough conditions and a tunnel-vision belief system, anyone can end up following orders that violate his or her own humanity and hurt other people. *Anyone.* With a yawn, Iris concluded that it all comes down to compassion for the human condition. Feeling peaceful from her toes to her hair, she curled up, stretched, and slept.

She often thought about Israel. What were they doing over there? It looked like, as a rule, the Israelis assumed the worst about Palestinians. They have an opportunity to build a true peace, and they're blowing it. Was the price of peace a series of hulking apartment buildings stacked around Jerusalem, spreading outward? Who were they locking out, or in?

Maybe the fearful ones were right: How do you trust a group of people ganged up just outside your hard-won borders that are sworn to destroy you? What do you make of their rage-filled glares and opaque stares as they whisper about you in a language you've never learned?

Israel was so far away. When she would phone her Aunt Rebecca in the Israeli town of Ashkalon, it was ten hours later—night when the sun shone here, and day after night had darkened the California sky.

How could she even dare to envision some kind of enduring peace in a place so far away, when she couldn't even manage to find peace in her own churning heart?

12 Ochre

Emerging from a sweat lodge at dawn during a Native American spiritual retreat in southern Oregon, Iris saw a blurry, jostling crowd of Indian people wearing buckskin forming in the morning mist that rose over the Sprague River.

Later that day, the retreat leaders instructed the encampment that ancestral ghosts of the Klamath tribe were to be fed that night. The people at the retreat were told to leave plates of food by the river for the spirits.

Iris had seen them herself, these spirits, before she had known anything about them.

Rick Walkinghorse shifted his hefty frame in the chair. His office was cluttered, with stacks of paper piled on every desk, and it was alive with intense energy. His assistant pushed a paper in front of his face, and he signed it without stopping to read it. His assistant had a certain presence, but who could have known that five years later, this woman would be elected traditional chief of the Cherokee Nation?

Iris told Walkinghorse that she had dreamed about bears the night before.

"Now, don't freak out, Miller," responded Rick, "I'm a member of the bear clan!"

She asked him if she could attend the upcoming all-night peyote ceremony.

"You ever had peyote before?"

"No."

"Think you can handle it?" Walkinghorse turned and consulted with Raven Wolf, who was casually slouched in an armchair across the office. "Think she can?"

"It's OK," said Leo Raven Wolf.

That evening found Iris stooping low to enter a giant tipi in the Walkinghorse family's backyard in Oakland's Fruitvale District, and then walking/crawling, bent forward, to take her place inside a double circle of seventy-five people who sat on the ground along its vast perimeter. Because it was a circle, the space felt uncrowded.

Iris scanned each face, surprised to find herself the only white woman present. The other non-Indian there was Raven Wolf's lawyer, who was Jewish, like Iris.

She heard a whisper from her friend Felix, sitting cross-legged beside her. There was hurt in his voice. "Do you realize I'm the only California Indian here?" It was true. A significant number of Lakota (Sioux) and Ojibwa Indians had recently appeared in local Indian country, bringing their sometimes-brash approaches and their unique ways of conducting ceremonies. Often they forgot to acknowledge the California Indians whose ancestral lands they were using for their sweat lodges and arbors, or to specifically invite local tribes to attend the ceremonies.

Leo Raven Wolf lit the central fire and spread coals into the shape of a water bird. Soon he was moving around the circle with small cylindrical green slivers of the special medicine-cactus, the *peyote*.

"Chew it all at once and it won't be so bitter," he advised, handing a sliver to each person in the double circle.

For Iris, ingesting the medicine and entering the altered state felt like entering a synagogue where a smiling rabbi offered you a joint.

Combining the sacred with the psychedelic was not the unusual mix, but here it felt right. Raven Wolf mentioned Daniel Firesmith's absence, and Iris sensed he was hurt that Daniel wasn't there. Firesmith's image faded away as the *peyote*'s earthy taste filled her mouth.

The tipi circle fell absolutely silent. Once in a while someone would cough, or retch from the nauseating effect of the peyote. Iris drifted, and a peaceful dream ballooned around her. And then she traveled very, very far away, to the other side of time and space.

"How's the medicine? Do you feel it?" The Lakota medicine man squatted before her, his voice concerned.

"Yes, it's good. Thank you." Iris gazed into his sweet, strong face. She knew enough of his story to see a shadow of the pain and confusion once drowned in alcohol, and to recall that, for him as for all of the Indian activists, it took enormous courage to reach beyond their righteous paranoia and interact innocently in the non-Indian world, even embracing some white people with love.

For so many native men and women, it was still the middle of a bad cowboy and Indian movie. America had never managed to look behind its whitewashed facade at the federally-sanctioned land grabs, the decimation of the bison herds, the bounties placed on the heads of Indians, the horrors of child abductions to Indian boarding schools, and the abuses still visited on native people.

Under the surface, it all still roils and simmers.

Iris was amazed at how close to the center of her own conflicted drama this peyote medicine was taking her. Then a vision came to her about Middle East peace and how to secure it.

After that, her heart ached for her mother, Miragold. How do you begin to honor the woman whose body and intentions and dreams had brought your very self into being? That fact was so beyond anything else—and so laden with mystery, a mysterious cocktail of prayer and blood, the seam in the basketball of life—the doorway, the portal.

At dawn, she moved with everyone else in a slow half-crawl along the tipi's edge to the low door. After exiting in the first pink light of day, they lined up to shake hands as glowing newborn people and say "Good morning."

The *peyote* ceremony danced in her head as she left the giant tipi in Oakland and drove home to Marin County over the Richmond Bridge. She carried her vision with her.

She could still recall the crooning wails of Margaret Raven Wolf singing the peyote songs and softly tapping on the water drum. The songs stayed in her mind for a week, with Israel, Palestine, and the Indians' sacred pipe thrown in, and then faded behind her daily tasks of bill-paying and schedules, work assignments and what to wear and what to make for dinner. But the core experience lingered, and she felt an urgent need to write down her *peyote* vision about Middle East peace while she could still remember it.

Without acknowledging to herself her deepening A·I·A involvement, Iris signed up for a few classes at DQ, the native college located near Davis in California farmland.

An integral part of the school was the sweat lodge. Mixed sweats—men and women together—often were held, and DQ Chancellor Daniel Firesmith regularly ran a ceremony where whites and Indians converged to pray.

When she traveled to DQ for classes, Iris attended sweats.

She would enter the sweat lodge wrapped in a large beach towel, turn to the left and crawl over those seated around the edge to find an empty place to sit.

After the door flap was closed, you were in pitch darkness. Inside the lodge, each in turn, you spoke aloud from your heart to the Great Mystery, beseeching the Creator for guidance and direction and for the healing of those you loved.

The porous orange-hot rocks were pulled from the nearby fire and sent in one at a time on a pitchfork or antler. After each steaming rock's delivery, the fire man would close the flap, plunging those inside into darkness once again. Men and women sat crowded together side by side, instructed by the ceremony's leader to keep their minds and hearts on the Divine.

People would pray in English, drank water from a metal ladle when it was passed around, and, when invited, smoke the sacred pipe, the leader explaining that the pipe was an instrument of spiritual communication. Then everyone would join in to sing sacred songs in Lakota.

The songs, prayers, and smoke all rose into the sky. Iris would pray for peace of mind, understanding, the strength to deal with her problems, and healing for friends or family members who needed it. This ancient way of praying was freely taught to everyone there, including many urban Indian youth drawn back to their ancestral traditions.

It was very real, and very powerful.

But it was also confusing to Iris, because she couldn't help it—she felt strong feelings for Daniel Firesmith, who often ran the sweat lodge ceremonies and also held press conferences, taught DQ classes, and led the activists surrounding him. Their work consumed them, and they were electrified by the charisma of their fiery leader.

Inside the low willow dome in complete darkness, everything—God and politics and love and lust and compassion and cross-cultural bridges and ethnic walls— would merge for her. The heat rose, growing more and more intense. Sweat poured from Iris's face and dripped onto the warm earth under her naked body to run between protective sprigs of cedar and sage.

Iris used to imagine the wall between the non-Indian world and the Indian world as a red and white candy cane-painted fence. Inside the sweat lodge, that fence would melt un-stickily into human flesh, human tears, and tiny orange circles of light from the cratered rocks.

Inside the sweat lodge and centered in herself, Iris could finally relax into her confusion and feel it recede.

13 Cream

From Iris's keyboard there bloomed a story about Middle East peace, a story whose tendrils first emerged during an American Indian ceremony in California.

The SINGING STONES of JERUSALEM

The table held a festive array of dishes piled high with a mix of Middle Eastern and Polish Jewish favorites: bowls of steaming chicken soup sat crowded next to plates of falafel drenched in tahini, plates of hummus and olive oil, and chubby rounds of fresh-baked pita bread. Somehow, it all worked.

Sitting nearest to Rachel Cohen was the matriarch, her Aunt Bette, older sister of Rachel's mother, Lilian. Aunt Bette was still going strong at 94, crediting her longevity to the ten cups of boiled water she downed each day and her daily treadmill sessions. At the table were Rachel's first cousin, Arik, his wife, Shoshana, and their two grown children, each seated next to a boyfriend or girlfriend.

This was no Jewish holiday feast, but a secular New Year's gathering that Aunt Bette had organized.

Some of the guests at this table were not Jewish—one of them an Israeli Arab. The discomfort at his presence, palpable at first, had morphed into laughter at his sarcastic story about harvesting chickpeas near Jerusalem. The smiles softened the mood all around, and the group mellowed more with each sip of dry Israeli wine. The most unusual visitor at this dinner was not the young Israeli Arab but Rachel's own special guest— Native American leader David Nowa, here with three fellow American Indian Alliance (A·I·A) activists.

David talked of the traditional parched corn soup, buffalo meat, and venison stew gracing many Indian ceremonial feasts. He said Indians could hunt deer in America without a license, because—as he put it—the entire continental United States was Indian land. Things felt tranquil and cheerful here in Jerusalem tonight, reminding Rachel of the mythical first Thanksgiving that American school children imagine while sticking paper feathers, round black hats, or plain white bonnets on their heads. Everything seemed normal, even hopeful. This was a peaceful interlude, too rare in an overly-anxious Israel. Rachel slowly passed a bowl of tabouli *to her right. She had conveniently forgotten about the jostling layers of photographers and news reporters waiting for them outside Aunt Bette's Ra'anana apartment to grab a hot interview.*

Between the courses, jokes, and teasing, the itinerary of yesterday, the last day of December, 1999, sharpened into focus. That day, the eve of the millennium, was the day an event of Biblical magnitude shook Jerusalem. It was also the culmination of months of planning by Rachel and her friends.

In Israel to visit her Aunt Bette several months before, she had found herself trapped on the edge of a rock-slinging riot between outraged Chabad-niks and enraged Palestinian youths.

An IDF brigade started shooting rubber bullets into the crazed mob, and the air reeked of gunpowder. As she dodged another shower of stones, Rachel couldn't help thinking that something has to change, now! *It was a mantra filling her head as she crouched and then backed herself out of the maelstrom.*

Rachel turned left and walked toward the Western Wall, all that remained of the ancient Israelites' Second Temple. She wanted to touch the wall and ask the Creator why so much ugliness and danger kept arising, tarnishing this holy place.

Near the wall area, she placed her hand flat against a nearby stone building to steady herself, and then she pulled it back in shock—the stones had vibrated under her hand! She touched the rock again and felt a tingle again. It was the same thing when she touched a different rock. The walls here were alive, and they were singing!

Rachel slowly walked toward the massive Western Wall, heading toward the women's side of the gender barrier.

Lost in thought, she felt a pulling deep inside her throat, and then huge gasps and sobs erupted from her, until she was drenched in tears. So this *was why people called the Western Wall "the wailing wall." She reached the wall and tenderly rubbed the surface of the large, smooth-edged block of stone directly in front of her. Then she pulled out a scrap of paper and a pen and scribbled a note to God, asking how she could help to bring peace to this land. Shoving the note into a crack between two of the boulders already crowded with many other notes, she wondered whether apprentice rabbis or their female assistants secretly came by at night to pull the tiny folded notes out of the cracks, to make room for more.*

Two names popped into her mind as she wound her way out of Jerusalem, Jonathan Minot and David Nowa. Why those names, and why now? She couldn't figure it out. Okay, so Jonathan had money. A former Catholic with a generous heart, he had been a healer to her during several tormented occurrences. She knew that he wanted to make a difference in the world. He had said he wanted to make his life count for something bigger. He wanted to make a difference, and he had money. But why enter her mind now? Rachel scanned the real world for a sign. She spun like a panoramic camera, alert for God to appear and vibrate like Jerusalem's walls. She had asked a question that was not focused on her own problems. This question was for the world, especially this city of peace, Yerushaliyim, that stood today. The truth was that Jerusalem could easily sink into rubble if the inflamed rage on either side of their endless conflict should ever reach kindling temperature.

Exhausted from fear and from the long walk, she spotted a bench near a huge sculpture and grabbed it. The sculpture commemorated victims of the Holocaust. A flat metal arm and hand reached up to the sky out of a huddle of slumped forms. Rachel turned Jonathan Minot around in her mind. Yes, he had money, but so what? How could that fact help this? He wants to make a difference. So did she, the desire burning inside her like an eternal flame.

Her gaze idly scanned the commemorative sculpture near her bench. The hand was grasping at the air, as though wanting to hold something. A baby? A goblet? A pipe?

A pipe! A sacred pipe of peace, the holy instrument of communication between living men and women and the spirit world in the American Indians' worldview, reaching the Great Mystery with heartfelt human prayers.

She had learned that the pipe connected the world of matter with the universe, the unseen. Traditional Indians taught that when you prayed with the pipe, your prayers went to the spirit world and were heard.

That was what David Nowa had said in the pitch black prayer lodge with the glowing rocks. Nowa tossed and turned in her head like an unpolished gem in a tumbling machine.

Reconciliation with the oppressors, the transformative idea touted by so many New Age forgiveness advocates. If such *a reconciliation could actually come to pass—here in Israel, wouldn't that be the very best thing in the entire world?*

Rachel envisioned some kind of a spiritual summit, filled with representatives of the Abrahamic monotheistic triad: Muslims, Christians, and Jews—a calm meeting of minds. She remembered reading that centuries ago, such a meeting had been called together by enlightened religious scholars in Persia.

Yes, a spiritual summit here! Or maybe she could land a guest-host spot on a regional radio show broadcast in English, and invite a popular rabbi, a respected minister or priest, and a ranking imam to sit at the same table and duke it out verbally

Seeing these images of peacemaking, her heart warmed.

In the Torah—*to Christians and Moslems, the Old Testament—David and Jonathan were best friends … David's courage and Jon's money … reconciliation with the oppressors … a reaching hand upholding a sacred pipe … .*

A dance of images and ideas followed Rachel back to Ra'anana and her local home, as she sank into a hot bath that evening, and as she slid into bed in Aunt Bette's guest room. Outside her window, date palms, tall hibiscus bushes, and tulip trees swayed in a warm breeze.

When Rachel awoke, a rose-gold sunbeam was pouring through the trees and the open window onto her face. Raucous brown and black birds that looked like Egyptian hieroglyphs argued in the trees in their raspy version of the desert language.

So many kinds of birds flew over this bottleneck of land beside the vast Mediterranean Sea. Rachel had once scanned a nature atlas only to discover that it was Israel over which all migrating birds on this side of the world converged and diverged, from Europe and Asia to Africa and back again, following the seasons and their inner directives.

She felt a rare urge to go outside to pray, and followed it. Facing toward each of the four directions, she sent her prayer into a sky into which millions of prayers had wafted before and from which trillions of visions had poured forth—a sky where there must be a direct conduit to the Divine.

This place, this land, surely a power spot and a natural pipeline. There it was again, in the center of her thoughts: the pipe. The sacred pipe. Like the tobacco pipe floating in the middle of that Magritte painting with French words painted below it that read, "THIS IS NOT A PIPE." If not a pipe, then what? Oil paints on canvas. The artist's will. Thoughts turned into painted words via suspended minerals. Minerals—tiny rocks, little crushed stones. Stones. The singing stones! A power spot of singing stones.

Later on, as soon as the time was right—about 6:00pm in Israel, equaling 10:00am in northern California, United States—Rachel made some calls. First she called Jon Minot and breathlessly shared her idea. She told him she figured it would take about $8,000 to pull it off, with plane tickets, hotel rooms, and cargo charges, and the rental of movie trucks and a portable sauna. Jonathan Minot told her she was crazy. "What do you mean, a sweat lodge? An American Indian prayer lodge? Over there? You're nuts!" he cried. "And anyway, how do you know David Nowa will go along with it? Who do you think you are?"

And so on.

"I don't know who I think I am, Jon, but I don't want to wait. This is now, and I'm here. I haven't even asked David yet, and I have no idea how he'll respond. I didn't want to say anything to him about it until I knew we had the finances in place. Can you do it, Jon? If not for the world, then for me? Or if not for me, then for world peace? Or would it embarrass you?"

Now she'd gone and done it—why had she said that? But Jonathan saw the light somehow. She told him to think of it as a loan. "Sure," he said, "A loan. I'll think of it as a novena." What is that? Rachel wondered. But never mind what it was, the Christians had to have a hand in this thing. Christianity was one of the three Abrahamic religions and remained an integral part of the stories and rules and myths that had coalesced into the mess happening today.

Many Muslims still resented the Crusades from the middle ages! That's religion for you, she thought. 'My faith is the best, I'm the best, I get to go to heaven and you don't! Nyah nyah nyah!'

She made another call, speaking rapidly across the world, her telephone receiver a deep well. "Everyone wants a piece of this place, David. I know you've called me a space cadet, and maybe sometimes I am, but I had this vision. It was a real vision, a true one, about the sacred pipe of peace coming over here to Israel, and you were part of it!"

Then she filled him in on her idea. "What do you think? Can you help us with this?" Rachel didn't know who was meant by 'us.' But she could hear that all of the passion in her soul, all the love and heart she had directed elsewhere, was in her voice right now.

David Nowa heard it, too. He thought it over and then thought some more, while a minute of very expensive silence stretched halfway around the globe.

"All right," he said finally. "We can do this, I think so. Except who's going to pay for hauling all those rocks?" He chuckled. The enterprise struck him as funny!

"We have that covered, David. I have this rich ex-Catholic ex-boyfriend who says he'll wire us and you guys the money for this action as soon as you've given it the green light."

"That's a lot of ex-es, Cohen," growled David.

"Yeah, I know. Whose pipe will it be? Yours?" she asked.

"You should remember this, Rachel—any consecrated pipe carrier has the authority to conduct an *inipi*, a prayer lodge pipe ceremony, and every pipe can be a spiritual conduit when connected together. It's the same power, it's all the same thing!"

She pledged she would remember that and then told him more about why she wanted a sweat lodge ceremony here. "It's to shake these people awake to where they are—and to their responsibility to this land and this power place called Jerusalem. The walls, the very stones here—they're singing!"

"OK, when and where? You work out the details. Let us know when it is that you're ready, and we'll be there."

"Soon," Rachel answered, "It will be very soon."

Three weeks after their conversation, a small cargo plane flown by a friend of Jonathan's landed at Ben Gurion Airport.

Eighteen mysterious packages were gently lifted from the hold while four traditional American Indians descended from the cockpit. David Nowa was there, along with Lakota singer Blanket Man, Yurok artist and storyteller Lorenzo Caba, and Creek/Apache medicine woman Salina Sacheen Blue Bird.

David Nowa, travel bag flung over one shoulder, held a small bundle wrapped in fringed suede in both hands.

Rachel imagined it contained the disassembled sacred pipe of peace.

"Welcome, shalom," she cried, beaming with pride as she met the travelers. "Thank you for coming!"

They all stayed up very late that night in Aunt Bette's flat, reviewing logistics, obstacles, and strategy, and laughing all along about the craziness of the plan.

It will definitely be a wild ride, thought Rachel, biting into a falafel sandwich with tahini sauce as the excited exchange bubbled up around her.

The following afternoon, they worked to set up a generator and portable sauna in the back of a rented truck parked on an empty street near their two other rented trucks. Then they heated the 18 volcanic rocks flown over from the prayer lodge at California's Indian-run DQ University. Driving into Jerusalem's Old City, they lined up the trucks near the Western Wall and the Temple Mount.

The Israel Defense Force (IDF) guards were curious, but they had already been briefed by a member of the Israeli Parliament (Knesset) that these Americans were here to film a movie. Aunt Bette had done her part, requesting a favor from a judge she had dated in pre-WWII Poland before he was elected to the Israeli Parliament and long before there was an Israel.

When the IDF officers saw the sauna rig inside the truck, they laughed about it, joking to one another in Hebrew, "These crazy Americans! Some kind of touchy-feely religious movie!" and then quietly retreated to their posts to keep eyes out for the usual crazies, the 'Armegeddonites.' Inside a second truck, a dome of willow branches was woven together and tied with sinew or cordage, and the lodge-covering blankets were readied.

Then the woven dome was placed on a mound of soil piled in the center of the holy plaza—a mixture of soil they had dug the day before, half from the Palestinian Territory and half from Israel.

Appearing next was the crew of filmmakers hired by Jonathan Minot to document the event and act as decoys, so observers wouldn't realize too early that this was anything other than a movie set. Crowds of the curious gathered behind barricades, jostling one another. Jews and Arabs tried to explain to their neighbors what was happening, while international tourists crowded around them. Theories flew.

Out of a third movie truck descended David Nowa, Blanket Man, Lorenzo Caba, Salina Sacheen Blue Bird, Rachel Cohen, progressive Knesset member Ramona Eshkol, and Abu Tor, a well known and much-admired Palestinian poet, each of them wrapped in a giant beach towel.

Most bent in turn to enter the low prayer lodge. One by one, volcanic rocks glowing fiery orange were delivered through the lodge door on a pitchfork wielded by Blanket Man.

This was the best they could do on short notice, reflected Rachel. Ideally, heads of state and leading religious figures would be a part of this. There had been no time in the last minute rush of preparation to educate anyone new about the significance of an American Indian prayer gathering set in the spiritual center of Jerusalem and including the pipe of peace.

But it was all right. This was no symbolic ceremony dependent on worldly hierarchies. It was, honestly and simply, the real thing. People were gathered to pray—to the One they named the Great Mystery, the Creator, God, Allah—amidst the singing stones of Jerusalem.

The Indians had taken great care to pile deep soil underneath and all around the domed structure, eliminating fire hazard. Inside the dome, prayer songs in the Lakota language began.

A sense of tranquility seeped into the square. There in the middle of the Middle East, in the middle of the ancient Biblical center of three religions, in a power spot centered inside a power spot, the sacred pipe brought by American Indian traditional spiritual people was connected stem to bowl, joining the worlds of matter and spirit. Prayers for peace were uttered with heart and sweat, songs and tears.

Outside the lodge, a low murmur ascended to raucous cries. The people behind protective barricades sounded angry: Israelis, Israeli Arabs, Palestinians, and tourists cried out in protest: "What are these Americans doing here on this holy place, Jerusalem's Temple Mount?"

Then a soft vibration shook the square. Somebody shouted that the stone walls around the plaza were tingling! People ran to any wall built of stone to feel the rocks.

"Yes!" the Israelis yelled. "Yes!" cried the Palestinians. "The rocks are vibrating!! What is this?"

And then night fell. It was the eve of the Millennium,

*according to the Gregorian calendar: New Year's Eve of the year
2000. Though the dates and times were artificial conventions,
the smoke from steaming rocks and consecrated tobacco was
genuine, ascending through the top of the prayer lodge into the
square and curling up into the sky, and the songs and tears
and cries for peace continued inside the lodge, every one of them
natural and real.*

An Israeli in a tallit *(prayer shawl) broke out a bottle of
kosher wine and a silver cup and passed it to those around him,
whether Jew or Moslem or Christian, woman or man. An Arab
brought out a* hookah *and shared the smoking herbs with those
around him, whether Jew or Moslem or Christian, woman or
man. The plaza grew calm as the moods of gathered onlookers
relaxed. And then it rained.*

*Out of a clear and starlit sky, it rained. A small cloud
had floated unnoticed to a place directly above the sweat lodge.
And suddenly a downpour drenched the square and the people.
Jews, Moslems, Christians, non-believers, and tourists began
falling on their knees. Everyone there seemed to recognize a holy
moment and a miracle.*

*It grew silent then, except for the splashing of the rain
and the sounds of prayer songs swelling out from the blanket-
covered dome set on holy ground in the middle of the plaza near
Jerusalem's Temple Mount. The praying and singing continued
on throughout the night.*

As dawn broke, the rain stopped. People emerged from the sweat lodge. Cameras rolled. Everyone in the surrounding crowd wanted to be interviewed to voice his or her reactions and questions and thoughts.

A sense of excitement and hope filled the air. David Nowa picked up an electronic bullhorn and spoke, his deep, strong voice very gentle. "What you have here is not a new religion but an ancient religion born of Mother Earth, just as your religions were born from this holy ground out of human hearts connecting with the Creator.

"We come in peace and we bring peace, but this holy peace is not something made up by us. Your prophets have told you this again and again. Thanks and no-thanks to Christian missionaries during my childhood in boarding school, I am familiar with some of the religious thought originating here.

"Know that you live in a power spot. If you doubt it, feel the rocks that make up these walls. Respect this place. Grow up. Quit fighting among yourselves for a piece of the magic. It's a circle, and you are all in it. There's room for everyone. It is a circle and cannot be owned by a few or broken into pieces.

"Happy New Year, and happy new Millennium. You can start fresh now. Peace. Shalom. Salaam. For all my relations."

David Nowa put down the bullhorn and walked toward a movie truck. He climbed in, and the driver slowly rolled away. When he had gone, some of the other Native Americans started *methodically dismantling the prayer lodge. They loaded the dome, rocks, and soil into the back of a rented truck, completely clearing out the site. Not even footprints were left behind.*

There were tears in Jerusalem that morning, and hugs. People whispered about the miracle of the rain, and other things. Boundaries and barriers were tentatively crossed.

Rachel thought the major miracle was the hugging. Black-clad Lubavichers embraced kafiyya-*wearing Palestinians, and western-outfitted women grinned and hugged robed women. Teenagers shyly exchanged cellphone numbers, and children from both sides of the wall started to play new games.*

The food brought into the plaza was tasty and bountiful, turning the area into a picnic that lasted all day.

Rachel's heart overflowed. She couldn't stop smiling.

"So, why aren't you married already, a pretty girl like you?" asked one of her cousins. Rachel Cohen was 55 years old, not exactly a girl. But she girlishly blushed and smiled, passing the bowl of tabouli *toward David Nowa.*

It always happened this way, she thought, slicing into a slab of brisket. Why did it always boil down to the same question? Maybe it was the survival gene.

In the back of her mind, other questions still whispered. But all Rachel wanted to hear right now were the stones that sang in Jerusalem. Her fingers gripped a pink-gold Jerusalem stone. She could feel the tingling.

Green Vines

14 Chartreuse

For several weeks after the intense peyote ceremony, Iris had laser-focused on getting her vision's tale of peace in the Middle East typed, edited, and then printed out. When she felt the story finally sing like the stones, she enjoyed a nanosecond of parental pride. Then she realized she had something new to wrestle with: what was she going to do with this?

She squirmed like Moses did when he hefted the stone tablets carved with ten commandments to carry down the mountain. "Why me, *Adonai*? I–I–I can hardly speak!"

Spring had appeared early this year, its subtle carnival infusing northern California. Baby leaves sprouted from parent branches everywhere. On a Sunday glimmering in translucency, Iris forced herself to trudge up and down the hilly blocks near her home. As she swung left around the next corner, she ran into her neighbor, Susanna Marcellus, trotting toward her down the sidewalk, the dark gypsy curls and bouncy walk unmistakable. An "ancient hippie," Susanna now worked in the corporate world. Despite the nature of her day job, she proudly kept her rebellious edge.

Different as they were from one another, Iris saw her own deeply personal child-yearning mirrored in Susanna. Baby-hunger had little to do with the presence or absence of a man; the impulse to mother was an obsession all its own.

While each of them kept an active dating life going, each struggled with granting her own inner permission to be intimate or to commit.

They rarely discussed this with one another. Layers of shame covered up a sense that they had failed to meet their biological clocks' deadlines. Suits of armor cloaked them both. The unspoken consensus was that it was better to stay casual neighbors than attempt a dubious co-therapy. Their invisible chains and straitjackets prevented them from sharing their stories and allowing a catharsis of their pain. They were sister non-mothers venturing forth sans strollers, each carrying only a laptop computer and an invisible empty cavern for babies to incubate and grow into their hearts.

The desire to make a baby and mother it had lingered long after Iris's mother, Miragold, had passed away, taking her own anger and mystery with her. Missing your own unborn children was like longing to be a ballerina while you watched your life slide by and your dance skills shrink away, or craving dark chocolate in the middle of the night with none left in the house, or not winning the lottery and knowing you never would. It was an unrequited love for nature's ultimate gift of grace. Iris and Susanna turned around and speed-walked the two blocks to Peets' coffee house, their gaits matching.

"I have to tell you about a vision I had about peace," said Iris, her voice urgent.

"What is it? What *happened*?" Susanna responded, her steaming mug of tea in hand. They were hovering over the condiment table in the comforting dark of the wood interior.

That was the thing about Susanna: she had studied psychology and retained her sensitivity to the complex human story. So Iris knew she would be taken seriously.

"Well, there was this all-night peyote ceremony that an American Indian activist invited me to, and I was the only white woman there."

"An authentic peyote ceremony? How did you get invited to *that*? Do you know how rare that is?"

"I do know. And that's a long story. Anyway, in the middle of the ceremony, in the middle of the night, I saw a path to peace in the Middle East!"

They found their seats. The coffeehouse din faded as Iris's vision danced on the table between them. Susanna sat in silence while Iris spun the tale of the singing stones of Jerusalem, the sacred pipe, and prayers inside a sweat lodge built on the Mount, the center of Jerusalem's most holy site.

After a long sip of green tea, Susanna finally said, "You know what this means, don't you?"

"No I don't! *What does it mean?*" Iris cried.

"You need to get this out there, girl! You were given a message that's not meant only for you."

"I did get it out—I wrote it up as a short story. But how do I get it out after that? I'm not going on the road for tent revivals and TV interviews!

"What else can I do, take the manuscript to Israel and bury it in a sacred place? Rent a public address van over there and park it near the Western Wall? *What?*"

"I don't know, Iris, but you'll figure it out. Maybe that's your mission."

This had been a different conversation for them, not their usual confidential analysis of current suitors. The two strolled over to Susanna's place, and then Iris headed back to her cottage to mull things over.

15 Viridian

ngaging both sides of her brain, Iris wrote and painted. Painting was a place to go that the literal mind either skipped over or held no key to. It was a trance place.

Squeezing a tube of paint to get the pigment out could hurt her fingers. So much time often passed between her painting sessions that the pigment would harden around the cap, and her fingers would get pinched when forcing open a paint tube or squeezing to encourage a gummy line of pigment to extrude onto her palette.

As a child, she had noticed the word "pain" sitting neatly tucked inside the word "paint," but no one—parent, teacher, or colleague—had ever said a word to her about it.

She tried to place the paints on her paper palette following the spectrum, the way they taught you to in art school: red, then orange, then yellow, squirted in little piles around the edges. Green, then aqua, then blue, then indigo, then purple. White paint in a big blob took up its own area at the top, with space left around it for color mixing (the original white space).

But today she toyed with the colors, swirling them together on the palette and stroking the resulting hues onto the canvas in wide swaths. The yellow brightened the adjacent green, and the purple changed the hue of the red surrounding it. After stroking a wide indigo field across the top, she caught herself staring at it and noticed her residual anxiety draining away.

With colors, you got different feelings from different hue combinations. Why is that? she wondered. There's got to be a story there.

The greatest thing was that the colors you used were your choice. There was no rule about having to use up every pile of pigment. The fact of the matter was that with art, there were hardly any rules at all.

That was what she liked about it. Art was the safe place, the sanctuary she could run to when the rest of the world got to be too much. Which, as a child, it often did.

Iris realized that her art school years had taught her nada-zip-zero about colors. She decided to start researching color. Maybe then she could discover why staring at a large flat area of indigo had helped fade her anxiety away.

At her easel, she began to construct a landscape, the lines of the under-painting brush-sketched first in yellow ochre, the art school standard. Echoing one of her favorite painters, Wayne Thiebaud, Iris then painted the outlines in colored edges, shifting the hues that contouring each white shape. After a while, a meadow stretched back in one-point perspective to a horizon set below a Maxfield Parrish-like gradient sky, while a gingerbread roof on a white Victorian cottage took shape in the foreground, bordered with its own shifting colored edges.

After painting until the work felt finished, Iris cleaned up, happy that the water-soluble oils allowed her to use water to wash her brushes instead of turpentine.

She put some water on to boil. With a cup of healing turmeric-ginger tea steaming on the side table, she hunkered down in the gray leather sofa to wrestle with words.

Still at play in hues and tints, she used the compressed language of poetry to distill the bright flavor of colors.

What emerged was *A Pack of Lifesavers.*

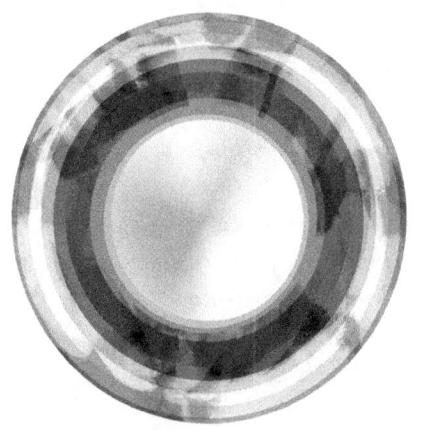

A Pack of Lifesavers

Red

Crimson roses and naked ladies
form perfect crescents on Valentines' dresses,
tracing hidden slits
where shiny organs slither inside skin.

Appendages carting diplomatic packets
seek out the red light zones
where multiple blood types
sort wartime envelopes,
and scarlet stamps proliferate.

As for her own rosy manuscript,
a message pops up stop-sign bright:
her book is red-tagged,
discounted, remaindered,
and returned unread

to America.

Orange

Flaming dayglow,
a bowl of warm ripe globes
centers the table like a bullseye.
Buried inside each fruit,
seeds carry their trees like promises
trajectoried through your mouth
into the Earth.
We are each
bright orange tubes
for one another's destinies,
waterslide-rides home.

Yellow

The yellow jumps! snaps Professor Priss.
Her brass-flecked eyes rake his painted landscape
where sunstruck aspens quiver wind-pierced leaves.
Hovering over campus ponds, his lightning bolts singe the
faculty parchment. His life doesn't sit quite right on the page.
Bareback astride every palomino roundelay
he grabs for the brass ring
swung once again from a bronze ark.
Over and over and only golden tea will ground him,
leaves pointing back to that scrapbook-citrine kitchen
still aglow in morning light,
where billowing creamy curtains
frame the oatmeal promise of another day.

Green

Winter sun warms their faces
like a candle-flame space heater.

Lying here away from time, two women
could be anyone and her friend, and any age

Up here, out on the edge of millennia
a Renoir oil of young girls
all rosy-cheeked and full of hope.

Rolling hills, khaki-furred down to the sea cliffs
above an ocean full of satin-painted light
drifting-in in wrinkled waves
so lackadaisical, as if time didn't matter,
life stages no matter, gray and grinding singlehood,
loves lost, unfulfilled ambitions, gilded guilts
and the whole damn schedule, no matter at all.
Left far behind, below in the loaded lowlands.

Even the wind pays respects to this spot
by keeping still.
And the stew of blame and fear
sinks down, becalmed
before your serene highness,
you promontory
with no name.

Blue

Night through shades. Chill wind.
Loss over loss
peering down deep wells.

Indifferent cerulean sky
or cobalt glass you bend to,
the deep blue transparency
morphing your visual field
into precious dusk, and royal thirst.

You want more;
you want less of now.
You want what was,
the hues and cries of the past.

You repeat your cadences of regret,
sad sharp notes spiraling down to zero.
You will feel this way forever
or until morning.

No one wins. Everything ends
and even your widest smile and giddiest laughter
mask horizons forever receding
to where you wish you could go
to start over, but

too far to go.
Too cold. Too blue.

Purple

I am Abraham. God sent me back.
I have to talk to you—
boys, stop your fighting.
You are shaking the Universe.
You are giving the only God
such a headache.

Stop the killing.
Stop the hurting
and the anger and the fear.
See the truth that you are blessed to be here.
Cease the death embrace, the lethal circle dance.

How many times do I have to tell you, boys?
Put down your mirrors, boys. Now!

I made some mistakes, I admit it.
I was only a father, only human,
feeling my way, praying for a sign.
I denied my love. For your mothers.
For my own better judgment. For you.

I was ready to kill you both.
Then where would you be?
But God stopped me
in a grand intervention,
and now God falls
in a gentle rain from the heavens
on your raging faces.

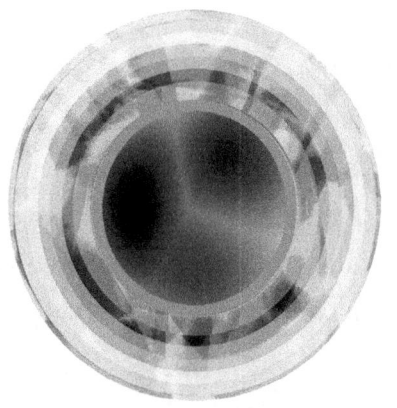

16 Khaki

As her daily grind ground on, Iris's memories of the *peyote* ceremony faded. She was glad she had managed to write down her singing stones vision as a story while she still could. For the moment at least, it sat locked inside her digital keyboard.

Iris had dreams that were doozies. She awoke from another midnight epic one morning in her chilly Mill Valley aerie; the landlord had neglected to heat the bedrooms, even after repeated complaints. One way to stay warm was to snuggle back under the comforter, go over some scenes from her still-fresh dreams, and write them down.

In part one, I sat around with the sister of a potential lover, discussing Monica Lewinsky's psyche and her motivations regarding the alpha male. I revealed my theory of the 'unattainable man' as one manifestation of a traditional woman's power search, equal in intensity and drive to a military attack on a threatening country.

The dream meandered to New York City, where Monica entered and offered me a beautiful dress, only slightly worn, for

$20, which I embarrassedly declined because I was so strapped that spending $20 on a dress felt unbearably extravagant.

I communicated my empathy and understanding to this distressed woman so recently painted scarlet by a rapacious media and left to sit all alone by a cold telephone.

Then the houseboat I lived on started peeling away from the dock, and I had to get busy saving it.

In part two, there was my houseboat, again inadequately tied to the dock and piling, and pulling out from its moorings in winter's whipping winds. Not too far away was my real houseboat, a domed wonder with diagonal wood siding, wrongfully taken away from me by a neighbor without either proof of consensual sale or any legal paperwork.

This was the familiar feeling of displacement: myself as ignored, unrecognized, deposed royalty.

Another night, another dream: I admired President Clinton and was attracted to him. I was one of his staff. He asked me for the notes I had taken at a prior interview. I told him they were all accounted for, and no note was just floating around.

He appeared disappointed but didn't press it.

I never actually gave him my notes, since I didn't know where they all were. Then I felt guilty and started looking for

them as though they could save him. He was putting on a brave
and calm front at the office. I liked feeling that he needed me.
    I was riding inside of, and then returning, a small fast
jet ski car, and then arguing with a stupid attendant. My
boyfriend was missing. He had gone off alone to test-drive
a fast black sports car.

After jotting down her newest dreams, Iris felt warm
enough to get dressed. She ate a quick breakfast, sent an
email to her latest romantic interest, and set off to work.
    The Golden Gate Bridge was her daily commute
partner. She knew that if things ever got too bad, it would
be awfully convenient to have that bridge handy—not a
scary thought at all, simply a given. Local color, she smiled.
    Woven through the events skittering around her life
was a thread of obsession. Iris could paint a picture of
obsession and how it took over, rings over rings of similar
thought, an itch that scratched itself and grew more and
more intensely itchy. Maybe the Shen practitioners were
correct: They said your emotions get stuck in your body,
and shells of numbness grow around them. They instructed
you to dig through those shells to get at the deep splinter of
hurt and squeeze it out.

In northern California, there was a drift and a flow. Friends got busy, missed appointments, forgot to call, made new and more fascinating friends, and, especially in San Rafael and Berkeley, were offended at politically incorrect remarks, tending to over-analyze everything. Love didn't seem too likely or even very possible out here.

New York City, by contrast, was bedrock-solid, with sparking conversations constantly under construction inside the magical spaces carved out of decomposing urban cliffs.

There, your friends stayed your friends, no question and no doubt. In New York, the human face was the landscape of choice and the desired human body was the exotic destination of your dreams. Once you learned to tune out the surrounding chaos and ugliness, your mind was free to create beauty. Also, you felt as though you were at the very center of the world, so why leave? As long as you didn't mind breathing air the equivalent of smoking three packs of cigarettes a day, or descending into the tedious hell of the subways between every meeting or tryst.

As a journalist, Iris had metaphorically sworn to tell the truth, but as a storyteller, she suffered. She was finding the writing of fiction, the making things up, wrenchingly difficult. She could manage it only by navigating a tangled, twisting path and controlling her drive toward truth-telling.

Similarly, Iris sometimes found daily living on the left coast extraordinarily hard. On impulse, she decided to move back east. The word 'back,' she knew, was a semantic hook that kept east coast émigrés 'out west,' since once they had moved 'out west,' they could hardly go 'back east.'

Some coastal emigrants did move east again, while others morphed into mutations known as 'bi-coastals,' dividing every year into segments between coasts. That was a great solution if you could afford it.

Extricating herself from the nests of objects, people, and interactions she had built in California would not be easy. Maybe she wouldn't do it. She might just stay where she was, where the tides of politics and her ancient passions had dropped her.

When she did move away from her chilly home, it was not to New York City at all but to a shingled house, older but warmer, located eight miles down the road. Packing up, she was amazed at the amount of stuff she had accumulated in her travels, every item holding a memory and requiring a decision. Each piece carried a story taking her somewhere else. Sorting the objects into bags was a glacial process, but she knew it needed doing. She sat in the center of her piles and piles of things, riding her emotions.

17 Olive

Addiction and drugs. Fame is a drug. Once you touch someone the way a celebrity touches his or her fans, the fans think you're their own, and they want more.

Iris recognized that. She also knew that if a star weren't cautious, that star could become addicted to getting all those strokes. 'If they want me and love me, I must be worth something,' the star would think. That would be exhilarating for a while, but then he or she could lose the thrilling feeling of audience adulation and urgently need to re-create it.

It was a drug! Face it, she thought, fame and glory were a form of substance abuse.

> *If you want to keep your song*
> *don't play the chords of fame, my friend.*
>
> —Phil Ochs

Iris saw that, but she still desired fame, whether her own or somebody else's. The desire for that substance was what made living an ordinary life so very hard for her. Iris needed to convince herself that she deserved luxuries, celebrity among them. And before that, she needed to start believing in herself—before it was too late to manifest anything at all.

18 Lime

Giving birth must be something like dying. You reach the end of your endurance and your old shape, and then you morph into another form, a form called 'a mom.' For Iris, childbirth was a missed boat and a blown opportunity, for the presumed excruciating pain and then a new forever-friend (or so one would hope).

Childbirth for Iris was never-never land—the doctors had said her tubes were blocked, and that was it.

No kids. No morning sickness, no cravings, no hyper-hormonal surges and interminable labor, no bulging, living form kicking you from inside—a real other little person within you, yawning, sucking its thumb, or shifting into upside down position to emerge. Not for her.

When the geriatric cat died, Iris had been there to see it, holding her orange and white familiar and watching the eyes dilate to huge saucers and solidify and the mouth bow into a toy replica of itself. Her soft and stubborn companion turned to stone in her arms, and Iris's heart broke, again. She and that cat had been together for twenty years. And now no more bumps of forehead and undercover snuggles and nuzzle of noses and the purest of pure love.

That was the part of life you could depend on: one thing or another would come along and pierce your sense of well-being and tear the living guts out of your heart. You had to be a combination witness and cockeyed optimist to survive that kind of onslaught, and you could count on its coming around. Amazing that so many people do hang on.

They say that pessimists are realists, and that it's the optimists who wear rose-colored glasses. They also say it can be healthier to see things rose-colored. So the upbeat people who seem sane are all actually slightly nuts, and the downbeat, bummed-out people are the ones who really tell it like it is. Go figure.

Great, thought Iris, that's just terrific. Maybe that's why Mother Nature put endorphins into our bodies, to give us a little drug lift when life gets to be too much.

A hot flash suffused her body from her stomach up into her neck and face, a blush on the inside. Her internal thermostat was going haywire. This was menopause. She found herself wondering if any man would ever desire her again. In her fertile years, her intensity about wanting children and her ambivalence about who their father should be had scared off or driven off a number of likely candidates. Now that childbearing had become academic, she wondered if she still emitted sufficient pheromones. It couldn't be too late for love, could it?

Each morning she took an estrogen pill, adding a ball of progesterone to simulate the monthly cycle of her childbearing years, and she gobbled down *tofu* and steamed soybeans almost daily for their phyto-estrogens.

Slowly her body regained its balance until she often felt like her old self again.

The up side was that now she found herself living in the real world instead of in some fantasy land where she was an iconic artist like Anias Nin or Ayn Rand, a mature yet seductive female creative who took lovers—while simultaneously running from and desperately yearning for a painless pregnancy and the idealized baby messiah at the end of the tunnel.

The morning was chilly and overcast. Iris had a fight with Bettina over the phone. It was ostensibly about a borrowed jacket, but she could feel the sharp edges of hidden knives piercing the folds of their short conversation. There was an edge between them. Menopause was in full force for Iris, although she looked the same on the outside.

Bettina had not yet begun the menopausal change and spoke of her periods' heavy flows and her monthly malaise in the careless tone most women of childbearing age use when referring to these cyclical things that were as close to them as moon-rise to ocean.

But once you had aged out of that cycle, reflected Iris, you saw the whole picture differently.

Like having children. As a free single woman during the first half of her reproductive years, Iris had fought tooth and nail against the manifestation of an unwed pregnancy. But now, at the swan song of any chance of biological motherhood, she ached for the healing rain of new life to moisten the parched desert inside her.

19 Jade

Today the *Jerusalem Post's* submission window was closing for its peace story competition. To meet that deadline, Iris had to get her entry to San Rafael's main post office before 6:00pm for the time stamp.

The Singing Stones of Jerusalem was Iris's entry. It was a fantasy, but its core was the vision she had been given during an indigenous *peyote* ceremony in Oakland.

Iris had written a tale of glorious possibility in which a few traditional American Indian people went to the Holy Land and climbed up to the sanctuary where the ancient Israelites' Second Temple had stood. On the plaza they erected a simple sweat lodge and entered it to pray, inviting the warring factions, Israeli Jews and Palestinian Arabs, into the lodge to pray for peace. These two peoples who dwelt right next door to each other were by turns invisible, fearful, and violently enraged one to the other. And each spoke a similar language that remained opaque to the other.

Inside the prayer lodge, the American Indian leaders, their friends, and some representatives from the Middle East prayed for peace, and for the spirituality born in this desert to shine forth. In her story, the Creator heard and maybe the people heard as well, because peace was born that day for the whole Earth.

Sliding into the driver's seat of her micro-van, Iris pressed the satellite radio button as soon as her engine growled awake. On the way to San Rafael's main post office, an old-time radio mystery kept her company and lifted the pressure to beat the clock. This was only the latest round in her familiar ongoing wrestling match with time. Time often didn't feel like her friend.

She ran into the post office, pushing by a harried postal worker. They can never get fired, they can only go postal, Iris snickered to herself. She'd made it!

Sliding the manila envelope over the counter, she demurely requested a receipt with a time stamp. Although as unlikely to win this competition as to fly to the moon, she appreciated the fact that now, at least, she was in the game.

"You have to play to win," she whispered to herself on the way out, and then she looked around sheepishly, hoping no one had heard her.

She found her way across busy Bellam Avenue to a local *taqueria* for a cooling plate of *flan*, taking comfort in the sweet slither of custard-y caramel down her throat.

"Save the world and save yourself, save the world and save yourself," she quietly chanted aloud between bites. She peered around again—no one was watching.

20 Aquamarine

Displaced east-coaster though she was, Iris finally recognized that this place, this Marin County plunked on the continent's far-western edge, had gotten under her skin, growing into her home-place.

She was sinking roots more and more deeply and reaching out to build a life here.

It wasn't easy finding a kid to adopt. After her own eggs had gone bye-bye, she had to jump through California's institutional hoops. She might never get to be a mother, in Marin County or anywhere else.

Adamant about finding a boy baby to raise—her very own son—Iris eventually conceded to the adoptions facilitator that a girl would be fine, too, and admitted to herself that every human being was a miracle.

For two weeks before her matched birth-mother, the controlling little bitch assigned by the facilitator, dumped her because inadequate support money flowed from her pockets to the pregnant teen, Iris had walked around happy, wrapped in a holy cloud of virtual pregnancy, the future mother of either a boy or a girl.

After the birth-mother had rejected her, Iris was too disheartened to find out whether the fetus had come out as a girl or a boy, leaving that fact to populate her overcrowded psychological netherland of lost desires.

But at least she had moved beyond her ambivalence. She had really wanted this boy or this girl and had opened her heart to the reality of that new child as part of her life.

Getting her heart slammed shut couldn't negate that. In her mind she had named that baby, now lost to her and the child of a gay adoptive single dad with deeper pockets. She had named the baby Chase, as in "wild goose chase."

21 Turquoise

The season was autumn. Spring's disappointing taste of motherhood had almost faded. Felix Moss was with her now. His love had brought the American Indian world home, into her heart and her bed.

Their new baby's name was Lorenzo. That was what his birth-mother had named him. The adoption facilitator had phoned Iris excitedly with the news that a young woman in Sacramento had given birth to a little boy, part Hispanic and part Irish, who needed a home now. He was full-term and healthy. Was Iris interested?

Her emotions teeter-tottered between delight and fear. She scanned her tiny bank account and glanced at her mid-fiftyish face in the mirror. Did she dare risk loving and losing a child again, after what had already happened? Something in her said yes, and she repeated, "Yes."

The adoptions facilitator, all business, admonished her for her hesitant tone, demanded a can-do attitude, and then gave her the contact information.

This birth-mother sounded shaky over the phone. But she told Iris she'd been impressed with the way her "dear birth-mother letter" spoke from the heart, and liked that Iris was an artist with a flower name.

"Lorenzo's father is an artist and writer; he writes comic books. But he's married," she added sadly. "Can you come get the baby tomorrow?"

Iris swallowed, thought about her magazine's deadlines and production schedule—and then said "Yes." For a nanosecond she was the hummingbird, shiny in the sunlight, cheeping, *Yes, yes!*

Driving up to Sacramento with a new car seat in the back and a pile of hastily-purchased blankets. newborn diapers, and onesies, plus bottles and formula packets, Iris had plenty of time to second-guess herself, her motivations, and her energy level, and to wonder whether she genuinely had anything to give a baby now, and a child and teenager later. But she shoved those thoughts onto the back burner and stepped on the gas.

Stopping at a flower stand, she chose a bunch of nodding Iceland poppies for Eileen, the seventeen year-old birth-mother. The blossoms fluttered in peach and yellow splendor like little Asian fans, and the buds with their hairy bulges underneath looked like fat or pregnant little animals.

Iris found Eileen alone, sitting up in her hospital bed and busily putting together an intricate jigsaw puzzle alive with tiny flowers. She welcomed Iris with a dazzling smile and then got up and walked her into the nursery.

And there was Lorenzo, ready to become Iris's little boy. He smiled up at her from his tiny crib, and his eyes, dark blue, sent a beam straight into her. She felt a heart pull she never could have predicted.

With Eileen's OK, she scooped him up and pressed him close to her, feeling his little heart beating against her own, and she made a silent promise to him to stick together and ride the rainbow of this world side by side from now until forever. "You do your part and I'll do mine," she whispered into his tiny ear.

22 Teal

Iris lowered Lorenzo into the crib, gently down and down, until his feet swept the sheet, and simultaneously scooped his body backward until midnight-brown curls met pillow.

Her hands lingered on the baby, squeezing his arms and stroking his face until he relaxed and yawned. She felt a fullness blooming deep inside, not like a mother who had birthed someone—how could she ever know that feeling? More like a healer whose medicine is helping bring someone back to wholeness.

She tip-toed from the baby's alcove out into the hall and entered the room she now shared with Felix Moss, bending forward to brush his sleeping face with her cheek.

Felix stirred, grunted, and abruptly pulled her down onto his chest.

"Don't ever try to surprise an Indian," he murmured.

"I didn't know I had any surprises left," she replied.

"Oh, you're full of them, my ageless white woman," he teased, his strong arms surrounding her in feelings of home.

"And you are so very full of it, my indigenous prince," whispered Iris.

"Prince? Hey, you said I was the King of Marin! That's what you told me," Felix replied, pouting.

"You are! You're the actual king, the real thing. You're an ethnic throwback wonder and landlord of all you survey, but it's a secret. It's such a big secret that even you didn't know it, so s*shhh*," she whispered.

"Lorenzo OK?" he asked.

"Oh, yeah, he's great."

"Let's sleep,"

"Yes, sleep," Iris said. Her eyelids lowering, she pushed closer to Felix under the comforter and drifted contentedly into dreamland.

White state capital buildings and sleek red cars made in Israel sat inside a Coast Miwok encampment surrounding tightly-woven baskets holding hot rocks and simmering acorn stew for the Big Time feast.

Outside their safe and sacred circle, curling smoke wafted upward, blurring the shoreline between hill and sea. The smoke shifted into pastel rainbows, then spun into one big white ring rising slowly to the sky.

23 *Cyan*

The world took a disastrous tumble. Lorenzo's birth-mother turned eighteen and had a change of heart, deciding to reclaim her baby. So now Lorenzo was gone. Her timing was within the law's window, so there could be no argument.

Iris still had an occasional foster care placement to anticipate, though. And she still had Felix Moss beside her. No one could have been more supportive.

But then Felix found reason to regret having ignored a cluster of early symptoms. He was diagnosed with colon cancer that had metastasized into the liver. Half of his large intestine was sliced out. It shocked everyone, nobody more than Felix himself, who adapted but could not believe it.

She offered him her two cents: a long-rumored cure using Essiac tea ingested twice a day for six months. Essiac, reputed to be an Ojibwa Indian medicine, combined equal parts of slippery elm, burdock root, Turkey rhubarb, and sheep's sorrel. The formula was given to a Canadian nurse named Rene Caisse, who used it to cure her own patients but kept it a secret as she had promised. Her nursing assistant made sure it went public after her own death.

Iris bought a pricey bottle of Essiac concentrate called FlorEssence at the health food store and gave it to Felix, and later bought him a second bottle. After that, she located a big bag of Essiac in powder form that came with strict instructions on how to distill the tea into stainless steel.

Felix moved back to Novato, a few miles north of San Rafael, to be closer to his family and his own children.

Months later, when he told her he had slipped off the Essiac wagon and was getting chemotherapy alone and following his doctors' advice, Iris's heart hit her stomach. She gently urged him to jump back into the Essiac routine, but he was distracted and barely heard her.

After many decades of doing good works for his tribe and others, and living for today as though there were no tomorrow—and, more recently, sitting in the back of his antique shop like a royal personage while buyers and well-wishers buzzed in and out—Felix Moss sank into a rapid decline and was soon gone.

Some time after losing Felix, Iris herself was almost gone. The cause of her brush with death was a psychic attack by a woman in whom she had put her faith, a woman whose actions revealed a cold-hearted, viciously sociopathic bully.

For a year after baby Lorenzo returned to his natural mother, Iris had worked with the adoption agency social worker Candace Malotte, with whom she shared her deep desire to parent and a great deal of personal information.

Her reward was a brutal betrayal. Never before had Iris felt so frustrated, so disempowered. How could Candy judge one forgetful and impulsive act so harshly? And how could she then 'diagnose' Iris with 'boundary issues' and proceed to destroy her good name with the Bundle of Joy Fost-Adopt Agency? Candace Malotte was no doctor and had no authority to diagnose anyone!

What have I done, Iris asked herself, to bring this firestorm down on my head?

She remembered that on the afternoon of the adoptions matching picnic, she had been swept into the children's reality. She had given her business card to Ian, the 10-year old bipolar boy Candy had urged her to adopt. With her card she also slipped him the golden dollar coin she'd loaned the boys for a game of finger-board.

She had forgotten the taboo drummed into the adults' heads earlier that day, that adoptive parent candidates must give nothing to any child in order to protect the other children from becoming jealous.

Iris had not understood that active spying (agency-termed 'observation') would occur at the matching picnic.

That was how naïve she had been and how ignorant of the fost-adopt agency's menu of questionable practices.

Candy Malotte had matched Iris with Ian, a boy Iris picked from a faded and incomplete photocopy, without mentioning his bipolar disorder. But red flags kept on popping up until Iris knew that this boy could not be a positive part of her dream family. Still, she wanted to meet him in person, so she went to the picnic where he would be. After that day, she wished she had not attended.

She and Ian, the bipolar boy, did make a connection, with Candy urging Iris to do that. Iris, knowing there would be no further contact, wanted to say goodbye to him. Her business card and the golden coin helped her do that. She smelled soap in his ear as she whispered goodbye. The taboo against giving a child anything had slipped her mind.

As it turned out, heavy-set black worker Candace Malotte, the agency's only minority social worker, had zero tolerance for her plans being upended by a client and zero room in her rigid worldview for adoptive parent candidates to screw up. She pulled Iris aside and screamed at her as though she were a criminal. Iris looked away—she wouldn't look someone in the eye while being screaming at!

Because her plans to match Iris with the bipolar 11 year-old had been thwarted, Candy kept pushing her false diagnosis. She disparaged Iris's motherly feelings toward a different 10 year-old boy she met at the picnic, Eli, and refused to help match them instead. And she denied her own hysterical on-site interrogation, claiming that Iris, damaged goods, was making it all up.

None of the agency supervisors listened to Iris tell her view of the incident, nor did they take at all seriously her written report about Candy's out-of-control outburst. Candy claimed Iris's refusal to look her in the eye exhibited furtiveness and said another adoptive parent candidate told her Iris was acting overly-friendly with Ian. But Candy herself had been urging Iris to stay connected with the boy!

Convinced by Candy that Iris was flawed, the agency's supervisors turned their backs on her without a word.

Iris never received a fair hearing from the agency, which meant that as an adoptive parent, she was out. The supervisors chose to side with one of their own, their token ethnic worker, against her, a five years-proven successful foster parent.

Demonizing someone by sticking that person with a vaguely-defined mental disorder or character flaw is an ugly and horribly dirty trick, since any emotion displayed in her own defense, such as tears, will surely be read as a symptom of that same disorder or flaw!

Bound and gagged: *voila*! In this way, the social worker both defamed and silenced Iris.

How did Iris learn her foster-parenting privileges had been revoked as well? She didn't. The agency simply stopped placing foster kids in her home. And since many child services organizations are networked. Iris realized she basically had been blacklisted by them all, in the present and on into the future.

Inside Iris, an infuriated animal paced. Imagined waves of rage steamrolled Candace until the woman and her excess bulk were flattened and completely erased from the world. Iris could not accept that all respect for herself and her good five-year foster parenting track record had been thrown under the bus—her good name trashed. And all future links with children who might need her had been torn away, with no recourse!

Her former therapist, to whom she ran when this disaster hit, was willing to refute the adoption worker's allegations and to stand up for Iris's sanity and her parenting credentials, but the agency never did call that doctor. All memory of Iris was apparently erased. It was the perfect crime, and Candace was the criminal. She had probably done this before. Iris's heart went out to the children, the birth-parents, the potential and actualized adoptive parents, and the foster care-givers whom Candy's self-serving judgments would surely ravage in the future.

Iris had felt too emotionally fragile—she would have wept wildly—to take advantage of the agency's narrow window in which a fost-adopt parent could file a grievance.

Ultimately the traitorous social worker's targeted campaign triggered a revisit of Iris's own hell: depression.

Depression sandbagged Iris.

Although she would eventually learn about the ways psychic trauma and mental pain can travel down into the body, she now was experiencing nothing but a series of pounding headaches and the sapping of energy accompanying her obsessive thoughts.

With what remained of her thinking mind, she attempted to tamp down her anger at Candy Malotte and censor its eruptions, but she could feel the rage burst through again, leak back into itself, and spread.

Feeling her basement floor sink under her, she ran for antidepressant pills and cognitive behavioral therapy to try to get herself in gear and purge the poison of the adoption worker's dirty bomb.

She had to battle her way up from the tendrilled infestation pulling her brain further and further down into a massive mind melt.

Iris struggled to regain—or retain—her footing.

Driving home from a talk therapy appointment in a mist of tears, she tightly gripped a slender bottle of antidepressants. She could see no way out of the grossly unfair railroading that had launched this sickness. She felt the heat of her mind catching on fire.

Psychically raped! Her mind reeled. The vision of world peace harvested from the *peyote* ceremony had faded into a pastel shadow. There was only so much loss she could take, and her meter rose to the top of the red zone and then beyond it. The sense of shame was so overwhelming that she frightened herself by considering suicide.

For weeks and then months, she slogged through inner swamps of depression, barely doing what she needed to do to keep going, dragging herself out of bed each gray morning until that too became too much.

After a while, her soft gray leather sofa was only an ugly lump in the room and too difficult to push herself down into, and she had trouble staying inside her own skin.

It's time now. She will have to hurry to outsmart the anti-suicide guard trundling up and down the walkway in his little electric cart. If they want to save women jumpers, why don't they have women guards?

Pointless thoughts. Tourists troop across the span, their white sneakers and skimpy shorts giving them away. Locals never dress so flimsily to traverse the moody icon that signals art deco to some, and to others, an arrow pointing to the end.

Wandering along the walkway to the center of the span, standing there, thinking about jumping. She thinks about how things haven't worked out for her, and about the city of San Francisco, that uncaring bastard!

She gets up enough courage to take action and then chuckles about the smart-phone camera in her pocket. What does she want to do, shoot a video of her decent?

Then why hasn't she bought a waterproof case?

Why is the technology revolution not enough for her? Why can't she just cocoon herself in her bed and binge on a series of TV shows until the storm clouds clear?

Screw it! Someone else can go ahead and change the world. "I hereby bequeath my task to that person," she says out loud.

The uncaring city skyline is a faraway sugarscape that glints like a row of stale marshmallow Peeps. The antidepressants aren't doing a thing. Her head is a blur.

This time it really must be time.

Time trips, time traps, time tripping up her trip. There isn't any more time and no reason she sees for time.

She climbs over the low international orange railing and stops on the ledge.

Fear paralyzes her, but her last dregs of courage propel her past fear. She doesn't stop to pull the camera out to shoot the show, she just goes. Feet first, she jumps into the record books.

Not the dent in the world she wanted to make, but hey, who's looking? Who is ever looking?

What barrier? No one ever mentioned a suicide barrier! She falls and falls, twisting and tumbling, terror ripping at her throat, wind tearing screams from her lips, and dies a thousand times and has time for a thousand second thoughts as love and regret intertwine into a tight noose.

No, no, STOP!!!

And then it stops.

And then she finds herself dry and unbroken inside the soft metal net of the new Golden Gate Bridge Suicide Barrier that has just been installed. The one emotion that surfaces in her roiling stew of a mind is—embarrassment. She must look like a fool!

"Just hang tight, Miss, the rescue crew is out on their lunch break. We'll get you up here on the snooker as soon as we can."

Embarrassment crimsons her cheeks. She feels like a total idiot, bruised and scraped and ashamed. She stands up and unsteadily walks, not knowing where to go. The net is springy and soft, pulling her down to her knees with each step. It's the kind of net acrobats use, only deeper and more metallic, and she can't find any place to flip it over even if she wants to, which she definitely does not. *Caught like a sea turtle in a gill net, she sits down to wait until the bridge guards deign to rescue her—with a snooker!*

Her backpack purse sits solidly on her shoulders. There is plenty of time to think about how she got here as groups of tourists point down at her, wave, and yell indecipherable words from the walkway above.

Notably, remarkably, the half-plunge has pushed her depression right out of her, for the moment anyway. Her head is clear again. A life-montage floods her resurrected brain. She is relieved, happy even, to be alive.

Some alternative therapy.

Blue Streams

24 Sky

Therapy and more therapy, along with some jobs of babysitting and some respite work not entangled with either state or agency 'child protective' systems, helped loosen the depressive straitjacket strangling Iris. Slowly, slowly, she emerged from the dark. A visit to a foster parent association event connected her with former colleagues not poisoned against her, and that helped as well.

In time, Iris gained sufficient perspective to re-frame the adoption worker's aggressive rejection and see her in a somewhat different light.

Time's merciful fog eventually sanded down the psychic attack's sharp edges, calming the violent waves of rage at Candy for her misjudgments in denying Iris fulfillment of her long-held maternal desire and potential.

The pain finally faded so Iris could venture out of her own bubble of awareness and witness the social worker's take on things, seeing its schism through the other's eyes as a gruesome cartoon projection from a separate and totally unrelated agenda.

Candy's way of doing her job skirted actual one-on-one communication with her 'cases.' Even when things seemed to be proceeding well, she would peek out at Iris through a curtain of clichés and pop-psych conclusions.

Before the rift, she had termed Iris both 'old' and 'smart,' as though assigning two weird attributes. During the toss of Iris under the bus, she complained to her supervisor that, although the agency had 'thrown her a bone' by letting her actually meet the adoptable boy pre-adoption, Iris still could not follow through.

A *bone*? What was this, a dog show?

Iris had hoped the social worker would remember the positive home study she had co-written, and the scores of other good interactions along the way, and eventually come to her senses.

Candy mentioned by phone that Ian would be freed-up for adoption in two months, as though that could still happen. And although she had assured Iris that this glitch would not stop her foster care placements, one supervisor at the Bundle of Joy agency chose to remove Iris from the foster parent roster without a word, triggering the blanket rejection from parenting assignments Iris had feared and traumatizing her further toward depression and suicide.

A minor taboo slip that caused no actual harm to any child had exploded, bringing out the institution's claws.

As the months passed and her sense of calm increased, Iris worked to soothe the residual pain woven around her traumatic humiliation and to recognize the inevitability of an explosive clash with a woman drunk with power and quick to jump to inaccurate conclusions.

In time, Iris accepted the end of her foster parenting odyssey, actually feeling relief that she was no longer under the thumb of an agency running under militaristic foster parenting regulations. To 'protect' children ripped from their natural homes—for either rational or questionable reasons—child protective agencies forced hired caregivers to jump through convoluted hoops, testing and retesting them and periodically writing them up with "deficiency reports." They were constantly watched and measured, except, oddly, during the time of each actual placement.

Foster parents feared losing their standing and their facility license, so they quietly endured the ongoing official intrusions for a paltry monthly placement salary and the 'privilege' of taking care of a wounded, traumatized child.

Another problem: foster care-givers received little information on a child's physical and psychological history or the reasons for their removal by the social workers, who hurriedly dropped the child off and moved to the next case.

After an indeterminate time living with a foster parent, the child was suddenly 'moved on' by the agency. Despite whatever love and attachment bonds had formed, the foster parent from then on was offered no contact with that child.

So what if the boy or girl felt abandoned by the foster parent and wrenched away again? Kids' feelings didn't count. The power these social workers wielded over the lives of children, parents, and foster parents was extraordinary.

Reflecting on all this, Iris ultimately saw that foster parents in the United States are treated by their agencies as indentured servants held in thrall. This insanity continues on, unreported and unquestioned: an American tragedy.

It was OK for Iris to be Iris, artist and free spirit. In an ideal world, she could accept and even celebrate her choices.

But this was the real world. To find self-acceptance, she saw she had to revisit her past and face the havoc that her worship of freedom had sometimes strewn around her.

To find her own peace, she needed to wade through the battlegrounds of her prior inner wars looking for collateral damage, answers, and forgiveness.

One night during this period of reflection, she dreamed about Angelo and Vicky in Belize and woke up remembering the sensual fling she had enjoyed with Angelo on the edge of the rainforest during an exotic vacation when she was 21 years-old and traveling with her radio engineer.

Her real radio man, her mentor and secret lover Robb Mast, had chosen another woman again—and she had felt the need to put miles and continents between them. In seducing Angelo in Belize, Iris had shown little respect for Vicky, his wife, and no regard for their large family.

A light bulb went on over her head. Could the vicious betrayal by the adoptions worker have been karmic revenge?

Iris called Bettina and reported the connection between her thoughtless affair in Belize back then and the social worker's ripping out of Iris's heart now. She also told Bettina that Candace Malotte, as it turned out, was not an African-American but a Belizian. Had this disaster been Iris's guilt-ridden subconscious erupting to sabotage her, or was it Afro-Indian vengeance magic after all these years?

Karmic tit-for-tat. In a strange way, the thought of that was a comfort, layering order on top of chaos, a possibility that felt like the lifting of a curse instead of a manifestation.

Bettina lectured Iris that it was masochistic to dwell on old guilts and sins. "Let it all go. So *what* if Candy's family was from Belize?"

After hanging up, Iris silently prayed a blessing for Victoria and Angelo, who surely after all these years were great-great grand-parents and ancestors of their own tribe.

She could see how her early worship of her own young freedom could have wounded other people and had done so.

> *If I can make it there, I'll make it anywhere.*
> *It's up to you, New York, New York!*
>
> —*New York New York!* Lyrics by Fred Ebb

The world wasn't always like that song. Iris's ego had grown overblown in New York City, with her own radio series, graduation from a great design school, and an outlaw affair with celebrity Robb Mast. She loved what was possible for her on Manhattan Island, loved the feeling that on some level she had 'made it' there.

But then she traveled far beyond that city's borders, and on a trip filled with numerous positive experiences, had caused considerable pain in a small fishing village on the coast of Belize by feeling so free to love a stranger and acting on that feeling.

She had been drunk on her own freedom. Facing those repercussions was another step on her slow trudge back to land and away from that uncompleted leap off the Golden Gate Bridge.

Six months later: a stocky figure with wavy chestnut hair squatted in one corner of a geometric maze: Iris sat among the stacked boxes from her recent move, artifacts of her existence and her journey.

"Too much stuff!" she exclaimed, feeling a headache coming on as she pawed through untidy piles of garbage bags and stared at crooked stacks of cardboard boxes.

She began to unpack and sort. I want it, she would think, and place an item over here. I don't want it, she would decide, and fling or toss another item far way, over toward a corner. I don't know if I want it—that rated a third shaky stack. Then there was the category of "someday it may be useful," and that was turning into a huge pile.

It was the only way she knew to cull her possessions.

This move to a different house was her chance to lighten up and take inventory. She wanted to get a handle on what she was carrying around and why.

For several hours she sorted, tossed, and bagged, and the original piles and stacks began to shrink.

Then she came upon a mass of photographs, and the rest of the afternoon was lost. One snapshot after another took her on a carousel ride of personal history.

She and her little brother Harry posing in front of their parents on the edge of the rocky river below Great Falls, Virginia, picnic items at their feet. Big smiles. Another picture: Harry and Iris with Heidi, their collie-Samoyed dog.

Miragold, their mother, always elegant, standing beside their father, U.S. soldier Meyer Miller, before he went off to Europe to fight the Germans in WWII—just after she was conceived and long before Harry would appear.

A war baby, that's what Iris was. A war baby who was still at war and forever embattled. When would her personal Allies appear to liberate her?

In a garden in Eastern Poland, Miragold wore a *kimono* and smiled coyly at the photographer. The sun cast white highlights on her smiling face while the apple tree behind her flickered with silvery blossoms. In another picture, Miragold wore a sailor dress, stylish even on no money.

In black and white documentary stills of piles of confiscated shoes and eyeglasses, the voiceover voice never informed you that many pre-WWII Polish Jews had dressed stylishly. Now their gray snapshots were fading and the anonymous people in them were much less substantial than their flimsy pictures. Miragold's sense of style survived her escape and the subsequent massacre of her family in Poland.

She could still smile coquettishly, capture a soldier's heart, marry him, and have his babies.

But something inside her had perished with news of her family's murder.

Iris was the child of a traumatized woman who walked around with a stunning sense of style, and who honed her acting abilities so everyone would be fooled by that effervescent persona and ignore her trauma.

Streams of impassioned criticism from her parents molded Iris into a good debater, while her mother's habit of interrupting pushed her children into becoming quick thinkers to slip their words in and be heard.

The true toxin for Iris was her father's rage. He claimed that she provoked him to it. Sometimes she *would* say something to trigger him, hoping for a different, kinder response. It never came. At other times clashes happened by accident between exhausted parent and exuberant child. And Iris would again run for her life, her heavy-breathing father chasing her—she ran for sanctuary behind a locked bathroom door. And where was her mother? Miragold thought parents should appear united in front of a child and would do nothing until privately chastising her husband later. To Miragold, marriage was a binding deal. 1950s mothers didn't sever purse-strings lightly. Miragold never stopped the war between her husband and their daughter. For the rest of her life, Iris would shake when she felt a heavy tread coming up the stairs or heard the pounding on a door. It was in her cells.

25 Slate

After stumbling upon a piece of chromotherapy software, Iris dove headlong into color therapy. The program she had discovered addressed healing of the skin and provided screens of different hues to be pointed at various symptoms, each screen filled with one pure color.

She found herself thinking, if green feels healing to me right now, I must have too much red in my life—like anger?

Numerous systems and theories crowded the color healing arena, and although not everyone would practice color therapy in the same way, this kind of work on balancing the oppositions made sense to Iris.*

The skin therapy program definitely stated that red improved micro-circulation and orange increased energy. Yellow was prescribed for detoxification, and green for relaxation. Blue was good for soothing the skin and the treatment of pain, while indigo alleviated allergic reactions.

Skeptical, Iris decided to experiment with the all-red screen, holding her outer forearm very close to it for three minutes as instructed. Her arm slightly reddened and grew warm where the red light fell, while the screen remained cool to the touch. She was hooked.

She ordered chromotherapy books and a set of color healing cards.

* *See page 333.*

Sitting on the floor surrounded by color charts, color cards, and colored scarves, she was overwhelmed by the cacophony. It was like eating an entire pack of assorted Lifesavers at once and trying to taste one flavor. Not that she had ever done that, but she could imagine! Even so, she started to think that getting all of the colors inside of her simultaneously could be some kind of mega-balancer.

For three days, Iris spoke with no one and hunkered down, bathing in the marbled swirls of color healing theory.

She made lists of disorders that healers both ancient and modern had connected with either an insufficiency or an overabundance of one hue or another. What kept surfacing for her was that either an absence or an overload of a particular color could present physically as a disorder, and balancing that color with its opposite hue could harmonize the body and spirit and neutralize the disorder.

The chromotherapy student was constantly cautioned to look for the underlying source of the disorder and treat that cause, since treating symptoms alone would, at best, constitute a temporary fix.

From the lists of disorders she compiled, Iris picked problems that troubled her now or in the past, plus a few others that either sounded familiar or piqued her curiosity.

Then she matched each disease, disorder, or affliction with a color that was linked with it on the disorders lists.

After that, she connected that hue with its opposite hue, and there it was—the healing hue for that disorder. Delving into her chromotherapy books, she copied down some glittering gems of color theory thought.

○○　○○○○

Color can express the way we are thinking and react back into us from our surroundings, raising or lowering our spirits.

○○　○○○○

Energy follows thought and circulates through the chakras. *Blockages or overstimulation of those energies can cause disease.*

○○　○○○○

Spectral color functions:

> *Red* **warms.**
>
> *Orange* **energizes.**
>
> *Yellow* **stimulates.**
>
> *Green* **harmonizes.**
>
> *Blue* **soothes.**
>
> *Violet* **transforms.**

○○ ○○○○

*An ancient belief is that color is life, the One Light,
the Divine Mind, expressed in the play of its parts. Disease
is the want of harmony and of balance. Using color rays,
chromotherapy restores that balance.*

○○ ○○○○

*Metabolism (balance) is made up of anabolism
(building up) and catabolism (elimination of toxins).*

○○ ○○○○

*Colors are chemical potencies and higher octaves of
vibration. Color rays can restore balance. The red ray
stimulates blood and liver. The violet ray destroys old blood
cells and stimulates white blood cells that combat bacteria.*

*The green ray is the balancer of red and violet. It
harmonizes via the pituitary gland.*

*Red, green, and violet are the central colors of
chromotherapy, restoring life potencies via chemical atomic
attraction and repulsion.*

—D.P. Ghadiali, *Spectro-Chromemitry Encyclopedia*

One post-rainstorm evening, cozy with her new-found bounty of color healing lore, Iris drove across the Richmond Bridge to a lecture in Berkeley. Her car nearly slid out of its traffic lane when her eyes beheld a most astonishing giant rainbow pouring its dayglow spectrum into Point Molino Park. After she had, regrettably, driven beyond its view, she caught sight of the other side of the rainbow through the passenger-side window, pouring its screamimgly bright colors into Point Richmond Harbor.

Iris continued to gather lists of illnesses that various colors are said to heal.

Along her kitchen windowsill, she arranged a row of spice bottles filled with colored water in spectral order. Backlit bottles of liquid red, orange, yellow, green, aqua, blue, indigo, and violet glowed in her dark kitchen.

Although not ready to share her colorful new treasury with the outside world, she had to admit to herself that she was feeling better in general, if only because she believed that through color she had a hand in her own healing.

She went further, starting to listen for a color's unique voice. Red spoke the loudest.

RED SPEAKS.

Exciting and energizing, I am growing you and flaring up within you always, every second of every day. I make you fiery and thrusting, wild and endless. I am unconquerable, and if you can see me and grasp hold of me, I will carry you over the top of any obstacle and bring you to your heart's desire. That is, if you will let me in to warm your loins and give you courage. Fly with me and live forever!

Use the harmony of green or the calming distance of blue after I am with you, to protect you, since I can get carried away.

If you ever feel intimidated, remember the fire in your belly that I am, and realize the worth of your ambitions and the unrepeatable flame of nature that you are.

Remember how long it has taken to bring you into the here and now. No one can be yourself but you, and there is no better time for it than now, in the red-hot light of the sun.

Iris kept listening for the voices of other hues and shades. In terra cotta, or Indian red, she heard the voice of Felix Moss, her late Coast Miwok Indian partner: what he might have said as he gazed down at the soil of his homeland.

TERRA COTTA SPEAKS.
The soil under my feet, the dirt, the Earth. The way things are and the way they have always been. I come from this place, now surrounded by a species of human that climbed up here after long boat rides or plane rides. Aliens, foreigners—bringing their own legends and mythology and morality, making some strange assumptions and jumping to conclusions. They call me 'an Indian.' I never called myself that. They started out saying we were savages and heathens, putting bounties on our heads. They are more open and tolerant now, when we are so few and wear the white man's clothing and speak the white man's slang.

We Indians still know one another. We nod to each other in the malls and at the gas stations. We joke together when we can. And we pray, always, to the Creator who made us. In our bones, we are in love with the Earth. It is our passion.

Some have grown old here with that love still in their hearts and those prayers just behind their eyes. Others have had their lives cut short.

Like the roots of a great tree that sink very deep and are unable to drink the light without help, our hearts grip and

sing so the tree can climb and bud and drink the fog and sun.
We keep Mother Earth stable and our lifeway solid. Some see
nothing at all in us. To this day they treat us like leaves under
their feet.

But we reach for the sky always, and we hold tight forever
to our love for this Earth that bore us and will take us back.

For aqua, the color of imagination, Iris thought of a visual
artist. She concentrated and could hear the voice of her
Asian friend, Kylie Chang. She didn't want to bother Kylie
in her secluded retreat, so she invented the whole interview.

AQUA SPEAKS.

It feels so free to be an artist! Sometimes that's the only safe
house and the only door out of the structure of concepts people
like to fling over you. They speak loudly with their "always's"
and their "never's," as though they come from some higher
place and have the right to judge and condemn you twice
before dinner. Sometimes your art piece says it all and makes
everything worthwhile, standing all alone in dignity as a
monument to the wild child inside of you and of everyone, and
what that child sees.

To have actual children and give up the center-stage of my imagination? No. I am the artist, the dreamer. My works are my dreams, they are my paintings on the refrigerator door. They are my offspring, and myself. Although I concede it might be glorious to be a mother—the all-knowing, the protector, the saint and shaman worshiped every day. I might have adored the adoration from a being I birthed. But right now, all I want to do is paint! And yet, having silent monuments standing alone, husks of trees cast in lava? Ah well, I don't need to tell you everything. You only get to see my free spirit—in my art!

To locate the voice of blue, Iris stared into a translucent deep cobalt vase, holding her gaze down there at the bottom long enough to sink into the blues.

BLUE SPEAKS.

You feel the water forever contained in its gravity cup, tracing edges of beach and bank. You feel the up side of blue, noble and tranquil, oscillating in ripples and rivulets. You want to drink cold water, your throat swallowing the sacred liquid and absorbing its vitality into each cell. You know that when you lift water out of its matrix, the liquid carries no color at all, only reflecting the sky or mirroring your face or the ceiling or random landscapes, as invisible as the air that sustains you along with everyone you love and know.

Hidden deep in the creases between worlds are the ones who have gone before, dying in the arms of your mind or the cracks between recollections. Imposing neither love nor anger, they dance on the edges of your trajectory. Having popped off the game board and out of the running, they still remember to swing to the blues. Sad that they were and are not now. Sad the way their outlines melt and all that filled in fades to white. What they are is only what they leave behind and what you remember. But they can still dance.

The following weekend, on a pristinely sunny Sunday, Iris and Ephraim put together a simple picnic and drove out to the tiny beach at China Camp Park. They unfolded low beach chairs and spread out their goodies and gear on a bumpy chartreuse towel draped over the pebbly sand. While Ephraim settled in to read the Sunday *New York Times*, Iris stared at the peaceful waterscape and daydreamed on the voices of green.

GREEN SPEAKS.

I swing my head to see a cliff crowned with trees and a hill sitting further behind, each of them still green despite the approaching summer heat that will dry non-native grasses golden brown. Still green despite global warming and pollution and despite a series of greedy companies competing for more and more green land to plow under for their cheaply-built condominium complexes with minimal-to-no greenbelts and zero environmental protection for the evicted or extant wildlife.

Green is alive. And green means life—from the bunches of glossy newborn pale green leaves to the mature dark green foliage or needles that drink sunlight and carbon dioxide and breathe out oxygen the four-leggeds and two-leggeds need to live.

Some American Indian people have called plants "the standing-up people," as though the only difference between plants and animals were the restriction to one location that a plant's roots require.

Any stop-motion film of blackberry vines tendrilling out to wrap around the woody stems of neighbor plants displays an active instinct at work, if not an intelligence. And why not an intelligence? Would it freak out hikers and gardeners to see living proof that the plants surrounding us are actually thinking, feeling beings?

How did the standing-up people learn to absorb sunlight and transform it into chlorophyll they could store? How did they learn to live? And without the standing-up people, how would animals have come to be? Or how would we have come to be? What if animals had never evolved from sea to land? Would the plants, which also came to shore from the ocean, by now have their own cellphones or writhing networks of neighborhoods?

Probably not. Everything depends on everything else, and we are entangled in so many ways today, caught in our nets of obligation and frustration and our layers of desire.

Green is harmony, and peace. Soak inside the green hues for too long, and you can grow lazy. Hammocks are especially relaxing when slung above the green undergrowth between trees.

A couple strode by, the young man gripping a yellow-green Frisbee. Iris continued marinating in the color green.

She wondered why so many Americans without a sprig of Irish ancestry celebrate St. Patrick's Day every March, passionately wearing green in its honor. Could it be the joy of draping oneself in green and drinking green beer and counting it a sin to go out in public that day without any green clothing?

Or is it all a primal celebration of the green we eat and the green we spend and the green we breathe and walk upon and dream about for holidays, while stuck in gray cubicles typing gray facts into our gray computers?

Green is a sanctuary. Green is a living destination. Iris sipped her coffee, a drink brewed from the fruit of a green bush—addictive but not illegal. She and Ephraim divided a power bar made of seeds and fruit bits held together by sugar syrup, each and every ingredient the offspring of a green plant: sugar cane stalks, almond trees, coconut palms, and grape vines.

Ephraim stood up and walked around, his sandals loudly crunching pebbles. He was still here with her and wasn't going anywhere until she did. She knew that, and relaxed. No more cougar on the prowl for her. For the moment at least, he seemed like her sanctuary and her destination. He was a green garden oasis on her long and winding road.

A small blonde boy in a striped green and blue shirt ran by them, gripping a chartreuse bucket and dayglow green shovel, determined to join his family, his tribe.

A lone egret lifted off and flew in all its whiteness around the point and out of sight, likely in search of greener pastures a-brim with flashing fish.

The tide was turning. It was starting to come in.

26 Ocean

One warm evening, Iris outlined for Ephraim the vision of Middle East peace she had received at the Native American *peyote* night and the story about it she'd written.

Inspired by this approach to peace, Ephraim urged her to get out there and spread the word. "Maybe you could connect with some Middle East movers and shakers on both sides of the Israeli wall, plus the media outlets over there," he enthusiastically suggested. But Iris, recalling prior conflicts and afraid to reach out now, resisted the idea.

"Maybe. But before getting into any of that, I want to tell you about the two weeks in my 20s I spent as a guest of Napa State."

"Napa State Hospital? You? *Really*?"

"Yes, really," she said. "But I don't know where to start."

"You could write it down for me," said Ephraim.

"No, that's too clunky," said Iris. "I know, I'll tape it as though I'm somebody else."

"Somebody else?" Ephraim echoed.

"You know, like I taped that description of my early dating life—in the third person," said Iris. "'Iris did this, and Iris did that.' It'll be easier to get it out that way."

"OK. If you think that works, go home and record a tape. I can meet with you tomorrow at Leeds Café at 1:30.

If you've got something done by then, you can play it for me. Or else call me before that, and we can get together another time soon."

The next day at the appointed hour, Iris handed an ear bud set to Ephraim and plugged a second set into the audio splitter plug for herself.

She had struggled to retrieve the snippets, shards, and fragments that bubbled to the surface. This twisted piece of her past had not been simple to reconstruct.

Over twin coffee cups, they bent their heads to listen.

"Hey Brother Comic on the Golden Gate, Golden Gate, Golden Gate Bridge ..." Over and over sing-songed the woman with the black hair three beds down on the observation ward of Napa State Hospital's Building A. "Hey Brother Comic on the Golden Gate, Golden Gate, Golden Gate Bridge ... Hey Brother Comic on the Golden Gate, Golden Gate, Golden Gate Bridge ..." until her eyes lit on Iris and she suddenly stopped. "Got a cigarette, honey? she inquired, her voice in a normal tone.

Iris hadn't been a smoker before Napa, but soon after her arrival, she started to smoke tobacco under the influence of Debra, a depressed young woman with slash scars on both wrists. New pals, they started hanging out together on the ward.

One day a funny thing happened to both of them that pierced the pain of Iris's persistent headaches. A group of professors came through the ward on a tour. As the well-dressed group straggled in, Iris and Debra were standing near the door. One of them happened to ask his colleagues an erudite question about symptoms. Iris, historically no slouch in the academic department, answered his question with a tumble of multi-syllabic words, throwing in a few complex concepts. The professor listened raptly until Iris went on a little too long, and he then realized she was not a fellow post-doc but a patient!

That encounter brought the pair a good laugh later and briefly eclipsed her world-ending grief over her loss of Nathan.

But it descended again. Without Nathan, there was no future, no hope. He was Hawaii, he was royalty, he was her soulmate, for God's sake! How could he forget her? He apparently hadn't agreed with her on that point, or else he could sense her inner vacillation, her oscillating ambivalence.

The sad fact is that she had feared her mother's negative judgment if she were to bring home as her life partner an exotic non-Jewish man. She had been afraid to make a commitment that risked her being disowned, and imprisoned by that very fear. Nathan must have picked up on her conflict and its fearful core, because he suddenly vanished, taking a college girl on a Valentine's Day road trip—a girl Iris knew he had deflowered.

Desperate and furious, Iris let herself do what she'd never done since she was three years old. She threw a tantrum!

She lay down on the hardwood floor of her Russian Hill flat and kicked and screamed and sobbed and pounded her feet. She put maximum energy into her fit and lost herself in it. Literally. Because in the middle of all that kicking and screaming, she tried to will herself to stop, and her brain short-circuited. Something switched off—that was exactly how it felt. Like a punctured boat in a hurricane, she felt her very being get sucked into a whirlpool.

A sudden constellation of symptoms overwhelmed her. Sleeplessness, repeated wakefulness at 4:00 in the morning, a sick headache that would not lift, listlessness, inability to complete a sentence, and a loss of interest in everything.

She would refer to her papers and paintings as though created by another, saying, "She did good work."

Iris was inconsolable, her sharp headache persistent and unending. Without Nathan, she was lost.

Freaked out by these sudden changes, she forced herself to trudge to different doctors. Seduced by her extensive vocabulary, the doctors could find nothing wrong. Until one day, a new doctor noticed the flat monotone of her answers and diagnosed her correctly. Iris was suffering from clinical depression.

Nathan called her once during those weeks, surprised that she was ill. A week after that, he called in the evening and implored her to drive over the Golden Gate Bridge to his Sausalito house immediately, saying he needed her.

But for Iris, it was too late: she was already socked into a very low and very dark place.

She did go to him, though, uncertainly braving the Marin Headlands fog bank in her questionable car. She found Nathan in the middle of tripping-out on a psychedelic substance.

He said, "I should marry you," sounding as though he thought he ought to do that. She agreed. But then he realized that something wasn't right with her. Like most people do in such a situation, he acknowledged zero responsibility for her state, saying only, "You've been eating too much candy lately."

Committing herself to Napa State Hospital was her idea.

A male friend (who meant nothing to her because he wasn't Nathan) drove her north to Sonoma County.

Once at the hospital, Iris self-committed, which, during that era, meant that she could also self-release. The asylum campus overflowed with characters. The hippie population, male and female, hung together at one table in the observation cafeteria as if they were a distinct ethnic group in a schoolyard.

On her first day, a disheveled Iris carrying a lunch tray was headed toward the hippies, sure they were her people, when a bearded man in a paisley scarf, a man the others called Dr. Zoom, slid over to make room and yelled out, "Welcome to the arena! It happens to the best of us!"

Twice a week, the hospital gave Iris an hour of private therapy. During one session, when she kept moaning on about Nathan, she looked up to see the therapist with his arms stretched out like a crucifix. That grabbed her—although it might have made a stronger impression had she been Catholic.

Mandatory group therapy took place every afternoon, the staff struggling to get silent patients to speak.

And there were the meds, distributed in tiny fluted paper cups in late afternoon by nurses who did everything they could not to look you in the eye.

After a week and a half at Napa, Iris was surprised by a visit from Nathan Paniolo himself, her obsession and her love. He had gotten permission to take her off the grounds and drove her to a leafy country spot for a picnic. She begged him, "Marry me, Nathan, marry me!" He stood and stared off into the trees, replying, "Not today, not today."

Eventually Iris earned a Napa Hospital campus pass by helping serve food to the lunch line. With the pass, she could go outside, even all the way to the edge of the campus where a small store sold real banana splits. That was the golden dream of the patients, and many hopeful pilgrimages were made there.

A few 'inmates' sold marijuana joints outside for a dollar. In retrospect, those might have been the best meds offered at Napa State Hospital. Other drugs seemed to be distributed no matter what the patient's diagnosis. Those meds, with "zine" at the end of their names and seemingly tailored to schizophrenics, tended to induce zombie-like side effects with a dose of tardive dyskinesia *thrown in*. Patients sluffed around in slippers with tremors or limps to accompany their blank masks.

If it hadn't been for the dentist list a week later, Iris might have stayed longer at Napa, since her headache and her Nathan-obsession were continuing on in full force. A young girl whose bed lay directly across the aisle on Iris's ward returned from her appointment with the hospital dentist with all of her teeth pulled out. When Iris was told her name was on the dentist list for next week, she said these immortal words to Debra, "I may be crazy, but I'm *not* that *crazy!*" and immediately wrote a letter to the hospital requesting her release.

A few days later, a special staff meeting took place. Iris and a group of well-dressed doctors sat around a conference table. After it was agreed that she was "neither a danger to herself nor others," they said she could leave, and she left Napa State Hospital with all of her teeth.

Dr. Zoom, the scarf-wrapped mad chemist of Haight-Ashbury and now her friend, wanted to leave as well. Iris convinced Joanna, an old friend from junior high who had driven up from Southern California to Napa State Hospital to spring her at her parents' request, that Dr. Zoom needed a ride to San Francisco. Halfway to the city, Joanna realized that Dr. Zoom was in the process of escaping. She kept on driving.

Dr. Zoom vanished into the Haight-Ashbury district, and Iris never heard from him again.

"I guess you can chalk that guy right up there on your list of disappointing men," commented Ephraim, unwinding his legs from the table leg, his arm from around her shoulder, and her extra set of ear buds from his ears.

"Present company excluded," Iris grinned.

"Of course, of course. Want a refill?" asked Ephraim.

"Eph, is that all we're *ever* going to do in this world, drink coffee?" asked Iris.

Ephraim stood and stretched. "I'll bet you could have used a good strong pot of joe at that Napa place," he said.

"Thanks, but I'll wait until tomorrow for my next cup," declared Iris. "At least I feel better now that I've winnowed all that trauma down into the contents of one little audio cassette. ”

"A true accomplishment," Ephraim agreed, walking her to the café doors. "I can't wait to hear how you ultimately returned to the living."

"Maybe tomorrow I can tell you," she responded. "I'll make another tape for us."

"See you tomorrow then, same time? Or call me, and we'll convene when you have part two."

27 Azure

To wrap up her odyssey of depression and recovery, Iris recorded the second part of her narrative and met Eph a few days later on the patio of yet another coffee house, her two sets of ear buds and audio splitter in hand along with the cassette deck, so they could listen in tandem.

This place sold interesting finger foods. She munched on *dolmas* as they sat with their heads close. Again, Iris had dictated the narrative in the third person—as though it had happened to somebody else.

After her parents flew her to D.C. from San Francisco minus her belongings, which she had left behind in the care of a former roommate, she continued in her clinically depressed state—the same interminable headache, the same lack of incentive, the same slow responses, and an inability to hold onto a thought or complete a complex sentence. Alarmed by the changes in Iris's behavior, her parents arranged for her to see a therapist at a university medical center.

She was extremely grateful for that, and grateful as well that one day her father returned from his court reporter work assignment with a message from Humphrey Osmond, a British psychologist and writer whom Iris happened to have read and admired. It was rumored he had dropped acid with Timothy Leary. Iris's father certainly had never heard about that.

After recording the medical interview, Meyer Miller had confided to Dr. Osmond that his daughter was depressed and "speaking of ending it all." The doctor's response was, "Be sure to tell her that acute depression is time-limited, and she will come out of it."

Those words, repeated to Iris by her father, were a sliver of sunlight in the dank cellar of her mind. The depression was time-limited! Who knew? None of her other doctors had told her that. Either they hadn't known or they hadn't bothered.

Remembering the link to sanity her father had brought to her, she thanked him, sending him a smile of love inside a prayer directed toward the deep space afterworld. This was the first time she had done that. Some might have branded her an uncaring bitch of a daughter, but her memories still overflowed with his rageaholic rampages and the terrifying poundings on the door of the bathroom where she had run to lock herself in and hide. She was grateful to her father for his years of support and for his pride in her art work, but she was even more grateful for the strength of that bathroom door lock, along with the fact that after he cooled down, he had never removed the lock for better luck next time in reaching her with his fists.

In her parents' house again after her wild years in San Francisco and her wounded weeks at Napa State Hospital, she remained depressed. Her father and mother bought her a puppy after she asked them for one, letting her choose it and name it. Iris chose a blonde cocker spaniel, the saddest-looking puppy at the shop, and named him Kimo—Hawaiian for James. Her mother fell in love with Kimo and kept him long after Iris had her sanity return and moved up to New York City to resume her life. When Kimo died, Miragold mourned the dog bitterly.

On a day in mid-June, a week after the puppy came to live with them, he did something cute and Iris laughed.

Standing nearby, her mother turned to her and said, smiling, "You just laughed!"

That was the first time Iris had laughed in months. She later read that an attack of acute depression usually lasts for four months. Just as Dr. Osmond had predicted to her father, the disorder lifted, and she slowly came out of it. Over a few days, the headache flickered on and off and on and then faded away. Her personal sky went from gray to blue, as though after a thunderstorm.

Color reentered Iris's world, along with her intellect and a mega-dose of perspective. She still missed Nathan achingly, but with a lessening of that desperate intensity. One week after her return to normality, Iris flew to New York to rent an apartment and then moved away once more from her childhood home.

Ephraim handed her back the ear buds. "Can you ever forgive Nathan for leaving you?" he asked.

"Maybe," she responded. "I mean, basically, I *have* forgiven him by now. He needs to forgive me too, though, because it was really my fault he left me. I hate to admit it, but it was my ambivalence that pushed him away, and the cultural bigotry rearing its ugly head in my family, or maybe my buying into my parents' thoughts that they had so much to say so about who my life partner would be. All of that. I still do miss him sometimes."

"Let's go." Ephraim walked out to their cars with her. He was quiet and then asked, "Could you ever forgive your dad for terrorizing you?"

Iris stopped walking and turned to him in tears. "What happens to the fear and the agony and the pain?"

He replied, "I don't know, kid, but you wouldn't want to build a sculpture to it, would you? *Uggglyyyy!*"

Ephraim hugged her.

"I guess not, no," Iris replied. "No sculpture."

He was right. She didn't need to carry the memory of all that ugly stuff around forever. She wouldn't. It was over. Even her father was over now, gone into history—the parts she knew of him and the parts she never knew. She could shake it all loose and let it go, and even send her dad love for giving her a life out of his passion for her mother, the beautiful Miragold.

"You're going to make a really fine psychologist, Eph," she said, and kissed him. "I'm feeling so much better!"

"I love you, too, Iris. Bye. See you soonish."

"Yeah, I know, 'We have to stop now.'" It was the classic shrink's goodbye.

"You can leave your check on the table," he responded in kind. When he drove away, she was smiling.

The air felt fresh and breezy, with a slight chill. The Golden Gate Bridge gleamed burnished orange in the flickering light, with cotton candy wafts of fog adrift across its towers. Clouds speeding toward Oakland began covering the aqua sky in layers of gray.

Iris shivered as she headed for San Francisco and the Apple Virtual Vacation Center. Appropriate weather for a trip to Eastern Europe, she thought, gray. She had always envisioned WWII as taking place in black and white, since most of the photographs she had seen of the battles and the Holocaust were gray-scale and muted.

She remembered how startling it was to recognize lush green woodlands behind her mother's family photo in a fading gray snapshot and to realize that eastern Poland, or *Poyln*, as Yiddish-speaking Jews pronounced it, must have been suffused in color as vibrant as the bright and varied hues of Marin County, California. Unbelievable, but true.

Reviews of Apple's Virtual Vacation Center had rated it extraordinarily high. People reported that their experiences rivaled reality. Iris wanted that to be true. She could not afford an actual round trip excursion to eastern Poland and Ukraine, but she knew going there was what her inner doctor was ordering. She had to see where the tragedy had happened and stand up for her murdered family members, and this virtual vacation was the closest she could manage to doing it.

Big teardrops of rain pelted her as she pushed open the heavy door of the Apple Store. The space was that company's usual spartan metal and glass cube. A big glass staircase sat squarely in the middle of the high-roofed arena, with the usual buzz of device buyers, window-shoppers, and black-shirted associates clustering around it. The genius barkeepers were busily solving hardware problems along the back edges of the cube. Envy wisped through Iris when she thought about Apple's Steve Jobs, someone younger than she was and with less design education, who had managed to change the world.

Maybe that was because he hadn't spent his formative years seducing movers and shakers, she sardonically told herself as she climbed up the glass stairway to the Apple Virtual Reality Lab.

Gear on. Stand inside the corral. See the IMax surround melt into real space before and behind your eyes.

Eastern Poyln/western Ukraine was green and hilly, with trees swaying in a late summer breeze. The train's engine pulled a string of small cars, chugged along, rickety-rick, clickety-click, along the narrow-gage tracks into Rufalev Station, once the pride of the Jewish *schtetl* town of Rufalev, located near Sarny city in what was then Poland. Iris sat stiffly on the hard bench and shook to enter this space. Now was now and not 1938, when her mother's friend succeeded in obtaining the needed papers for her to flee the increasingly anti-Semitic oppression and set sail for America.

Her mother had intended to stay in America, with cousins in Baltimore, for only two years and then join her pioneer sister in Palestine, but circumstances had intervened— ghastly circumstances. She received a letter soon after the war reporting that her parents had been herded to the edge of town under gunpoint along with the rest of Rufalev's Jews, and then forced dig a massive trench. And then all of them were shot dead inside that trench, by Ukrainian soldiers drafted by the German Nazi authority.

There went her mother's brilliant mother and scholarly father, her sweet sister-in-law, and her dear little nephew. After learning this, it had not mattered to Miragold where she went, where she stayed, or whom she married.

Iris could have virtually experienced the time of that horrific disaster, September 9, 1941, while seeing the location. She could have witnessed it all inside an invisible bubble of safety. But she chose to stay in present time and see the

Rufalev of today, now a sleepy agricultural town, and no longer a part of Poland but set inside the newly-drawn borders of modern Ukraine.

Walking around Rufalev, Iris was shocked to see blocks and blocks of razed land, flattened dirt where buildings had once stood. The site of the schtetl? Apparently, nothing else was ever built on that ground. She saw some simple bungalows nearby, a few older buildings, and several Russian cars and pickup trucks. The place was still poor, its current inhabitants mostly peasant farmers and merchants. Rufalev projected a tawdry liveliness. Clusters of gossiping women and beer-guzzling men dotted the plank sidewalks. On a church wall, a bronze plaque glared in the sun, its words in Polish, Ukrainian, and Russian.

> HERE STOOD THE RUFALEV JEWISH CHURCH
> DESTROYED IN SEPTEMBER OF 1941
> BY UKRAINIAN SOLDIERS UNDER NAZI COMMAND.
> NO RELIGIOUS SCROLLS WERE FOUND.

Through her digitized glasses, Iris could read a closed-caption English translation that ran along the weeds.

No scrolls. She already knew what had become of the Torah scroll from the *shul* that church had been. Found by Jews after the war in the soggy mud of a stable, it was reverently escorted to Israel, where it sat now in its own ark in the center of a synagogue, *Beit Chaim* (House of Life) built to house that rescue-Torah.

She studied the landscape through her VR glasses and communicated her instructions to them. The GPS led her to her destination, a long, flat meadow carpeted in wildflowers. This was the site of the mass grave of Rufalev's Jews.

Iris sank down in the soft grass and sobbed. Her family! Maybe they didn't speak the same language and wouldn't have understood one other, but they were her blood, they were hers! She knew for certain that if she herself had been a baby in their house within the exact same time frame, she would have been bayonetted by a Ukrainian Nazi thug and buried here, too.

Her bath of tears did not bring the curtain down on her inner holocaust as she had hoped. It was the howl and sackcloth-rending of a frustrated soul unable to set right one of the world's most evil and hideous wrongs. Her rage erupted. If the Ukrainian murderers who did this were to pass by now as old men and she were certain of their identity, she would shoot them, stab them, or water-board them into admitting their guilt and then submerge them to drown! She had no doubt she would do that. What does that make me? her reflective mind whispered. Just as bad! The answer came too rapidly to censor.

The hilly Ukrainian scenery faded into pastel snapshots as she hurriedly walked to the train station in the center of this flattened town of Rufalev, or Rufalevka, to ride away on the train and end her journey. She was moving so fast that she nearly missed seeing the sign: "KOSHER-STYLE DELECTABLES" on the front window of a small café constructed of wood planks in the Jewish schtetl style. She stopped in her tracks. On the picture window painted below the words was a very large, very yellow six-pointed star, this retro café's logo. On the star. painted in crude rust-colored strokes, was the word "JUDE." This 'kosher-style' café came complete with a gaggle of Polish and Ukrainian teenagers slouching at small sidewalk tables in front, munching bagels stuffed with bacon or washing bulging down pastrami-on-rye sandwiches with big glasses of milk. Yeah, sure, *kosher*-style! thought Iris.

The Star of David on the window echoed the yellow cloth star the Nazis ordered every Jew in countries they conquered to sew upon their clothing. Weeks or months after that branding, local Jewish families were jammed onto cattle-cars on trains bound for gassing or slave labor, or else shot dead where they stood. It was the same way Native American nations had been treated—genocided across the United States, tribe after tribe derided, diminished, or destroyed—and later mythologized in a red-white-and-blue version of '*kosher*-style.' It is said "*der feurer*" got the idea for Nazi concentration camps from studying American Indian reservations.

The order had come down from Hitler's Alpine retreat to quickly clear this Polish border railroad town of its Jewish population. *Schtetl* residents were to receive no warning.

ACHTUNG!

CLEAR RUFALEV STATION FIRST!

This railroad station stood in exactly the same location as the one the Nazi leadership had circled on their maps—an early part of their "final solution" people-moving system.

Iris boarded the small train, sat down in a passenger car, and rode away from this place, rickety-rick, clickety-click. Away from a grave with no headstones, a destroyed synagogue with no sacred scroll, and a Ukrainian or Polish town with no Jews and no memory, only razed blocks and blocks of dirt and a *"kosher*-style" café.

After leaving the Apple Virtual Vacation Center, Iris drove through San Francisco. Although she was certain that there was no one chasing her to kill her, the ancestral thread had been broken, utterly and violently.

Iris's mother grieved for her family the rest of her life. Yet she had managed to marry a Jewish-American soldier and raise their children. Iris prayed, "Thank you, Mother, for my chance to live. Please forgive me for the hurt. Please be at peace. I love you, and I turned out OK. You were a *great* mother!"

She drove home exhausted from her crying and raging on the virtual tour. The Holocaust was now no longer black and white but filled with the reds of anger and bloody flesh, the browns of war and murder, the soft greens of Poland/ Ukraine, and the glaring yellow of a giant six-pointed star.

She almost phoned Eph to describe her visit, but something told her not to. Instead, she stood in her kitchen sipping tea and staring at the cobalt blue drinking glasses aligned like transparent troops and the colored jars of water glowing in the afterlight of day, until it grew too dark to see.

28 Cobalt

When Kylie Chang's paintings exploded in flames and her Mill Valley rental instantly sank into ashes like a cardboard Western movie set, a thick cloud of drifting black smoke stopped the football game at Tamalpais High School.

All of the players from both teams stood silent, their heads bowed as though in mourning.

A horse rode off into an aquamarine sky while a perfect ear of corn split into a thousand atomized kernels and burrowed into the crevices of the boy athletes. A caped woman ran across the redwood tops, and a Native American baby grew up, became a leader, and after a good long life, died of old age. A tiny dancer emerged as the most graceful person in the world, twirled around in the sky and then shot upward in a huge pirouette, while giant graceful Hebrew letters spelled out flaming prayers. Three horses ran their first and only race.

Meanwhile, twenty-five years of radio shows spoke among themselves while atomizing into a rusty heaven.

Decades of videotapes of cable TV programs Kylie Chang had produced instantaneously reached the eyes of a million dead viewers, who were so thankful something could finally penetrate the afterworld where they dwelt without corporality or cable.

A closet full of clothing from the 1960s, 1970s, 1980s, and 1990s evaporated into a too-quickly obsolete fashion show, while, crossing the Richmond Bridge, an architect who had experienced great loss witnessed the huge plume of black smoke shooting up and drifting oddly over Mill Valley. He was so moved that after reading the newspaper report about the house fire, he mailed Kylie a check for $100 along with a note of sweet compassion.

On receiving that note at her temporary retreat in the psych ward at Marin General, Kylie's tears erupted, the first since the fiery holocaust destroyed her home and the artifacts of her creative work, and she began to heal.

She tried harder than before to stop beating herself up for leaving two scavenged sofa cushions stacked vertically near the dangerous floor grate heater, so near the grate that the skittish cat the landlord gave her might have jumped up and toppled them, and probably did. And for the mistake of letting herself get so down on her paintings because so few people seemed to care about them, that she found herself thinking that her paintings might as well not exist.

Was that thought toxic enough to singe her aura and provide kindling for the eruption of a giant fire?

It was this horrific explanation that rang true to Kylie. She'd had no inkling before this that a person's state of mind could bend reality, but now she knew better.

Even though deep inside her tranquilized hospital torpor, Kylie swore she would never again let herself twist into someone so blindly self-negating.

Over and over she tried to discuss her guilt and self-blame with the hospital therapists. But all she kept hearing back was that in order to move on, she needed to forgive herself for letting down her landlord and not taking better care of the property he himself had referred to, post-inferno, as a firetrap.

She could not seem to communicate to them how her warm-green-toxic thought about her paintings deserving to vanish because no one cared about them had possibly acted as a kind of mental kindling for their own fiery destruction.

The doctors just shrugged and upped her meds.

Psychiatry is still in its infancy, reflected Kylie wearily. It hasn't gotten into the body-mind connection very much yet, where the physical and metaphysical can collide so horribly and so catastrophically.

29 Sapphire

After their separate lives happened to dump them off at a random slide show documenting a trek through swamplands, Iris and Ephraim got in touch again, huddling in a back corner of the bookstore and whispering the latest news to one another. When Iris heard about Kylie's fire, she shuddered in shock. That Mill Valley house fire on the *Marin I. J.*'s front page—that had been Kylie's cottage? No!!

Back home, Iris threw her *New York Times'* and *Marin Independent Journal*s into a ragged pile and phoned the number she had for Kylie Chang, trembling as she imagined what had become of the giant painted canvasses stacked against her friend's walls.

A man's voice answered. Iris hesitantly asked for Kylie. "Oh, Kylie's over at Marin General for a rest," came the too casual reply. "Sure, you can visit her there."

Ephraim went to the hospital with Iris to see Kylie. According to the newspaper report, no one knew what had set the fire off. Kylie had barely escaped it. Turned to charcoal dust and melted glass were three decades of her paintings, along with treasures and heirlooms and archives and clothing, and priceless inherited dish-ware, and windows and walls and doors and beds and plants and landscaping—the staples of her life.

Iris and Ephraim entered the hospital's psychiatric area where the doors were too wide and the walls were too bright. They ambled slowly down a series of hallways to a common room furnished with eclectic castoffs and containing a small kitchenette where patients could brew tea and microwave snacks.

And there was Kylie, her long black hair draped over the teddy bear her therapist had given her. She told them the therapist said the bear was connected with "heart therapy" and re-parenting—that the pressure of the stuffed animal hugged against her heart would tell her unconscious that she was loved and not abandoned. Teddy bear medicine was probably at least as effective as some of the other drugs they prescribed here, thought Iris.

The ever-hospitable Kylie invited them both to sit down. Iris plopped onto the sofa while Ephraim claimed an overstuffed chair across the coffee table, but set close enough to hear the other two and to talk with them.

He and Iris listened as Kylie recounted her sleepless nights and fiery flashbacks, and the repeated tortuous episodes of self-blame.

The staff kept stressing to her that the fire had been an accident. She agreed that it was nothing she had envisioned when she woke up that morning feeling sick and chilled. But she insisted that her negative thoughts about her art must have contributed to a blurry lack of ordinary vigilance. No one could convince her otherwise.

She had felt cold that morning and, with a twinge of guilt, had turned up the hall thermostat to 80 degrees. She hadn't noticed that the cat had knocked the surplus sofa cushions onto the living room's floor furnace grate.

Voracious Mr. Fire noticed, however, and proceeded to explode her home, devour her work, solarize her mind, and in five minutes, reduce the wooden walls and everything inside them to a moonscape of cinders and shards.

Kylie recounted that after that blistering day she had withdrawn from all friends and activities. Blasted saucer-eyed, she and the cat both stayed in a motel for a few days courtesy of the Red Cross, and after that, stayed with a compassionate friend of a friend.

But the insomnia had become overwhelming, and she had admitted herself to the inpatient psychiatric ward at Marin General Hospital, where talk therapy and anti-anxiety pills attempted to ease her time of grieving.

To Kylie, it felt as though the house had been a part of her and that part of her had died. She was suffering phantom pain for lost walls and melted windows, precious art by her and others, and only-copies of super-8 movie reels and radio recordings that archived years of her work. But, thank the fates, her housemate had been away all day.

Rumination on her actions just before the fire, plus evidence of the insane power of her unconscious, had pulled the capacity for pleasure right out of her. Now even the taste of mint chocolate chip ice cream was water in her mouth.

As she mumbled and muttered on, Iris noticed Kylie's body language: her shoulders hunched inward, her head drooped down. But when she would recount the strength of her dreams and her gratitude that she and the cat and her roommate remained uninjured, her head would rise and her back would straighten.

A few times, Iris caught Ephraim gazing at their friend, his eyes bright with admiration.

Kylie smiled. "You can make changes in the world and think you've done something important, right? While all along inside you, the fires are still raging, you know?" She ruefully tossed her long hair.

"I *do* know," said Iris.

"One day," continued Kylie, "I stood in my rented house with all my stuff. The next day I stood on the very same spot on a pile of charcoal!

"The psychiatric ward is its own country," Ephraim said, scanning the robed figures sleepily navigating around their central oasis.

He gazed fondly at the two women, his friends. Beautiful. His eyes lingered on Kylie, still engrossed in reliving her hideous encounter with Mr. Fire.

In a reverie of compassion that unexpectedly turned sensual, he virtually stroked the twin mounds of her breasts. Leaping back to consciousness, he jerked with a guilty start.

"Did you ever feel anything like that?" Kylie asked him softly. His face flushed as his eyes met hers.

"Like what? Sorry! I wasn't listening."

"Oh. Never mind then. I was just telling Iris how it feels when you look into your living room from the hallway, and there's this gigantic orange cloud crawling over the ceiling in curling tendrils. It's like seeing a fish swimming through your bedroom. Impossible, you know?"

"Poor kid. You must have been paralyzed," he responded. "Hey guys, I think I need some fresh air. You take your time, Iris. I'll be right outside."

"Be back to see you soon, Kylie. You just hang in there. Things are going to get a lot better than you think they are. Don't let the bastards grind you down."

Ephraim surprised both women by crossing the seating island and pulling Kylie up for a hug.

He whispered to her, "Tongue the pills, kid, don't swallow them. No zoning-out right now. You're OK."

His breath tickles, thought Kylie. She giggled.

"See you guys later," he called at the threshold and then was gone, taking his disturbing male energy with him.

Although nothing was said about Ephraim during their next ten minutes together, Kylie and Iris had both felt a shift. Each sat in silence, nursing her own thoughts. Hurt and relief marinated into a strange stew for Iris, who was once again feeling drawn to Ephraim. She tried to cast her uncertainties aside and focus on Kylie, who needed as much energy as possible now. After all, no one owned Ephraim—he was a free agent.

Still, seeing Eph hug Kylie that way had stung. Maybe she'd been mistaken, and he was only pouring compassion into Kylie. He couldn't help being sexy, could he?

"Hey," exclaimed Kylie during Iris's solo visit several days later. "I found something of yours. It survived the fire in my metal filing cabinet. The edges are like—you know, that funny bread you guys eat at Passover?"

"*Matzoh?*"

"Yeah, like matzoh."

"The edges of what?"

"Damn Xanax, or whatever the hell they're giving me! I can't even finish a thought!"

"Be gentle with yourself," said Iris. "You're a genuine disaster victim, a survivor. Give it some time."

"Time to feel like a total loser, you mean! Damn, why didn't I just look at the floor grate before I turned on the heater that morning? Then everything would have been different. And why did I have to get so bummed that no one was buying my paintings that I had to think that thought?"

"*What* thought?"

"The thought that lugging around my paintings was a burden, and that nobody cared about them anyway, and that they might as well not exist!

"Do you think that caused the fire? *A poison thought?*" I seriously doubt it, Kylie. But even if that thought *did* open a hole in the shell of your protective aura or something ... In Judaism, we don't believe God punishes someone for a thought, no matter what the thought is. You didn't get up that morning and say, 'I think I'll set the house on fire today.' Right?"

"No, no way! I loved that house, except it was chilly when I moved to Mill Valley after living in San Rafael, and I wasn't used to the micro-climate change, and I didn't adapt well, either for me or for my pets, and my animals got sick, and then my old cat died from a cold. The two iguanas never recovered right, and then they died. I was mad at the house because I thought it had killed my animals, when really it was my own fault! The heat there was inadequate, even in the living room with blankets and a space heater on.

"I was mad at that house, but I loved it in other ways. So I kind of buried my rage at the house, which was really at its owner, because I had complained to him about the lack of heat over and over, and he didn't do anything about it. He said to use space heaters! Did you know the bedrooms weren't heated at all?

"I told him space heaters were a fire risk. Ironic, huh?

"Damn, I was always so careful to unplug those heaters before going to bed and before going out. I was very conscientious about fire safety. And look what happened!

"I know the landlord loved that place. He'd inherited it from his uncle. What did I *do*?" Kylie dissolved in sobs, alarming the two nurses hovering at the edge of the lounge. They instantly rushed over and pulled Kylie to her feet, patting her and gently directing her toward her room.

"It's good for you to cry," Iris told her. "Get it out, but don't beat yourself up. It was just the last day in the life of that house and probably meant to be. No one got hurt."

"Except for the plants! All of those camellia bushes, and the strange plants in the side yard, and my mother's lemon tree in a pot on the patio. They're all sticks now!"

Kylie quieted down to sniffles while one of the nurses went off to get more drugs. Iris let her thoughts swirl until she knew what to say. "Look, I'm not your shrink or your mother-confessor," said Iris, passing Kylie some tissues as they moved slowly toward her room. "I do have to say this, though. I know you, and I know you didn't mean for that fire to happen. Do you really think your unconscious is that powerful? That it could rise up and will the bad house and under-performing art to be gone and then manipulate the universe to manifest it? I'll tell you something, Kylie, if your unconscious mind is really that powerful—"

"Then I should be committed?" Kylie whispered thinly.

"No, damn it, then you should *not* be committed! You should run right out of here and start your own mystery school! You might have some extraordinary energy in there, and if you could channel compassion into it, then maybe you could save the world, or make it better, anyway! Look, nobody was killed or hurt and no neighbor houses were burned down—even that cat the landlord gave you got out OK! You should thank the universe for that."

"Oh, you really think so? Wow! It did show me there's a lot of love around. There I was above the fire, up on the street, and the house below was exploding and torching and roaring, and all the neighbors who had been hiding out in their hillside homes were surrounding me with such love. I said something like 'I always wanted to meet you, but why did it have to happen like this? I could have had a party.'"

She leaned back in her hospital bed and yawned.

"Time to go," said Iris, and then she added before she could stop herself, "Anything I should tell Ephraim?"

"Just tell him thanks for being here for me, and being my friend," Kylie answered faintly.

Then she sat up. "Hey, I never did tell you what I recovered of yours. What the fire forgot, you know?"

Halfway through the room's wide doorway, Iris turned. "The thing with the *matzoh* edges, you mean?"

"Yes. It was your story, '*Borderland.*"

"Oh that—my high-tech attempt to get pregnant story. You can keep your copy. I'm glad it didn't turn into toast, though. I never did send that manuscript out. I thought about it for *Ms.* magazine, but—too personal."

"Maybe the universe is telling you to read it again now that you're wanting to adopt a child," said Kylie, swallowing another wave of remorse to empathize a tiny bit with Iris.

"I'm not thinking so much about that now. There was this sociopathic adoptions worker who threw a big fat monkey wrench onto that idea."

"Oh, no! I never knew that!"

"That's a story for another time. I'm okay with it now. But maybe the universe *is* telling me to read my story."

"That universe, gets you every time!" said Kylie. It was good to hear Kylie laugh.

After the hospital visit, Iris needed to clear her head. She pulled out the step-though motorcycle she maintained for occasional back road jaunts, strapped on her red helmet, and kicked the engine alive.

The little bike easily climbed the neighboring hills, and the wind cradled her as she swept through residential blocks and past green lots, speed not to fast, not too slow, just right.

This motorcycle was an instant rolling respite from the pressures poking at her every day and the money dogs nipping at her heels.

She thought about Kylie Chang's hillside home, and a great sadness filled her for the lush camellia bushes and the plant with strange little blue fruits all in a row that she'd noticed and appreciated there.

On impulse, she turned the bike downhill and drove to the site of Kylie's house, slowly passing the charred ruin with a prayer for whatever needed a prayer in there

Something so very solid and now so totally gone. It showed her how evanescent things were, and how important it was to value every day and every person, and every hour, and every breath.

She pulled onto an empty straightaway. Kicking the little bike's gears up to fourth, Aarona Iris Miller screamed down the avenue at what felt to her like the speed of sound.

At the hospital a week later, Kylie and Iris hugged with real warmth and then sat down to trade small talk and insights. Kylie seemed much better. Iris offered her the pint of ice cream she'd brought, and Kylie eagerly shoveled it into two glass bowls, happy to play hostess.

Kylie said the pills and talk therapy were helping, along with support from a Red Cross disaster counselor.

"I've been taking stock," she said. "I know I still exist—surprise! I'm stripped of my belongings and also some of my burden. But I'm coming back to life. I know I'm strung out, but because I survived the fire, there's hope."

She said she was not going to let anyone's negative energy, including her own, make a mush out of everything she'd accomplished. More good was still possible to do, to contribute. She said her friend Phil had found slides of her burnt-up larger paintings in a rescued metal file cabinet.

Once she had accepted that her paintings still counted for something and found out they did still exist, at least as slides, Kylie decided to work on resurrecting the images and celebrating their continued existence on the Earth.

She told Iris that what mattered was where she would put her attention from now on. It was matter of choice, and a choice of matter.

She said she was remembering more and more that people mattered, her projects mattered, life mattered— and she mattered! That was all she had ever been given to work with anyway, and she had forgotten it.

It was what all the suffering was about. But she would never let herself negate her life or demean it again. From now on, she would remember her gift was still hers to give. She knew now that she had survived to share the fruits of her search and her journey.

Iris took it all in. She was happy to see Kylie coming out of her inner prison and getting better. But Iris was not comfortable hearing all this. It was like being claustrophobically trapped inside the tent of a born-again believer. Kylie's new inner fire was that intense.

As it turned out, Ephraim had been to see Kylie twice between Iris's hospital visits.

A twinge of jealousy tore into Iris when Kylie said something about his visits. But then, Iris had never taken Eph that seriously, and vice versa. Maybe she was too strong for him. How come the weak ones got all the attention?

Kylie wasn't weak, though. Walking back to the ward entrance, Iris felt ashamed of thinking so uncharitably about her friend. And it wasn't about strength or weakness anyway, it was about love. Maybe I need to have more love going out to get more love coming in, she reflected.

Iris saw her occasional interludes with Ephraim as welcome parentheses of peace in the turbulence of her life.

Feeling the wave of electricity surging from Kylie in their goodbye hug, Iris hoped Ephraim would not let his heart get completely swept up inside Kylie's blossoming.

Iris meandered along a creekside path in the park across from the hospital. It was low tide, a twice-daily phase she disliked because it made the air smell dank, salty, fertile—and depressing. She turned back to her car. Some environments brought her low. She needed to avoid them, or else counter them with substances, mantras, sunlit meadows, classical music, and/or intercourse of one sort or another with an upbeat person.

That evening Iris phoned Ephraim and asked him over. She knew her assertive tendency to call a man broke a social taboo and could be a turnoff, and she hated that. All of the liberation in the world, yet if the man didn't think of it first or think he thought of it, any move toward connection was usually doomed. But with Ephraim, it should be no big deal, since the two of them knew each other so well. Before he

213

arrived, Iris pulled together some cheese plates and opened the *pinot noir* to breathe.

Ephraim didn't mention Kylie that evening, and Iris was finally learning the difficult lesson of tact. They watched the sunset through her work room window, and after that indulged in some channel-surfing and undirected conversation. When the wine had blurred the edges of things, they slipped into a sweet round of lovemaking. She slithered out of her top and her camisole and enjoyed Eph's sharp intake of breath as her shapely full breasts poured into view and into his cupped hands. "Twin treasures," he murmured. The memory of how he'd looked at Kylie sent Iris a flinch of fear, and she held on to him tightly.

They writhed across her bed in a warm embrace very comforting to Iris, until his need turned urgent. She swam with him into the waterfall of his desire. Before drifting from their union into the surreality of her dreams, Iris thought about Kylie back there at the hospital, alone in her narrow bed. She was climbing out of the cinders of an atomized past to grab hold of pleasure and let it pull her back into the world.

"I heard you had a baby with you for a while. What was it like, playing mommy?" asked Kylie.

It was on Iris's next visit to see her hospitalized friend that the subject of Emilio came up. Baby Emilio had shared Iris's world for a seemingly endless time that really spanned less than two months.

"Oh, it was terrible and wonderful and ordinary and strange," she replied, "and expensive! Do you really want to hear about that now?"

Kylie picked at her throw blanket.

"Yes, I do. After what happened to me, it's hard to accept being comfortable and safe. But now that I'm coming back into myself and looking at my future, I've started thinking about kids myself. Maybe I can still have one. I'm not that old."

She glanced at Iris, who could not help wincing.

"Oh, sorry! Anyway, go on, tell me. I want to know everything."

"I can give you some highlights," said Iris, shifting her body in the lounge chair and then getting up to pour herself a cup of instant coffee.

After checking again that Kylie really did want to hear about her toddler, she pulled a notebook from her purse full of notes about Emilio that she still carried around with her, notes written while she was his mother.

Dear Mama Miragold,

You said when I was a mother, I would understand. So now that I've had this toddler with me for over a month, playing baby while I play mommy, I do see it differently. You never told me how that egomaniacal little "other" can pull your attention and suck at your energy. And keep on doing it and doing it.

But cute? My friend Bettina calls him a yumball. He's definitely a milk junkie—he has to have that bottle with him at all times, always filled. You should see how he shakes it back and forth disapprovingly when it's empty. He's a little pantomime artist. He knows so much! Speech will be the icing on the cake.

Only, now the birth-mother wants him back, or so she says. It's been a week, and she hasn't gotten herself over here yet to pick him up. My adoption facilitator says she's seen this before, and that the birth-mother will probably never show up.

Part of me is ready for all this stress and energy-drain to be over, to get my room back, and uninterrupted nights.

But another part of me can see some future for this kid and me.

As long as Emilio is with me, it feels like I'm not aging anymore. Instead of growing older, I'm going through the new mom thing!
Miss you, miss you.

All my love,
Iris

For Iris, becoming a mother had been nothing like the nine month evolution of a biological pregnancy. Instead, it was sudden and shocking, like plunging into a cold swimming pool on a blazing hot day.

She had wondered if it would be fair to impose her neuroses on the little Mexican-Irish tyke now encamped in her room. She didn't know if she had it in her to take up this challenge filled with ongoing commitments and isolating bonds, or if there were still enough nurturing tissue in her scarred heart to be the mother he needed.

One thing about him, though, he sure did know how to look after his own interests. He was tough, in his baby way.

The walls of the hospital disappeared for a while as Iris pulled Kylie into an unfamiliar maternal world.

The squishiness, the extreme smoothness of skin. The lines in the middle of his forearms and on the thighs for a fat wrinkle, as though he were right out of the box and still creased. The wrinkling of his nose when he smiled or laughed.

That smile like a sunburst through clouds when he woke up all cheery. The absolutely crushed and crumbled devastation of his face awash in tearful misery. The frustrated flinging of the toy across the room at me, the throwing of the bottle in rebellious rage. The biting of the bottle nipple and stretching of it—ouch!—with his tiny strong teeth until it nearly tore and I could feel his rage in the flesh of my own breasts—even at arm's length when he didn't get his way.

The shaking of his head and his whole body up and down to say "Yes!" when he understood me and agreed. The giddy, silly shaking of his head and body "No!" and the rolling of his eyes when we played at being dizzy at the breakfast table. The dizzying twirls in the living room until he fell down laughing. The dance of the diapers, one in each hand, around and around in an indigenous stomping. I danced with him.

*The tininess of his fingers. The way he smiled when
I called his feet "footsies." The gentle, embarrassed way he
gripped a naked breast when I let him see them, to see what he
would do. The way he tried to put his shoe on and peeled the
Velcro straps off and on, off and on. The writhing butterball
of his constant motion in the afternoons, when he was too full
of milk and stimulation. The milk addiction so pronounced
that he could never be without that full bottle and its nipple
very close by.*

*The accusing look as he shook the bottle to show me it
was empty or low. The sense of time—now, and now, and* now. *
The inability to wait, and the constant crisis of desires unmet*
NOW. *And, thankfully, the instant transition from misery to
curiosity when a new object would capture his attention and
catch his fancy. The way he said, "Oooohhhh!" when he saw
a big red ball.*

Iris shared more with Kylie, telling her that Emilio came
into her life and showed her by his demands what is needed
for a life, any life. He would express delight or tolerance or
impatience or rage so clearly. His voice would ring out like
a clear little bell, "Ma! MA!!" to get her attention. "YEAH?"
she would respond in the same tone. And when she would
drift over to the computer to get some work done, taking her
attention, he would come up and slap the keyboard! BANG!

As long as she had him in her house, she was magically transformed into a new mom with childcare concerns and a tight schedule. Her time alone became expensive and precious. Each day, it cost her between $25 and $40 to buy the time to work undistracted.

Sweetest of all was his dropping the big ball in his hands at daycare and sticking out both arms to be picked up, with no doubt whatsoever that she was his Ma. And that radiant smile in the morning as she left him there.

On the mornings when he woke up neither grouchy nor tearful, he was a smiling, moon-faced *Buddha* standing up in his crib across the room and gripping his blankie and bottle, the kit he needed to meet the day.

One afternoon, he was playing with his toys outside the low kitchen window, safely visible or audible, while she sat at the breakfast table working at her computer.

When it had grown too quiet for several minutes, she rose to check on him on the other side of the window. She found him curled into the fetal position on the welcome mat at the kitchen door, in the cute overalls and little running shoes she had bought for him, gripping his milk bottle and blanket, fast asleep.

Her heart gushed open to love as she lifted all 25 pounds of him and gently laid him in his crib, still tightly gripping his blankie and bottle and still deeply sleeping.

At the drugstore after her visit with Kylie, Iris paid for her hormone replacement therapy pills with a check she hoped would clear and walked slowly into the crystalline California day.

Later, changing channels with the remote to find something decent on TV, she finally found a classic old movie and lost herself in it.

After the movie came the news: national, international, regional, and local. And there was Jefferson Stetson sitting at his council desk, opining on a current San Rafael crisis.

Seeing him still rattled her feelings. Shaken, she had to admit to herself that she didn't know how long she could stay away from his vortex. That was what he once said a friend of his had called it, "my vortex."

She got up, entered her kitchen, and dug two scoops of butter pecan ice cream from a frosty carton.

A wonderful refurbished laptop computer she had just purchased online for a song was winging its way to her, Jefferson was still out there almost within reach, and Ephraim was only a phone call away, as were Bettina and Kylie. She let a spoonful of the buttery frozen delight melt on her tongue. Maybe, just maybe, things were looking up.

After her fire-induced trauma had calmed somewhat, Kylie left the hospital and moved in with someone advertising for a roommate: a Mill Valley lady with a reclusive teenage son.

Part of the move-in deal was an instruction to Kylie to ignore the boy hiding in his room with his computer, and to ignore the consistently silent mother and son interaction.

As a trauma survivor, Kylie felt she might be able to offer both of them some help. But the lady, both her landlord and her housemate, refused to hear a word about it.

So at risk of eviction, Kylie held her tongue.

That was a good thing, since she needed to focus on her recovery. It was going to take her months to sort her tattered belongings, particularly the items that had escaped the fire but had gotten drenched in the fire hose floods. She liked the physical and emotional space this hilltop house was providing.

Over the winter, she ignored the boxes salvaged from the basement of her former home, now stacked on the earthen floor below this house. When she finally felt up to sorting the things she had formerly deemed extraneous enough for subterranean banishment in the rental that burned down in October, she was rudely awakened to the damage suffered by her valuable papers, drawings, and clip art collections. Even the papers supposedly tightly sealed inside clear plastic cartons had been soaked through.

One morning, she took a deep breath of the aroma of mold and plunged her hands into the nearest carton. But it was an impossible struggle for Kylie to extract even one folder from the semi-solid pulpy mass.

She turned the plastic carton over and shook it. Like an upside-down cake in a buttered pan, a solid block of paper pulp slipped onto the basement's dirt floor. She picked up the block, wincing as slimy strips came off on her fingers, and carried it outside into the sun, where she proceeded to pull layers of folders apart from one another.

The old magazines she tossed over to a trash pile. But the papers were precious, laden with evidence of her life's journey—sketches, poems, essays, even old love letters.

Kylie pretended to be an archival museum worker restoring the Dead Sea scrolls. It made this work feel better. Slowly and carefully, she peeled one sheet from the next and laid it out to dry.

Although delicate work, it was strangely tranquilizing. The physicality of it and the immediate reward when one sheet after the next of fragile and translucently wet paper came out of its matted nest in one piece, calmed her. She enjoyed the resurrection of a poem, essay, or drawing.

Kylie saw it as a gift and something of a miracle that these penned or typed images and snippets of thought—and, indeed, she herself—still existed. The sub-floor gas furnace had exploded a few minutes after she ran out. The monstrous Mr. Fire had come so very, very close.

Now that she was awake again, she needed to simplify her life. Even after the furious flames devoured eighty per cent of what the fire marshal termed "the fire load"—a.k.a., Kylie Chang's material possessions—she *still* had too much stuff. The declutterization imp tried taming her and failed!

She laughed in surprise as a tiny multicolored newt fell out of a lump of sopping news clippings. The newt was slick, curvy, and plastic-looking, with large, alert eyes and four puffy out-sized feet. At an inch and a half long, the entire animal resembled a two-month human embryo.

After scooping up the newt with a dry sheet of paper she slipped beneath it, she gently slid it into a glass vase.

She later washed away the bits of inky paper that clung to her hands, her face, and her long black hair, and drove down the hill to the coffee shop. Along the way, she set the little rainbow-hued newt free at the base of a bush on a marshy inlet near some *tules* (bullrushes). Before she let it slide down and out, she held the clear glass up to see the little creature one last time. Unafraid, it moseyed toward the edge of the tipped vase and the location of her mouth, pulling back in alarm as she kissed the glass in front of its tiny face.

When Kylie returned to the hillside cottage and opened the front door, her telephone was ringing. She ran to her bedroom to answer.

It was Ephraim, her new sweet love.

Today was warm and glorious. Birds swooped down from the trees along the mountain roads. Iris gunned her motorbike, speeding across the empty intersections and down the byways. She could still get to the meadow in time to meet Ephraim inside their ten-minute window.

It was hard to know what to say to him. Their recent dates had been thick with emotion, mostly his. He was softer somehow, and tense with unspoken despair. Iris recognized it as love. He must be falling in love with her, deeply. She should be thrilled.

Her hand banged down on the handlebars as she recognized once again the rebellious core of her hidden self, never satisfied with the world's gifts to her. Why was she always and endlessly reaching for the brass ring dangling just beyond her grasp?

It was the hope. She suddenly recognized that the real addiction was hope itself and not hope's object, not even the human love object. Hope and the thrill of fear, the fear of rejection, the fear of failure, the fear of judgment, and the fear of being found wanting. Or else fear that the love object might turn on you and bite and scratch and devour you, reverting to a strange and lethal ogre.

It made the love object both powerful and terrifying.

Iris hated to admit, even to herself, that something in that fear made her feel more on the edge and therefore more alive. Was this her souvenir of a battered childhood?

She must have gotten an extra dose of testosterone in her fetal stage, she concluded, since acting as "the beloved" she often found boring. She would rather act as "the lover," the one who got to chose. She wanted the choice of who, when, what, and even if.

It amazed Iris how clearly her mind worked on two wheels! She leaned into a wide curve and felt her body lift in that lyrical motorcycle rider way: an indescribable high!

Then she swung into the meadow's parking area, geared-down to idle, and pulled the little bike up onto its kickstand. Anticipation and dread spiraled inside her.

The picnic with Ephraim was peaceful and satisfying. The turkey sub and lemon-lime soda he provided hit the spot. Ephraim shifted uncomfortably when Iris launched into a story about seeing Jeff Stetson on television and wondering what it was inside him that made him want to run the world. After that, she segued into admiring Daniel Firesmith and his leadership in Indian country, and the passion and genius in him she could recognize.

"I realize they both have Aries sun signs," she said, "and so did my dad. I wonder what that means."

"Any shrink could figure that out in three seconds," Ephraim snapped, the edge in his voice stabbing through their serenity. "Still working out that daddy thing? Still trying to win over the old man? I'm an Aquarius," he added.

"My water carrier," she murmured, reaching out her fingers to sift through his dark blonde curls. "My sweet, cool drink of water."

They leaned toward each other and kissed. But for her, something just wasn't there.

He drove to her place later on and ended up staying the night. They giggled and wrestled in her bed.

The next morning, he made waffles for her in an old waffle iron she never used.

He was being so sweet. Tentatively, she started to let him further in. So there was an extra sting when he finally came out with his secret, that Kylie had taken his heart and he was in love with her. She needed him now, after the fire, and they would soon be moving in together.

Hearing his story, his unanticipated truth, Iris felt her head nodding sagely and understandingly. But then her head started to ache and her chest began to feel cold, as though a flickering flame had gone out.

Generally on Saturdays, Iris tried to keep her mind away from paying bills or doing any work. Saturday was *Shabbat*.

She was not an observant Jew in the traditional sense, but had her personal ways of connecting with the Divine. Today, to honor her own history, she decided to dig into her collection of papers.

In her mind's eye, she could see the consuming flames of Kylie's devastating house fire where flash drives filled with backup copies of original art and design work had instantly vanished. The hard drives inside four computers had warped so badly that they were unrecoverable by the best drive-saver company.

As for Kylie's DVD and CD disks, cassette audio tapes, and film reels, they were all gone, atomized.

Any data not stored off-site had been devoured by the voracious roaring inferno, all within five minutes.

Astonishingly, papers, slides, even drawings on vellum compressed into metal flat files or filing cabinets had survived, some with charred edges but readable centers or images. Even papers out in the open, suspended in hanging folder files on a rack, made it through the fire, though the table under that file folder rack completely disappeared.

Kylie's fire was a shocking reminder of what was real and what was unreal.

With all of its bells and whistles, the digital world still wasn't real. If her friend had thought to store her data in cyberspace, what some called "the cloud," it would have been backed up on a server far away from her doomed home and would have survived.

Fortunately for Kylie, one small laptop had previously malfunctioned and was still in the shop awaiting a part, so some of her digital art and poetry and the bare bones of her novel received reprieves from a fiery demise.

Here was Iris with her own archive. Boxes and files of writings from her past lay piled on the floor all around her, with two brownies and a glass of milk within easy reach. She dug in, read, culled, and sorted.

Her rediscovered writing surprised her. Because she didn't recall having ever produced some of this, she was a fresh eye for pieces her younger self had churned out and believed worthy of typing up. Some of the writing was darn good, she thought, meriting a warm feeling of accomplishment and a well-deserved wrist-kiss from herself.

Seeing the reflection of a whole human being in her forgotten words, someone who lacked nothing and could do anything, nourished her. It was a soothing fiction, helping compensate for skills such as rapid typing and fluid bike riding, that took a type of bodily coordination foreign to Iris. Maybe it was the way she was wired, something that accompanied her left-handedness.

Although thoughts of Kylie's beautiful and fulfilling continuing adventure with Ephraim frequently disturbed her nights, time and distance were helping Iris to lighten up, back off, and accept their reality as reality.

Reading her rediscovered words today felt especially comforting, like having a cuddly shrink in your pocket.

Indigo Clouds

30 Dawn

Dipping into the study of color therapy was like eating one potato chip—Iris wanted more. Hunched over her laptop, she built a circle of color slices that followed one after the other in order, with each hue like a section in a full-color "half-grapefruit," nestled next to an adjoining grapefruit section: the next hue in the spectrum.

She set the full-colored 'half-grapefruit' circle tightly inside a square. Then she created other squares containing three grapefruit sections, or maybe pizza slices—each color slice kissing two of its opposite-color slices so the points of three colored triangles touched in the center of that square.

This was repeated with all eight colors, each with its opposites, until there was a grid around the center square that held the rainbow-hued "half-grapefruit."

Together the squares made a quilt and a visual analysis of each color in balance with its opposites.*

Iris was pleased with her modular grid. She considered printing the squares one by one on a large-image printer, and piecing together a giant paper quilt.

*(See page 333.)

Or else she could print them on inkjet canvas squares to sew into a real cloth quilt.

One great thing about color therapy: there were no side effects to this medicine. Someone interested in using colors to heal could easily assemble a list of disorders and use this quilt chart to create a custom healing path.

Excited by the fruits of her research, she phoned Bettina and described the color healing quilt. Bettina really wanted to see it, so they arranged to meet in a café in Point Richmond, a little town on San Francisco Bay mid-way between Berkeley and San Rafael. Iris brought her laptop.

After placing her coffee and pastry order, Bettina launched into a tale of overwhelm and confusion.

Iris listened. She pausing her inner chatter to hear Bettina's string of complaints and yearnings, meanwhile recognizing a recurrent pattern lying beneath them. Bettina grew aware of Iris's deep attention and thanked her for it.

Iris told her she was picking up on the way that Bettina spent too much time analyzing herself and critiquing others who crossed her path, with the result that she was isolating herself and shortchanging her life.

She silently added that Bettina was becoming too bogged down in the blue and indigo range and might benefit from an infusion of vibrant oranges and yellows.

"What color do you feel like right now?" Iris asked.

"Purple. Periwinkle, I guess," Bettina responded.

"Do you want to drive over to Molino Park and see some flowers? There are masses of nasturtiums and African daisies out now."

Bettina lit up. "Good idea, Iris! What brought that on?"

"The quilt," answered Iris, grinning. "Let's go drench you in oranges and yellows!"

After walking for an hour among the brilliant flowers, the two parted, one toward the east and one toward the west, both of them happy.

At home the next morning, Iris thought about their sunny afternoon in the garden, and how good it felt to help someone else feel better.

Then it dawned on her: Hey, that's compassion! And she said it out loud, "Compassion! I wasn't even looking for my compassionate side, and it found me!"

She blew a kiss at her reflection in the mirror and left the shadowy domain of her front room for the sun-drenched hammock waiting outside.

31 Dusk

wo months later, feeling better than she had in a long time, Iris phoned Ephraim. She'd been out of touch and didn't know whether he was still with Kylie by now or not.

Today it didn't matter that much to her what the answer was. She simply missed him. He said he was on his own and free and invited her to drive over the hill to his Stinson Beach cabin for some *nachos*.

Accepting the tempting invitation, Iris headed over to Miller Avenue and turned left at the 2AM Club to start the drive up the south side of Mt. Tamalpais.

Marin County's local mountain was claimed as watershed and state park lands, with an abundance of trails criss-crossing it and a number of roads winding up and over the hill. "Over the hill" was how the residents of west Marin referred to their remote coastal area of rural foothills, vast rolling pastures, rugged ocean cliffs, and funky little towns.

Ephraim lived in a cabin above Stinson Beach nestled on Mt. Tam's western edge.

Iris loved the space/time jolt she received every time she pulled into Eph's driveway. Hopping out of the car, she turned around to inhale the vast oceanscape spread out below. The Farallon Islands were dots on the horizon. Out here she became someone else, someone gentler and better.

It was a treat to access this enchanting vista, and this man, again. Ephraim was busily hovering over two dinner plates piled high with organic blue corn chips. He shook a bag of grated Mexican-mix cheese generously over each pile and then sprinkled on crushed red pepper. "You can add more pepper if you want," he muttered. It's only a microwave thing, not the oven."

"That's fine. They look like they'll be great!"

Into the microwave went the plates, one at a time, for a minute and a half, until the cheese melted into a stretchy topping. After both plates were on the table, Eph spooned a small sour cream mountain next to each crispy pile and garnished the whole thing with chunks of mild green chilies and slices of avocado.

Nothing could beat those nachos, washed down with artisanal ale. Ephraim and Iris sat near the open French doors to catch the breeze, munching and swigging while watching a taped episode of *Fringe* on his big flat-screen.

Iris was confused about the plot of *Fringe*, even after the teaser at the beginning and Ephraim's patient attempts to explain the back story, the paranormal events, and the parallel universe populated by inexact doubles.

After the show, there was black cherry sorbet and fresh whipped cream, and then the two were drawn once again into one another's arms.

Iris felt so safe and well-fed. She put up no resistance in opening up to Ephraim, pushing all thoughts of Kylie far out of mind as she and Eph kissed passionately and touched new and familiar places, moving so close together that there was no space left between them. When he entered her, it was with a nearly impossible mixture of forceful and gentle. She loved that, and she loved him. It was something she was starting to know with greater and greater certainty.

Comfortably relaxed on his bed afterward, Iris moved into a recounting of her Apple Virtual Reality Vacation trip to Western Ukraine/Eastern Poland, a story she had never shared with him before.

Ephraim listened in silence to her description of the town of Rufalev Station, once located on the eastern border of Poland and now redrawn on maps as inside Ukraine. She talked about the railroad station, the razed *schetl*'s urban blocks of flattened dirt, and the mass grave where members of her family lay with Rufalev's other Jewish residents, none of their names marked on a headstone or plaque to this day.

Then she painted a word-picture of the clueless local café denizens chomping down bagels stuffed with bacon beneath a giant logo of a yellow six-pointed star with the word *"Jude"* painted on it in blood red.

Ignoring Ephraim's continued silence, she continued, sharing her discovery that it was Ukrainian conscripted goons who actually shot and killed her grandmother and grandfather, her uncle's wife, and the little first cousin from her own generation—a boy with no name, because no one alive would ever tell her what it was.

In his captain's chair next to the bed, Ephraim leaned forward. Iris noted the depth of his silent listening and thanked him for the respect he was showing her painful tale.

It was then that he dropped the grenade on her head.

"Did you ever wonder what my last name means?" he asked her in a low voice.

"Not really," she replied. "What does it mean?"

"'Kiever' means resident of Kiev, in Ukraine. That's where my ancestors on my father's side come from. I hate to tell you this, but I feel like I have to. My grandfather, Serge Kiever, was drafted into the Nazi army in 1940 without a choice—and—"

"Oh *no!*" cried Iris, suddenly springing to her feet. "It can't be true! *No!!*"

"It *is* true."

"And? And there's an *and*?"

"There is. The story in our family, which has pretty much been kept quiet, is that Serge was assigned with his platoon in the autumn of 1941 to clear out a railroad station town in Eastern Poland."

"To clear the place of Jews, you mean."

"I'm afraid so."

"*September* of 1941? Was the town Rufalev Station?"

"I think that it was, yes."

"*Oh my God!*"

"You should know that he didn't last too long himself. The Russian army came after the Ukrainian Nazis, and Serge was badly wounded in 1944 and died in Kiev in 1945. He had two sons. One of his boys was my father, who managed to emigrate to America after WWII. So here I am."

"You didn't ever tell me this before. *Why?*"

"I knew how you'd feel about it! His voice cracked.

"Iris ..." He reached for her.

"I can't, *I can't*!!" She stood up, shoved her feet into her shoes, and, feeling dizzy, said, "I need to go home now."

"Are you OK? Coffee or something? Advil?"

"Nothing! I'm going now. *I've got to go!*"

"I'm sorry, I'm *so* sorry! But that was 60 years ago."

"If that's the way you see it, *then you don't get it!*" Iris cried, running out of the cabin and down the path to her car without saying her usual farewell to the sparkling ocean below. Ephraim's grandfather could have been the man who murdered her family, the one she had sworn to kill! How could she love—or make love with—his grandson ever again? Back home, Iris downed a full glass of vodka and fell into a fitful slumber swarming with dark dreams.

32 Midnight

For three days Iris drowned her pain in vodka and ibuprofen. She even rolled and smoked a few "red and greens," an equal mixture of tobacco and grass that she once believed could balance marijuana's "upper" with tobacco's "downer" and therefore mirror normality.

Nothing helped.

There was no normality in the bomb Ephraim had exploded inside her head.

She felt torn open, blasted in two.

If she wouldn't let herself buy a Volkswagen or fly on Lufthansa or visit Germany in her lifetime for fear of not honoring her mother's family, how in hell could she take this Ukrainian killer's grandson as her boyfriend, or more?

During Iris's college years at Pratt Institute in New York City, a new friend, a Hungarian immigrant, had told her a strange story while they lay sprawled on the Pratt library's lawn in late spring sun. He painted a picture of an elegant retreat high in the German Alps where Nazi leaders gathered to formulate their plans, plans that included "the final solution to the Jewish problem."

In that ski lodge atmosphere, a young Aryan towhead son of a Hungarian Nazi officer played at the feet of the men, who would occasionally reach down to ruffle his hair.

It turned out that his grownup self was the very friend recounting his story here in the long shadows of a Brooklyn afternoon. She was stunned. "But you *like* Jews!" she cried.

"Yes, very much, and I prefer to date Jewish women. They're strong," responded the young man.

Iris could no longer remember his name, but she did remember letting the friendship dry up and blow away so it could never rise to the level of dating. She had told herself that he was probably overcompensating about Jews by liking them so much.

Is that what Ephraim was doing with her now?

On the fourth day, desperate for direction, Iris gulped down a tab of acid hidden in the back of her medicine cabinet for years.

As the LSD took effect, she grew calm. Sitting in front of a mirror, wearing only a robe over her clean, naked body, she brushed her hair very slowly. Then she heard a male voice deliberately and solemnly saying, "Fish or cut bait. Fish or cut bait." What did that mean?

After her hallucinogenic serenity wore off, Iris's inner storm resumed. Her belief system had been shattered into pieces, and she was deeply troubled.

Two days passed. Iris lay low, with no trips to the store or social interaction. Then she managed to slog through two magazine assignments to stay on schedule and meet her commitments, drowning herself in a binge of television crime shows when not at work. With *Law and Order*, you knew the situation would resolve itself in half an hour. Not like real life!

Finally the urge to get outside into the sunshine won out, and Iris filled her car's tank with gasoline and drove up the southern side of Mt. Tamalpais, not over to Ephraim's place but up to the no name promontory, her favorite mountainside vantage-point.

But on this day, the 360° views brought her no solace. Her emotions felt truncated. Better not to reach down into her well of feelings at all than to drown in it, she decided.

She stared out at the sweep of downslope and hills and foothills and distant city skyline and towns and bay and sea and sky.

Iris saw herself as infinitesimal, living out her daily psychodrama, essentially mindless amidst all of this glory.

Then she sat on a log at the edge of the parking lot, put her head into her hands, and grew still. After many minutes, she lifted her head and looked around.

Everything looked new—softer and more gentle.

The truth she now could admit to herself, which she

had struggled against hearing for all of these days, was that she loved Ephraim, certainly as a longtime friend, with bonds not easily broken.

Furthermore, she knew now she had genuinely fallen in love with him on that distant afternoon five days ago, just before his soul grenade hit.

And she continued to love him now, at the same time as she knew that his own grandfather may have shot her grandparents, aunt, and little cousin dead in eastern Poland on September 9th, 1941.

Diving deeper than that, she acknowledged to herself that this love of hers was not a dishonoring of her mother or her mother's family, even though it had felt that way at first. This love diminished neither her mother's life nor the fury in her mother's nightly tears.

She understood now that she could never bring peace to either her mother's spirit or her own soul through experiencing rage and extending pain over generations.

Although she had never given birth to a child and therefore, in Miragold's view, could not know motherhood, Iris did understand some things. She understood she did not owe Miragold's memory a continuation of hatred of entire nations and their innocent people and yet-unborn offspring.

Iris's soul had opened a tiny crack to let all of this in.

In her car rolling around sharp curves down the

mountainside, she unpacked the mysterious phrase from her acid trip: "Fish or cut bait."

She thought it must mean that she had to be what she believed and act to be one, or else leave the boat, life's arena. If she really wanted to end her inner war, she could no longer have it both ways. Because if you're fighting on both sides of yourself, your war can never end. The more you win, the more you lose, and you're always divided.

Iris turned onto Camino Alto from Miller Avenue and headed east toward Highway 101 and north to San Rafael.

"Hey, I'm not so dumb!" she said, giving herself a kiss on the wrist.

A well-known New Yorker, Flo Kennedy, used to exclaim, "That's a wrist-kisser!" and kiss herself on the wrist after realizing she had accomplished something good. Iris considered it a tradition worth keeping.

Arriving at home, she hit the bed and stayed there for a day and a half, until her headaches had completely lifted along with her nightmares.

She was tremendously, enormously tired, and her torn-open heart needed time to knit together and heal.

33 Periwinkle

Things started to change for Iris. The mornings brought pleasure, not dread. The mockingbird's mad riffs outside her window were for her amusement as well as its own, and the entire spring day was for her. Her inner colors grew brighter. She was finally invited to the birthday party in her soul, not locked outside to peer once again through the same grimy window.

It was a week later, at one of their café haunts, where Iris saw Ephraim for the first time since his bomb dropped.

After saying hello and then sitting down across from him as though nothing had happened, Iris suddenly stood up and cried, "*You didn't do it! It wasn't you!*"

She leaned forward to fling her arms around him. He rose as well to embrace her with humility and acceptance. She sent the latter back to him—acceptance.

Accepting Ephraim for who he was went a long way toward finally accepting each of her parents, and herself.

Now she was feeling safe enough with someone else to start letting down her guard. Not that her prejudices, hurt places, and disappointments simply drifted away in curling smoke rings of enlightenment. All of that was still there, an archive of scary lumps lined up for her later perusal.

But they had shrunk into miniatures. They became her tools, and she was no longer theirs—she was free.

Soon she dared to ask Ephraim about his relationship with Kylie Chang. He informed her that, though they were still close, some pretty major issues had surfaced. He said it was basically a friendship now.

Alone in her bedroom that night, Iris opened her arms and *pirouetted*, turn after turn after turn. It felt so good and so different to be free!

She pulled back her slumped shoulders, repeating a set of physical therapy exercises designed to re-educate her rock hard shoulder muscles and relax her neck.

"I've got you! I've really got you now," she growled, running up behind Ephraim and wrapping her arms around his. He dropped the *New York Times* and stood up, turning to face her and stretching up to his full height. "We'll see about that, kiddo," he growled back, "We'll just see about that!"

The rest of the world fell away, and only these two remained. They could hear the ocean breakers repeating pulsing chants in the distance as once again the duo learned to play the fine instruments of one another's bodies. By the time the sun dropped below the liquid edge of the globe, they were already curled into spoons on Ephraim's bed.

For Iris, time was taking a needed vacation. She turned her head, murmuring, "You know, Eph, I never realized how much of the past I've been carrying around on my shoulders all the time, and how bent-over I've been with it. And it's not even my own past!"

He sat up suddenly, saying, "We've *all* got that to work on, my dear. But now a bigger and more immediate problem presents itself."

"And what's that?" Iris inquired, yawning.

"Dinner!"

"Ah, yes, dinner. I forgot about dinner. Definitely a more delicious problem. Let's see what you've got to eat around here."

She slowly arose, pulled one of Eph's t-shirts over her thong, and headed toward the kitchen to work some magic.

It was a winding-down of the most peaceful day Iris had lived in years.

34 Denim

Later on in the week, Iris phoned Ephraim in the morning, breathlessly asking if he would listen to what had come to her fresh out of sleep.

"What is it this time?" he asked, his voice groggy.

"Nothing major," she responded, "just enlightenment."

"Why am I not surprised?" he smiled. "Wait, though." He poured his coffee, then said, "I'm ready now. Read."

This morning I woke up enlightened. I saw enlightenment not as a war between lightness and darkness but as a choice between lightness and heaviness. Enlightenment comes after pulling away the heavy layers that hide the original core. It aches to pull them off, but then it gets lighter. And the core of the matter is the original blessing, not the original sin. It is truth. And when the truth makes you free, consider yourself blessed. Blessed not only to hear these words but for hearing at all, and for being. For being, and for Being.

"That's a part of it. What do you think?" Iris asked. "You may need to see the words to really get it."

Ephraim stirred his house-made *latté* and responded, "Oh, I get it all right. You know, if you could bottle that stuff, you'd be rich!"

Violet Skies

35 Plum

For the following week, Iris nestled inside a brand new sense of tranquility. Ephraim kept on proving he was there for her, visiting her often and staying overnight as they began to establish a new pattern of closeness.

Iris didn't bring up Holocaust issues anymore, feeling there was no need for it now and enjoying the calm plateau they had reached. Eph's steady presence calmed her as they encountered the multiple events of their days.

Among other things, Iris shared her explorations in color healing with Ephraim. They both enjoyed gazing at the line of "water-colors" on her kitchen windowsill—little bottles filled with water, each saturated in a color of the visible spectrum and glowing in sunlight or moonlight.

She showed him how to create a duplicate set with food coloring, as well as how to choose the particular hue needed to counter a perceived problem area and restore balance, depending on what felt unbalanced in body or psyche.

Sometimes each of them would sip one chosen color of water and concentrate on visualizing the body's interior drenched in the energy of that color. Ephraim enjoyed these experiments, but he also teased Iris about her color studies.

"Damn fine placebo!" he would exclaim, grabbing her in a bear hug to kiss away her argument.

The *Jerusalem Post's* bilingual logo on the envelope in her hand made Iris's heart race.

Then again, this letter came in a thin envelope, and she recalled a truism about replies from colleges you had applied to—a thin envelope meant "no" while a thick envelope meant "yes." So you pretty much knew what was inside that envelope before you opened it.

This communique did not appear to follow those guidelines. In very formal English, it informed her that her short story, "The Singing Stones of Jerusalem," had won first place in the *Jerusalem Post's* first annual Peace Literature Competition. The letter further stated that in one month, the awards would be presented in Jerusalem at the *Post's* Reconciliation Summit, and that she, along with two companions of her choice, were invited to attend the conference and tour Israel and the West Bank for ten days, with all airfares and expenses paid.

Iris screamed. Ephraim, who had stayed with her the night before, came running out to the mailbox, afraid she had been stung or bitten.

"Are you stung?" he yelled.

"Stung by victory!" she yelled back. "*Wooo-hooooo*!!" He read the letter, and then they hugged and jumped up and down like two five-year olds.

The next morning, Iris drew up a list of companion-candidates. Because her dream was to somehow see her story come alive, Iris headed the list with American Indian leaders Daniel Firesmith and Richard Walkinghorse. Then she added Ephraim Kiever, and after that, Bettina Coates.

She mailed copies of her story with the *Jerusalem Post* winner notification and a personal invitation, to Daniel Firesmith and to Richard Walkinghorse. Within a week she had their answers in hand: both A·I·A leaders had accepted her invitation.

That was fine with Ephraim, who would have had to cancel attendance at an upcoming psychology conference.

Iris had not told Bettina about having won the writing competition and about the prize until after hearing from Daniel and Rick. She was surprised that the two leaders had decided to go, but she shouldn't have been—each A·I·A leader was already a seasoned statesman on the world stage.

36 Mauve

She climbed the wheeled stairway to the airplane flying her to Jerusalem for the presentation of her literary award at the *Jerusalem Post* Reconciliation Summit, something she hadn't dared to imagine becoming reality.

Such things seemed to happen all the time for her great friend, nonagenarian dance pioneer Anna Halprin, a woman with an original mind and an ageless spirit who broke new ground with every innovative project, and who in her 90s won an arts grant she never even applied for.

Anna had returned from Israel a month earlier, after directing her original Planetary Dance, a giant circle dance in which Palestinian Arabs and Israeli Jews expanded and contracted and prayed aloud in turn while their circles spun and wove around each other. Her dance had breathed fresh air and new possibilities into a tired, lethal, stagnant feud. Laughingly, she told Iris the trip had been well worth the effort in her sunset years.

Iris felt considerably less sanguine about her own looming journey. True, her story had won first prize in the *Post*'s peace lit competition. She knew the story was hers and took pride in it, but at the same time she knew it to have been seeded by a vision she received at an indigenous ceremony. So it was hers, and yet it was not hers.

At that vision's core was a cross-cultural transformation with the same chance of occurring in the real Middle East as a snowstorm in July. *What* snowed? she idly mused as the plane reached cruising altitude and leveled off for its long flight. *It* snowed. But what was the "it?" As meticulous as she tried to be with the English language, she had never asked herself that. "*It's* raining. *What's* raining?" That which is beyond our knowing and which we cannot name. We don't know, so we say "it."

It's OK, it'll all work out, whatever *it* is, she thought, asking the beautiful coffee-skinned flight attendant for both sparkling water and apple juice.

"Yes," she repeated, "both."

Iris and her two guests were flying to Israel on separate flights, so she was alone among strangers. It'll be OK, it'll be fine. she soothed herself, using the same rhythmic iconic words a mother sing-songs to a frightened child. She embraced her anxious inner toddler, murmuring to it, "It's OK, it's all going to be OK." Below her seat and the plane's thin metal shell, clouds were billowing in fantastic piles, some drooping down to hug mountain tops. Then came the prairie and then the tree-covered east coast, the Atlantic Ocean, Europe, and the Mediterranean Sea. Jet fuel and tailwind smoothly moved her east and more east and ever more east, all the way to *Eretz Yisroel*—the Land of Israel.

37 Raisin

Iris panicked. Not only were Walkinghorse and Firesmith important leaders, they were her friends. They'd traveled to Jerusalem at her invitation, and now they were missing and possibly in jeopardy. The indigenous world needed them, she knew that. For God's sake, America needed them, too, whether it would admit it or not. So how could she have brought them to Israel—and in doing so, put their very lives at risk?

Dizzy with anxiety and guilt, she skipped lunch in the King David Hotel courtyard and retreated to her room, where she stared out of the narrow window at a tulip tree's huge orange blossoms and the Old City's skyline blooming beyond it. She prayed hard for forgiveness and a miracle.

Once settled into their room at the King David Hotel, Rick and Daniel decided to venture out to explore Jerusalem's Old City. Because they knew the copious news coverage surrounding the upcoming summit conference meant that many people of all stripes must know about their visit, the pair donned *kaffiyah*-like scarves and moved cautiously.

After walking around for an hour, they took a taxi to the American Colony Hotel in East Jerusalem for coffee. The hotel's sumptuous elegance provoked a string of bad jokes and worse puns about U.S. and British colonialism.

Then several Palestinian men approached them and they all engaged them in passionate conversation. These strangers seemed to know who Daniel and Rick were.

Something tasteless slipped into their coffee caused them to go semi-conscious, and they were led, stumbling, to an older car with Israeli license plates and driven to the Old City's Damascus Gate.

In a command center set up in the King David's first floor conference room, Iris helped Israeli Defense Forces officers gather information to track her guests' whereabouts.

Her face was drained of color. "Where *are* they?" she cried out, both to her friend Dov and to the heavens.

Dov Levy, an Israeli engineer she had met online six months before, recalled noticing an IDF helicopter landing and then lifting off near one of the parapets at Damascus Gate approximately two hours after the Indian leaders were spotted leaving the King David Hotel.

Terror gripped Iris. These men, Rick and Daniel, both of them controversial figures known around the world, had gone missing. Were they kidnapped by the Israeli Mossad or radical Palestinians? And if yes in either case, *why*?

Or had they, like Indian braves in old movies, instead simply vanished without a trace, on the Old City's crowded, twisting streets?

Walkinghorse and Firesmith each regained consciousness in a locked room inside President Khalid Ararat's offices in Ramallah, Palestinian Territory.

They had been kidnapped for an unplanned meeting.

An intense discussion ensued between Ararat's group and the American Indian Alliance leaders. The Palestinians argued that peace could never come to this place as long as the duplicitous and racist Israeli occupation continued to hold Palestine hostage.

Daniel and Rick, international diplomats as well as 21st century Native American warriors, were already aware that the Palestinians identified with America's Indians.

After confirming the A·I·A's ongoing solidarity with the Palestinian struggle for independence and justice, they each expressed the view that in truth, it was the Jewish people who were the Indians on this land.

The Palestinian leadership sat in shocked silence as Firesmith and Walkinghorse recalled that it was ancient Israelites who had lived here first, long before Arab families and civilizations had existed, and that both contemporary Israelis and diaspora Jews possessed proof of that, historical as well as archaeological.

Although wincing at hearing this line of thought spout from supposed allies, the PLO leader did not dispute it. He proceeded to question them about the *Post*'s Reconciliation Conference, asking, "But what is in it for the Palestinians?"

The Indian leaders thought for a while before they answered. Then Walkinghorse said, "It seems to me there has to be something for you when you negotiate. No one should be equating peace with questions such as 'Does Israel have the right to exist?' That's not the question to ask anymore, if it ever was. Israel *does* exist."

"So get used to it!" Firesmith interjected.

Walkinghorse continued, "There needs to be something you both value to encourage you to cooperate, and there is. Under your feet—the land, the sacred, holy land! Mother Earth is confused now and crying out for the care she needs from everyone who lives here. That's *everyone*, from both sides of your dispute.

"Distribute water fairly, irrigate, farm organically. Insist that the Israelis include you in an ecological plan for the region. Insist that they act fairly and humanely.

"Let things grow naturally, and water the desert so it can bloom. Show one another your humanity, and help Israel learn to trust you. Stop teaching hatred to your kids. You eat the same foods—right there, that's a clue for your successful cooperation.

"And take the trouble to learn the other's language. Understanding is important."

Firesmith picked up the thread. "What if Israel offered you a premium for your contributions toward a mutual peace? They could provide checkpoint easy-passes and homes inside the old Israeli borders for immediate families of those who are peaceful, in the towns of their choice. Or you could earn timeshare stays there.

"Oh, and it would no longer be labeled the 'right of return,' an idea you lifted from the early Zionists. Instead, it could be called a resettlement privilege.

"Here's an example. After five years, of peaceful living and neighborly interaction between Palestinians, Israeli Jews, and Israeli Arabs, and a demonstrated acquisition of spoken Hebrew by Palestinians, there could be resettlement offered for extended family members in trade for an honest public commitment to aim for peaceful solutions to future disputes. It would be up to each Palestinian family to decide to make or not to make those public pledges.

"It is in this way that you could realistically regain a foothold on Israeli land. That is all I have to say."

Iris and her allies at the hotel command center later learned that the two native leaders had been whisked to Ramallah.

And Iris eventually found out, after her two friends swore her to secrecy, who it was that had actually taken Daniel Firesmith and Rick Walkinghorse. It was Bill Goldstein who had piloted the IDF chopper that spirited them away to the West Bank city of Ramallah, capitol of the Palestinian Territories, and had returned them unharmed four hours later, after their unexpected and secret talk with PLO President Khalid Ararat.

That same Bill Goldstein was now a high-ranking Israeli Defense Forces officer, a reward for his heroism in Israel's Six Day War and his extraordinary skill in the training of fighter pilots.

What the IDF authorities could not know was that it was the very same Bill Goldstein who had also trained the Palestinian fighter pilots! Bill was a progressive American

Jew with his own personal mission, that of helping build a free and independent Palestinian state. And he had also helped the Indians at Wounded Knee in 1973, flying food-drops past the FBI siege to support the A·I·A warriors there.

For the PLO's kidnapping of Daniel and Rick, Bill had carefully prepared a cover scenario. A Jewish settler family he knew in the West Bank agreed to help him with his alibi. The wife called the IDF that morning to claim the impending threat of domestic violence from her husband, and requesting that her long-time friend, Bill Goldstein, fly to her *moshav* in Judea to check up on the situation.

That gave Bill the excuse to schedule a flight to *Moshav Gan Eden* in the West Bank and to leave the chopper parked there for four hours, facilitating the taking of the Indians.

The two leaders would be drugged, helicoptered to the moshav, and then spirited across an overgrown field to a camouflaged Jeep for the ride to Ramallah, with the route reversed after the conclusion of Ararat's meeting. That way, there would be only one landing, one takeoff, and little to stir IDF suspicions.

Bill had asked his PLO contact why the Indian leaders couldn't simply be invited over the border without adding the drama of drugging and smuggling. The contact said there was only a narrow window of time for this talk and no room for resistance, waffling, or Israeli intervention.

"We know these things because we've been through it," said Walkinghorse. "Our people had to learn how to live with the white man. It has been hard. But our native culture is in a renaissance now. We've kept our rituals and our world-view.

"As for you, you can have your own Palestinian rebirth here. You can welcome those from the other side of the wall who dare to show you their hearts and who will listen to the stories of your lives with respect. And you can listen to their fear and pain as well. You can invite them in, listen to them, and show them your legendary hospitality.

"One of these days, Palestinians will attend the same schools and have the same opportunities as Israelis.

"You should destroy the anti-Jewish textbooks used in your schools for mind control of your children—the books that teach arithmetic by counting 'how many Jews are killed.' Hate breeds hate. Both sides need to destroy and ban and declare illegal the flaming racism in operation now.

"You can organize cross-cultural festivals rich with dance and cuisine and crafts, and show one another who you really are.

"You can share some fun together, and accept some help. And learn what each side has to teach the other.

"And now can we please go? Our friends in Jerusalem must be pretty worried about us by now."

"Yes, all right," Ararat responded, "Go in peace, my friends. Yours are the voices we needed to hear. There is hope in their echoes, hope for the future of Palestine. Thank you for the American Indian support for Palestinian voices over past years. We will attend this reconciliation conference and listen carefully to the Israelis for healing echoes from them."

Iris promised Daniel and Rick that she wouldn't blow the whistle on the IDF pilot, Bill Goldstein.

She was astonished when Daniel Firesmith told her he had met Bill Goldstein before. Several months after helping with air-drops during the Wounded Knee siege, Bill had visited Daniel in jail in South Dakota.

When the helicopter landed close to them and the pilot had jumped out and morphed into Bill Goldstein before their bleary eyes, it was OK.

Even in a drugged haze, Daniel recognized Bill and could then reassure Rick Walkinghorse. And off they had flown into Palestine.

"What does it mean when a Jewish groom breaks a glass at his wedding?" Walkinghorse asked Iris.

"It has many meanings," replied Iris, breathless with relief at seeing her friends back at the hotel in one piece. She continued, "It means sadness for the history of our oppression, and happiness too, like sparkling fireworks. It's also an ancient public announcement—a metaphor for sex with a virgin and his claiming of her as his own."

"Well, we need a diversion so our disappearance won't become page one news and sink the conference," declared strategist Firesmith. "We need to break some glass."

"And so our friend Bill can keep his job," added Rick.

Daniel issued an order to Iris, "Miller, you go break the glass on the hotel fire alarm while we head back to our room and lay low. We'll pretend we were deep asleep and didn't hear the alarm. Jet lag. That'll be our cover for these hours."

"OK!" answered Iris. "Will do. I never thought I'd get to play a bridegroom consummating his marriage!"

"If you want to make omelets, you gotta break some eggs," cracked Rick. "Old Indian saying."

The two leaders retreated to their hotel room while Iris and Dov walked to the fire alarm. Iris picked up the tiny red hammer. Covering her eyes, she broke the glass. A piercing klaxon sounded, and the hotel p.a. system crackled to life. In Hebrew and English, guests and staff were directed outside.

38 Purple

The First Annual Peace Literature Awards ceremony took place in an urban forest in Jerusalem's new city, on a stage set slightly higher than the semi-circular floor. Gently-banked stone seating held Jewish, Christian, and Druze Israelis, Israeli Arabs, Bedouins, bussed-in West Bank Palestinians, Americans, Europeans, Asians, Africans, Pacific Islanders, the two Native Americans, and journalists.

After benedictions in Hebrew, Arabic, and English, the story called "The Singing Stones of Jerusalem" was read aloud by a strikingly handsome Sephardic Israeli actor, first in Hebrew, then in Arabic, and finally in English.

And then its author, Aarona Iris Miller, was invited to the stage, introduced, and presented with the *Jerusalem Post*'s first-place plaque for her winning entry.

Iris, glowing in a long black velvet dress woven in muted purple vines and flowers, moved to the podium to speak. She pulled the wireless microphone close to her lips and began to address the crowd. There was pin-drop silence.

"Shalom, salaam, hello!

First I want to thank you for listening to me now, and for hearing my story. The story is mine, it's true, but it was also given to me. Last year I went to a Native American ceremony.

When I entered that huge tipi, the furthest thing from my mind was the Middle East. While I do think of this place quite often and do have family here, I was a guest in Indian country that night, and my thoughts were with them.

After taking the peyote medicine and praying for many hours, it was given to me to recall this power spot, Jerusalem.

When I visited here years ago, I felt the power seeping up from the Earth. The stones of Jerusalem really do sing, they vibrate. That sacred power has no brand on it: no Jewish brand, no Islamic brand, and no Christian brand. That power just is!

I came to Jerusalem in the spring of 1985. There was a lively energy in the streets. Hostility and distrust as well, yes, but in general the people seemed willing to interact across their cultural lines to share the day. I liked being a part of that.

The second time I was here, in the 1990s, the intifadas had happened, and tremendous violence. There was a very different atmosphere that I hate to say felt more like apartheid. Arabs no longer walked around freely in Jerusalem, and there was palpable fear among the Israelis. It made me sad for all of you.

Now I am here again, and an actual reconciliation event is on the menu! Hallelujah! I believe good things are possible for Jerusalem, beginning now. For the people of Israel, for the people of Palestine, and for the world and all our relations.

So that's some of my own story about Israel. What I want to give you now is something else, something I thought about in

the sky at cruising altitude when I prayed for the right words.
Things around here have to change. People throwing rocks and
shooting rubber bullets at each other—that's not the answer.
Neither is mind-controlling your young people into wanting
to explode the human beings around them and themselves.
Disrespect and destruction don't work. Bombings and intifadas
and jailings and occupation and avenging don't work. Neither
do walls. None of that gets you any closer to justice or to peace.

So what is the answer? I won't say that I have it.

But I will point out what we already know: we are each on
this Earth for such a very short time. Not until midway on the
learning curve do we latch onto our history and our inherited
rage. Learning about the Holocaust or the N'achbar amplifies
that rage, not to mention losses, and barely surviving either one.

So we build our own walls: physical walls and us-versus-
them psychological walls, using blind hatred as mortar mixed
with paranoia, expanding the targets of our rage from one
group and one time frame out to entire generations and whole
cultures. Our walls grow so high that nothing can ever scale
them. And on either side of them, we suffer.

So what do I suggest for you, so peace can seep between the
hairline cracks in our walls?

Change the channel. In my story, that's why a small
group of traditional Native Americans came here to the Holy
Land: to open another channel. Not a better channel, and not

for a conversion. For a transformation. These people recognize that their roots are from everywhere that grass grows and rivers flow. That means everywhere on Earth where there are four-leggeds and two-leggeds and wingeds and the standing-up people—the plants—who all struggle to live out their lives and loves under the sun, moon, and stars. Everywhere includes Israel, and everywhere includes the Palestinian Territories.

Switching channels could mean switching your focus to somewhere else, such as the very land under your feet both your peoples love so dearly and claim so hard. That sacred land, the Holy Land, is suffering. You could save it—together.

It's a wisdom-of-Solomon kind of a thing. Do you satisfy the claims of both mothers by cutting the baby in half? Or do you love the baby so much that you are willing to loosen your claim on it so it can live?

A Jewish woman is what I am. I will always be that, and I will always remember the Holocaust—to the extent that I can and still keep my sanity. I will not forget the murder of my family members in what was then Poland. I will not forget the turning away by America of shiploads of Jewish refugees waiting at our own shore, sending them back to certain Nazi doom. I swear I will never forsake my own people or any human being I can help!

I cannot abide the bulldozing of Palestinian houses and the uprooting of their ancient olive trees. I beg of you, IDF, stop *this grossly inhumane and disrespectful practice now!*

I have to say I find some things disturbing. The creep of Israeli apartment blocks into West Bank land and the mobile homes Israel has overstuffed with settlers there, specifically those Brooklyn Orthodox Jews who've moved in filled with entitlement and some cowboy fantasy. Their pools and lawns drain the water of Palestinian villages. And the barrier wall bisecting the land—is it still needed? Can it come down now?

What a miracle if these two cultures could call a truce and take time to teach one another and learn from each other! How much knowledge could be exchanged if we were to dare acknowledge the human beings we all are, and dare let go of the anger and fear for a while, and genuinely listen to the other's yearning for what has been lost and start to feel some empathy for the suffering of the human beings sitting across the table.

There are cross-cultural villages in Israel where Jews and Arabs welcome one another to live nearby, and where they treat one another with respect. We all know about these places.

Notice that families on both sides of your wall eat the same foods: pita *and* falafel *and* tabouli *and* hummus *and* tahini *and olives and coffee and lentils, all from plants that thrive here. Eat at the same table and share your foods.*

I discovered on my visits here that Israeli Jews, who may know a great many things, do not know what Israeli Arabs and Palestinians know about making a great cup of coffee.

If you pray, pray your own prayers. Or don't pray, if you choose not to. Learn one another's languages, and hear how remarkably similar, and how very Middle Eastern, they sound.

Argue in the media and debate over the internet, but do not hurt, humiliate, or destroy each other's lives anymore. Invite psychologists from both cultures to mirror your humanness for you, show you some better ways to express it, and help you make peace with the rage that can lurk inside each of us.

That's my two cents. I know all this because I've been fighting my own inner wars for years. I have only recently let myself recognize that peace can really be possible inside of me.

Peace is possible. Israel has a right to exist. Palestine has a right to exist. Your holy books speak about treating your neighbor as you wish to be treated. Some of those holy books are the same books! Let their verses speak to you. You are their best interpreter, not some rigid authority out there determining how you should think.

You can change the channel. Whenever that starts to appear impossible, you have only to reach out and put your hand on the side of a building constructed of Jerusalem stone to feel the stones sing to you. Change the channel. Re-frame what is real. Tell yourself that you have the strength to achieve peace, because you do. Dare to seek one another out. You are all beautiful people here, and you deserve to live in peace.

Shookran, todah rabah. Thank you so much!

In a swirl of applause, shouts, and ululations, Iris stepped back from the podium and left the stage.

Daniel Firesmith and Rick Walkinghorse were leaving for America. Iris stood with them at one of the Ben Gurion Airport's snack bars and shook Rick's hand, thanking him for coming to Israel. He pulled her into a bear hug.

Then she turned to Daniel and pushed through all of their remaining barriers to fling her arms around him and press her lips onto his. He responded from his soul, and their kiss continued.

After they slowly pulled apart, Daniel said, "We can't do this, Miller."

Iris replied, "It needed doing. I love you, Daniel."

"I love you too, but we have a different purpose together. You taught me that," responded Firesmith.

He smoothed her chestnut curls and turned toward the departure gate.

"See you guys back home!" Iris called out as the two Indian leaders waved and walked away, growing smaller and smaller until they disappeared into the vast, echoing dome.

39 Orchid

Iris stayed on in Israel, after deciding to move in with Dov in Jerusalem.

Dov Levy had responded to her personals ad on the internet's Jewish Ark Line six months before the literary award and awards ceremony had exploded into her reality.

With Ephraim and Kylie Chang entangled once again, Iris had reached out for a new companion. When she had placed the ad, she didn't know that the Ark Line website originated in Israel, and that the men listed on it were single Jewish Israelis, each one seeking his *bashert*, his intended.

In Dov's emailed response, she felt a tenderness seep through their cyberspace connection. Dov appeared to be a genuine person of high intelligence who might possess the ability to care for another and the courage to risk being real.

And so it happened that Dov flew to California to meet Iris and initiate a courtship.

This was different from her dating experiences with American men—less complex and more directed. Handsome bilingual engineer Dov Levy knew he needed a woman and knew he wanted commitment. He also understood that to be truly strong, a man needs to be gentle.

He did carry some Israeli abruptness and impatience, as well as an over-generalized bigotry about Arabs. But who could blame him for his prejudice against Arab neighbors who saw your Jewishness as reason enough to kill you?

He was tight-lipped about the Israeli occupation of the Palestinian Territories and the dehumanizing practices toward Palestinians by the Israeli Defense Force.

She came to the conclusion that Dov would never understand her or her viewpoint. But she decided that he was a dear heart all the same, a kindred spirit.

When Ephraim and she had grown close once again, Iris moved Dov's long distance attentions to her back burner. But after Kylie re-entered the scene, even thinking about Ephraim had grown painful.

Remaining at the King David Hotel for two weeks post-conference while dating Dov, she seriously considered his repeated invitation to move in together in Jerusalem. She finally decided to accept. She would "make *aliyah*," ("go up to the Holy Land") and try to build a life with him.

Ephraim was very, very far away. When she had learned about his murderous grandfather, she wrestled with that—and ultimately kept on loving Ephraim. More recently though, when he admitted to her that his attention was again drawn to Kylie, it was like a broken record in her ears.

The threads that bound Iris to Ephraim, to the U.S., and to northern California, were stretched and thinning. She released them.

Living with Dov in Israel gave Iris something she had yearned for: a sense of belonging, of being accepted.

The two shared good fun and soulful times, many deep talks, and a fair level of intimacy.

Dov treated her with kindness bordering on reverence. Sometimes his intense gaze became uncomfortable for her.

Over the following months, their roles fell into a pattern of gender-predictability. Dov went off to work each weekday while Iris shopped, studied color healing, and attended an *ulpan* to learn Hebrew.

His idealization of her womanly qualities eventually devolved into a soft prison for Iris.

That unwelcome shift, together with the sharp cadences of still-unintelligible Hebrew that often danced around her in public places, made her miss California's muted pastels.

She realized that back there, she felt more like herself.

On a spice run one afternoon on the crowded bus that trundled from their flat into the Old City, Iris stared through the windows at kaleidoscopic rows of blankets and bedding flapping on wash lines against the off-white and desert tan stucco walls of Jerusalem's apartment buildings.

Strange what happens when you get what you pray for, she reflected. It can turn into another bed you once made that you now have to lie in.

40 Lilac

In an email to her friend Bettina, Iris described her life in Israel and her continuing chromotherapy studies.

Hey Bettina—

Remember when we went to see the orange and yellow flowers because you were in an indigo funk?

We both felt better.

I won't say chromotherapy is the answer to everything that ails people, although I've been delving into it further and I like it very much. It's ancient and transcultural and new.

What works for me is to connect a color with the way I'm feeling at a particular moment. If I'm not feeling that great, maybe I have either too much of the problem color or an insufficiency of it, and I balance my insides using the opposite hue to the problem color. *

Of course, a colors isn't problematic in itself, but you can call a particular color "a problem" when it matches up with an internal problem you're having.

It could be a digestive problem, or a muscular problem, or heartbreak, or grief from loss, or a headache, or depression. It could be anything. I study lists of colors and the ailments that ancient or contemporary healers have paired with them, to identify my currently over-saturated or underutilized color.

* (*See pages 332-333.*)

As I told you before, color therapy isn't new. It was used in ancient India in Ayurvedic medicine, in ancient Egypt, and in China. But it's a new discovery for me.

Sometimes I let water sit for at least four hours under the sun in a colored drinking glass, so the sun's rays penetrate through the colored glass into the water, and then I sip the sun-water from the glass. It holds the color energy I need for balance and healing on that day.

The Israeli sun is very strong! If I feel I need harmony, I sip sun-water from a green glass. For greater spiritual balance, I sip sun-water from a violet glass. If my need is for a creative boost, I sip sun-water from an orange glass or from a magenta glass.

I don't care if an element of the placebo effect is at play, because the sun-water works and chromotherapy works.

One thing that's been really fun for me is to pull a few shuffled color healing cards at random and then look up the meanings listed in their booklet. For some cards, the booklet gives you short exercises to do, or supplications you can say.

If you happen to pull the ruby red card, for example, you see a beautiful closeup of a gleaming polished ruby. Since that card deals with rejuvenating the physical body, you're instructed to rapidly shake your right hand back and forth for 30 seconds and then let it rest for 15 seconds, do the same thing with your left hand, and then do the same with your whole body. And then you rub your palms together super-fast for 40 seconds. Do this whole set three times, and your body does *feel better, trust me. You should try it!*

I'm researching all this material and ordering books about it, and collecting notes for my own future color book.

The work keeps me inside for part of each day, which is really for the best—because ever since my Jerusalem Post *peace lit award got all that media coverage, I can be swarmed in the street. Sounds funny, huh? It's a strange feeling and not a hundred per cent welcome, even though I do admit there's a buzz to it. It's not something I thought I'd ever experience.*

Now I know how my old love object Jefferson Stetson might feel about his own celebrity.

Living your life as a famous person can feel like running a gauntlet of stalkers. Well, maybe a little more gratifying than that!

Things seem to be loosening up around here, as though an inside wall has started to crumble. I go to the West Bank for events with Dov or with friends, and I feel pretty safe there these days. Gaza, of course, not so much. As a Jewish woman, I wouldn't risk going down there even with someone else, not when murdering Jewish civilians is official Hamas policy!

But a cultural change may penetrate Gaza eventually, especially after they see that their more flexible compatriots in the West Bank are doing so much better than they are.

There are tons of conversational Arabic language classes around here, and across the Jordan River, conversational Hebrew classes. People finally want to talk to each other! Yay!!

I don't know what Dan Firesmith and Rick Walkinghorse said to President Ararat at their enforced meeting before the Reconciliation Summit, but it seems to have softened Ararat's stone heart somewhat about Palestinian policies. I wouldn't put much past Rick and Daniel!

America should honor them, in the same way cultural heroes are honored in Japan. Over there, they call a person like that a national treasure, and they give that person their own baseball cap to wear that says "A National Treasure of Japan." *How about that!*

Thanks for asking about Dov. He's doing fine.

Tell Ephraim and Kylie hello from me.

Take good care.

Shalom,

Iris

When the phone rang the following Saturday afternoon, Iris ran to answer, thinking it must be something extraordinary.

In Israel, people don't often phone one another on *Shabbat*.

It *was* extraordinary: an invitation from America to speak about color healing at an upcoming San Francisco conference, and after that event, to facilitate a mobile chromotherapy clinic—an elaborately outfitted pull-out bus for clinics, classes, and color meditation sessions. The color-shift lighting alone sounded phenomenal! The mobile unit had been pulled together by a colleague she had met during her months of color healing study in California.

There would be a good salary in it for Iris and funds set aside for advancement of the field, plus the opportunity to help heal PTSD survivors.

Iris thought about it all during the conversation and then impulsively jumped on board. After the phone call had ended, however, her buyer's regret surged.

Should she go back to America? Did she really want to trade the security of her nearly-married life in Israel for the shakiness of a solo existence on the far western edge of the North American continent? And did she want to leave Dov?

Although worried as usual about a suicide bomber on an Israeli bus, she hopped a local to Jerusalem's western edge, where she wandered through the little village of Ein Kerim that sat inside Jerusalem's borders. It was a biblical flashback of a town set at the base of a hill. Tall, slender poplar trees straight out of the illuminated *Book of Ruth* grew amidst the lush vegetation bordering a meandering stream. Small stone cottages whose walled gardens were overflowing with a profusion of flowering vines crowded the winding cobblestone alleys. For Iris, it was the Marin County towns of Sausalito and Bolinas with the Old Testament thrown in.

There was no getting around it. She missed northern California—and she didn't want to blow this rare chance to expand and share her knowledge of chromotherapy. Plus, she was becoming increasingly tired of Dov's generically worshipful ways as she filled "the woman-shoes" for him.

When you've been on your own for decades as a single person, Iris reflected, it didn't feel *real* to be spending each day in the role of "the beloved," constantly available for the realization of a man's fantasies. It felt idolatrous and boring.

It was dawning on her that her days with Dov had grown too soft. She needed challenges and deeper meaning in her life.

Dov was shocked when Iris described her sudden work opportunity, and even more astounded that she was actually considering heading back to California.

Iris felt a bit disappointed when he retreated into his cameras and computers and began to act more like a brother than a lover. She tried to convince him of the bright future that waited just around the corner for him, certain there were many ladies, local or online, who would be eager to provide the colors needed for Dov's romantic projections.

But after all was said and done, she did regret leaving him and moving away from her comfortable life in Israel. With sadness she prepared to depart and bring her color therapy discoveries and recently-acquired fame back to America, specifically to Marin County, northern California.

On her last day with Dov, he was surprisingly calm, acting aware that she had to do what she had to do.

He drove her and her luggage to Ben Gurion Airport. They each vowed that their mutual affection would survive, promising one another to stay in touch, and leaving open the possibility of an eventual reunification.

"I could pop over there again sometime," said Dov.

"You definitely could, probably with your own amazing conference to lead," Iris laughed.

"*Shalom, Neshama. Ahava. Todah rabah*," she said.

"*Bavaka sha. Shalom, Neshama*," he replied.

Outside the airport's winding security line, they kissed, kissed again, and parted. Iris didn't take much with her on her many-houred flight to America's western coast, only a few gifts and pictures, her books on color, her clothing, her laptop computer, and several artifacts legally obtained. It was little more than what she had brought to Dov's flat in Israel. She was brimming with memories, though, and that was enough for her. She had finally learned to travel light.

41 Wine

Scanning the yellow California hills through SFO's huge windows, Iris felt let down. As it used to happen for her, seeing this dry landscape made her miss the lush greens of her east coast late springs and summers. She still found herself wondering whether her decision as a young woman to sink roots in California had been the right choice.

After moving through international customs to the security gate, she was met with a surprise. Waiting for her with a big grin and a bunch of lilacs and irises was Ephraim.

"How did you know when I was coming back?" Iris gasped, taking the bouquet as he grabbed her carry-on bag.

"Kylie called and told me the whats, the whens, and some of the whys."

"How *is* Kylie?" inquired Iris. "Is she painting again? How are you two doing?"

"She's working toward an exhibit, a whole other avenue of approach including multi-dimensional photos. And she'll be showing rescued images of her burned-up paintings that she's enlarged from slides that survived the fire. Some beautiful stuff. She seems happy. Oh, and we're not an item anymore. She's got someone else now."

Iris flinched. "You're kidding me! I thought you'd gotten back together for good!

"We just ran out of steam. Honestly, I think your presence was a significant part of the mix. We haven't been together for six months now."

"It's really strange to hear that. Are you doing OK?" Her heart went out to him. He must have been through the ringer, losing Kylie.

"I'm OK with it. But it sure is good to see *you*!"

The subject felt like it needed changing.

"Hey, I need to pick up my luggage right now at baggage claims."

Following the airport signage, they headed left.

"So you know about my color healing conference?"

"I do, and also about the rolling chromotherapy clinic. Truly a colorful pursuit! That's only the first of many bad jokes you're going to hear, I'll bet. Thanks for not forgetting about us out here and our tremendous need for healing."

"These are so beautiful," she said, leaning forward to nuzzle the irises and lilacs.

"Yes, beautiful," echoed Ephraim, grabbing a sideways glance at her as they made their way downstairs to the baggage carousels. He lifted her bags from the roundabout, piled them on a rented cart, and led Iris to his car.

"I was going to take the Marin Airporter. Thanks for the ride, Eph. This is a truly fantastic surprise!" said Iris as Ephraim navigated out of the parking structure.

"How does it feel to be back in the golden state?"

"So far, mixed. I don't know how to feel. I'm already missing the Israeli stew of sounds, and the people from all over, and all the emotions flying around. And the desert sunlight, and the food, and the noisy brown-winged doves."

"It must be interesting now that the barrier wall is coming down, and people are making an effort to cross the cultural divide."

"That was in the news? Wow! It's definitely a trip and a half! It's the very beginnings of mutual trust. There seems to be an attempt to move toward a show of hospitality. Lots of cross-cultural dinners, mostly with the same foods! And there's less hostility, less boiling over."

"And you had something to do with all of that! Hey, maybe they should have a ceremony to rename *falafels* from 'feel-awfuls' to 'feel-goods' "

"You know, I thought of that once, but I never dared to tell it to anybody!" She stretched her arms out as far as she could inside his car. "Oh, I can't wait to get *home*!"

"So where is home for you now?" asked Ephraim. "It would help if I knew where to drive you to."

"Home to Marin County is what I mean. I'm invited to stay in Mill Valley with Bettina until I find my sea legs."

"She's moved to Marin from Berkeley? That's great! Then we'll be just over the hill from each other again."

They drove on in comfortable silence as Highway 280 veered left onto 19th Avenue.

The Golden Gate Bridge rose before them in all of its *art deco* glory. They rolled across it into Marin County without any words. Iris silently thanked God, the suicide prevention netting, and the bridge district's considerate blocking of jumpers' names, that she hadn't become just another statistic.

As they emerged from the Robin Williams Tunnel into the headlands hills, Ephraim reached into the back seat to pull out a package. "Here," he said, "something for you."

Iris stared down at a gift wrapped in shiny blue foil.

Then she peeled off the wrapping, opened the box, and pulled back several layers of white tissue. And there, wrapped in a purple velvet sleeve, sat a small Torah scroll.

"Eph! Where did you *get* this?"

"There's a Judaica store in Berkeley. I kept them on the lookout for it. It's in English, like you wanted."

"*No! Really?*" Iris exclaimed, rolling open the scroll from the right n the traditional manner and reading part of a sentence from "Genesis" aloud in English. The Torah was formatted in right to left columns, as were Hebrew scrolls, but it was printed in English, with the paragraphs within each column reading from left to right, as English does. It actually worked, as Iris had always imagined it would work.

"They told me this was edited by feminist rabbis," said Ephraim, "and all of the gender-biased wording has been changed to neutral, so God is called 'the Creator' in here, not 'the King' or 'He'—things like that."

"This is amazing!" cried Iris. "What ever possessed you to get this for me?"

"I wanted to do what I could to make amends for what my family did to your family. Not that I can do very much."

They drove through Mill Valley, pulling up at Bettina's shingled house. Ephraim set her suitcases on the front deck while Iris slid her hand under a jade plant to locate the key.

"See you soon, then?"

"Let's talk in a few days," she replied. "Thank you *sooo* much for the modern English Torah! I love it!"

"I had four trees planted in an Israeli memorial forest in honor of your grandparents and aunt and little cousin."

Iris's breath was a half-sob. "You're pulling at my heart now, Ephraim."

"You've been pulling at my heart for a while, Iris."

They embraced tightly, for a very long time.

Two weeks later, armed with a fish burrito and a giant cup of fresh-squeezed *taqueria* orange juice, Iris visited her old picnic spot on the bank of Richardson Bay. The food tasted divine in this paradise on the far western edge. She felt very peaceful, and grateful to be home.

The color therapy conference had gone well, and there was a chromotherapy meet-up group to facilitate, plus the mobile clinic to pull together and a new website to work on while she looked for her own place.

The confusing chaos of her inner war and her fading memories of betrayals and obsessions sank into weeds on the edges of a sunny new meadow of calm.

She decided to gather some notes together for a memoir before her past grew too sketchy to access.

Home felt wonderful, even though it currently meant borrowing Bettina's guest room. Mill Valley was the refuge she remembered, tucked so closely beneath Mt. Tamalpais that no one could see the peak. Hearing both English and Spanish spoken in stores felt right. She could comprehend the street signs at a glance, no longer needing to puzzle-out the meanings of barely-recognizable *Ivrit* (Hebrew).

Remaining unrecognized in public was a big relief, too.

She kept track of the happenings in Israel, glad to hear that psychologists had been pulled into the mix. After all, being human was everybody's club, and guiding human impulses ought to supersede all of those political posturings. If people would let themselves hear each other's stories and risk empathizing with one another's pain, maybe the main channel there could eventually change to a peace channel.

Iris had explored that idea in her *60 Minutes* interview with Leslie Stahl, taped on the plaza dividing Jerusalem's Old City and new city. *60 Minutes* included a camel in the background, of course. The ancient Arab camel man and his equally ancient, jewel-bedecked tame beast, Kojak, had been selling rides and posing for tourist snapshots throughout numerous Israeli administrations and Palestinian *intifadas*.

60 Minutes was broadcast in Israel as well as in the United States, and after it aired, people recognized Iris and reached out to her. "The Singing Stones of Jerusalem" and her awards speech were featured in the *Jerusalem Post*, touching a nerve. Then strangers started claiming her, and she ran for hiding.

Returning to America had lifted that veil, and now she could stretch out into her own expanded personal space, attend events with friends, walk the hills by herself, and not feel as though everyone she ran into wanted a piece of her.

Then she got the call.

"Iris?"

Her heart began beating wildly.

It was so surreal. The gravelly tone of Jefferson's voice was all too familiar, stoking a long-buried fire.

"Jefferson?"

"Ah, so you do remember my voice. I wondered if you would. So, how are you? I saw your interview you did on *60 Minutes*. Looks like the peace process has legs in Israel now. You should be proud of yourself!"

Thanking him, she told him she *was* proud, and proud also of those on both sides of the cross-cultural wall who had risked listening and heard some truth in what she said. It had came through her, but it wasn't hers. It was a vision. She had just helped uncover what was underneath all along.

"Oh, everybody says things like that," responded Jeff. "You know what you did! Enjoy it!"

Jefferson's tone swelled with confidence, just as she remembered. He thought he knew how things were.

Something odd hovered around this totally unexpected call. Jefferson sounded needy. Not as though he finally realized he needed her—nothing like that. It was more as if he needed something from her. She wondered if she had seemed needy and grasping to him before. Probably she had.

"Speaking of enjoyment," he said, "there's a California

City Councils' Conference, the CCCC, happening in two weeks up in Sacramento, over that weekend. Would you like to go? You could meet some influential people and network, and we could have some fun on the river."

Images of their sweet night on his little runabout boat flicked through her mind—followed by twinges of pain left over from his rejection as she'd waited to hear from him for so many months afterward and heard not a single word.

Why was he calling her now? He was making her old dream come true when it was no longer her dream!

Suddenly she got it. She realized what was bringing him back into her life at this moment. She was famous. She was more famous than he was, and he wanted some! It was the same aphrodisiac that had triggered her addiction when emanating from him. It was the celebrity drug!

"Listen, Jefferson, it really means a lot to me to hear from you, even after all this time. You touched my heart, and you're still in my heart. But I'm seeing somebody—"

"Is it serious?"

"Maybe."

"You didn't tell him anything about me, did you?"

"A little," Iris admitted.

"Well, keep it down to a cameo appearance, all right?"

"Certainly, Jefferson, will do. I have some things I'd like to send you about color healing. I've really gotten into that subject lately. Would that be OK?"

"Sure, that'll be fine. You remember my email address?"

"I never forgot it. Thanks for the invitation to the CCCC event. And thank you for calling me."

"You're very welcome, Iris. Good to have you back in the golden west."

"Thanks. Bye, Jefferson. Take good care."

"You too. Goodbye, now."

After their call ended, a flicker of regret zipped through her, buyer's regret. Or maybe non-buyer's regret.

Then she turned back to her work. There were some new writing assignments. And Ephraim was coming over later, so there was dinner to plan, and dessert.

Jefferson's CCCC gathering would have been a fine place to network and hand out her new business cards, especially with that magical Stetson vortex so close at hand. But the thought of an overnight stay with him raised too many red flags. She wasn't available for his kind of games anymore, and she didn't need them now.

Iris stepped through the French doors onto Bettina's redwood deck. A breeze from the hidden ocean wrapped her in coastal air, briny, fresh and familiar. She leaned into it.

Then she straightened up and stood tall, head held high and shoulders back. The shoes she filled, sage-green vegan leather sandals, were her own.

Ultraviolet **Rays** — BLACKLIGHT

hey danced behind her eyes: Kylie Chang's fire, baby Emilio, Ephraim and Jefferson, Dov Levy and Daniel Firesmith and Rick Walkinghorse. And her radio mentor Robb Mast, and her Hawaiian prince Nathan Paniolo, and her American Indian kindred spirit Felix Moss.

And Miragold, her mother, who had managed to carve out a life for herself and had given Iris her own life, singing to her, "You Are My Sunshine."

Aarona Iris Miller-Kiever wondered if her internal wars would truly end when the world vanished, meaning when she left the world—probably very soon.

A fragrant breeze drifted through the open window, bringing her back to verdant Marin County and reminding her that she was still a part of life here on planet Earth.

Gazing at herself in the mirror, she smoothed down her lined cheeks, pulling the skin back symmetrically to see the reflection of her earlier face.

After their long, love-filled, and drama-free union, Iris could not complain that her husband, Ephraim Kiever, had passed away and was gone. His end had been tranquil and fairly painless, and he had faced it bravely and calmly. For that she was grateful. She did miss him, but peacefully.

The world would continue, she realized, Iris or no Iris. A wave of fury rippled through her, fury that planet Earth would have the audacity to go on without her.

And then great sadness flooded in again, with the start of a headache that could pull her down into depression.

She saw the uncaring skyline of San Francisco from the edge of the Golden Gate Bridge as it had appeared on the day she had jumped. That hadn't worked, and she was very, very glad of that—glad for the rest of her life.

Now it wasn't about her alone. The world was a noisy newsreel of cultures overlapping and tearing at one other, and planet Earth was crying out for help for its butterflies and so many other threatened and assaulted creatures, and for its plants and its climate. Around Iris and inside of her, layers of the present, the future, and the past collided. She had danced along the edges of her own rainbow in a sparkling, kaleidoscopic flow, and now she was fading into history, as all do. She had to make herself acknowledge that.

Collages of images in grays, sepias, and washed-out pastels drifted through her brain, sticking to the walls of her mind in wrinkled, dog-eared snapshots.

But she wouldn't let the world get away so easily, she decided. She was still here today, and she would leave the world something to remember her by. She would paste her images into a slide show no one else could have imagined, and then turn that into a video to blow the minds of some cyber-surfers out there. And maybe another look at her color studies could help heal someone.

She realized she needed to coalesce it all first, this new project, while she was still present and the world was still her priceless gift of reality.

No one had lived a life anything close to hers, and no one else could tell it as it had been—in full-spectrum color. She could see it, bright and real as day, and prayed there would be time enough for the telling.

She would leave her material legacy, the meandering startracks of her own bright comet, to baby Emilio, her nearly-adopted toddler, to sort out. She had tracked him down, and her grownup Emilio was a regular visitor.

What you could see wasn't all there was, not usually, anyway. Thinking about that, Iris smiled. Her eyes sparkled and the years disappeared.

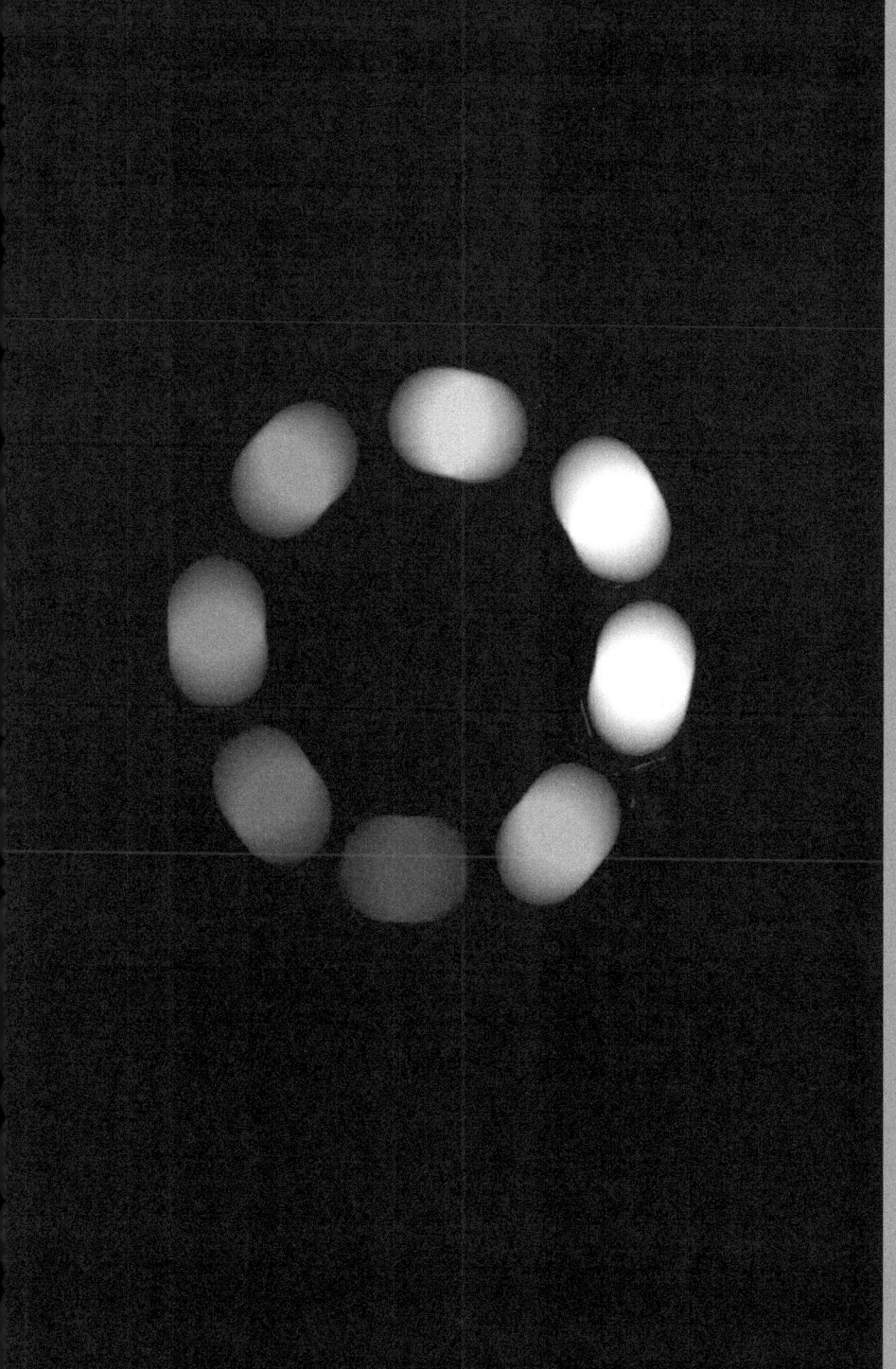

About the Author

SHARON RUTH SKOLNICK-BAGNOLI is a visual and word artist. She was born in Atlantic City, New Jersey, and was raised there as well as in Fairfax County, Virginia, and Baltimore, Maryland.

She earned a bachelor's degree in industrial design from Pratt Institute in New York City, and a master's degree in educational communications/ technology from the University of Hawaii, Honolulu.

Along with wide-ranging work as a visual designer and media producer, she has written three books. They are: *Dreams of Tamalpais*, a regional history (1989, Last Gasp, San Francisco); *Shiny Objects*, a poetry and fine art anthology (2009, Beatitude Press, Berkeley); and *Colored Edges*, a novel (2015; 2nd edition 2017, Spaceframe Press, San Rafael).

In 2004 she married Bruce Bagnoli, videographer and project manager. Their studio, Visigraf Communications and Design, offers promotional design for print and web, video recording and editing, and book editing and design. They produce and host a community television interview program, *Marinations* (cmcm.tv channel 26; www.youtube.com). With their companion cats and Russian tortoises, they share a rambling house in a grove of tall bamboo in Marin County, California.

For further information and to order COLORED EDGES: 2ND EDITION as an ebook or as a printed book in FULL COLOR or BLACK AND WHITE, go to http://www.visigraf.com or http://www.amazon.com. To contact VISIGRAF COMMUNICATIONS AND DESIGN, send an email to: srsb@visigraf.com.

MAGENTA *Globes—CHROMOTHERAPY*

Color Healing References

Anderson, Mary   *Colour Healing*, Aquarian Press, UK, 1984

Andrews, Ted   *How to Heal with Color*, Llewellyn Publications, NYC, 2005

DeGiorgio, Laura   http://deeptrancenow.com/colortherapy.htm 2014

Ghadiali, D. P.   *Spectro Chromemitry Encyclopedia,* India

Lilly, Susan & Lilly, Simon   *Practical Book of Colour Therapy*, Anness, Ltd., London, 2009

Segal, Inna   *The Secret Language of Color*, Simon & Schuster, NYC, 2011

Skolnick-Bagnoli, S. R.   ©2014 Visigraf Institute, http://visigraf.com

Color and Color Healing

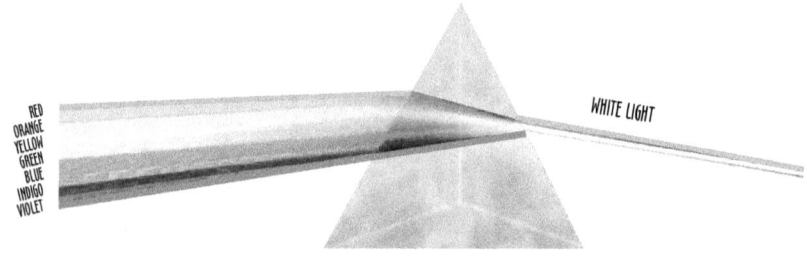

RED
ORANGE
YELLOW
GREEN
BLUE
INDIGO
VIOLET

WHITE LIGHT

CRYSTAL PRISM

Colors are certain wavelengths of electromagnetic energy seen through our eyes. The color we see is the part of the visible spectrum reflected back by an object.

Color is a form of non-static, nonverbal communication. Every color has a symbolic meaning, often culturally determined, that is instantly recognized by the human subconscious. Color is one of the languages of the soul and affects our way of perception. Color affects one's feelings, moods, and emotions. Colors influence the flow and amount of energy in our bodies. Color healing, known as chromotherapy, utilizes color as a balancer. It provides the color that one needs more of or else provides the opposite hue to a color one has too much of.

Chromotherapy provides an energy boost that mobilizes one's internal healing mechanism. Healing with color therapy is achieved through an inner transformation— the mind leads and the body follows. If the healing process relieves or masks only the symptoms, eventually the disorder that brought about a need for healing in the first place will resurface and manifest again. True healing occurs only when the basic cause of the condition or illness is addressed and transformed.

A preference for certain colors can point to two things:

Self-expression—You choose the colors that match your personality: for instance, green is chosen by a lover of harmony and nature.

Completion—You choose the colors you need more of: for instance, an active, passionate person may choose blue hues to cool down his or her nature.

Color and the *Chakras*

> *For health and well-being, we need all of the* chakras *and all colours, for only with access to the full spectrum can we reach our full potential.*
>
> —Susan Lilly and Simon Lilly

> *If we don't keep our spiritual, mental, and emotional energies balanced, they will eventually work themselves down into our physical bodies, manifesting disease.*
>
> —Ted Andrews

The *chakra* system originated in ancient India. In this system, it is believed that certain points aligned symmetrically on the human body are vortices of particular energies, and that each point is expressed by the color of its energy.

> *The One Light is expressed in the play of colors. Colors are all part of the One Light. The seven-fold nature of man equals the seven divisions of color in the solar spectrum.*

The higher body *chakras*, centers of individual expression, include green, blue, indigo, and violet. The life-supporting lower body *chakras* are expressed by red, orange and yellow.

Violet.
Crown *chakra* – above crown of head –
pituitary/pineal gland –
integration

Indigo.
Brow *chakra* – third eye/center of head –
intuition, imagination

Blue.
Throat *chakra* – neck –
connection, creativity, communication

Green.
Heart *chakra* – heart, lungs, arms –
balance

Yellow.
Solar Plexus *chakra* – lumbar spine, pancreas –
digestion, assimilation

Orange.
Sacral *chakra* – sacrum area of spine –
reproduction, elimination

Red.
Root *chakra* – base of spine –
survival, groundedness

Color and the Kabbalistic Tree of Life

During the early Middle Ages, a school of Jewish mysticism called *Kaballah* was developed by Torah scholars in the Holy Land. Within *Kaballah*, the tree of life is seen as a map of the human journey. Points of intersection on the tree, called the *sepherot*, embody the different aspects of experience. Each is assigned a color expressing that aspect. From the base, or foundation in the physical world, to the crown in the spiritual world, a journey through the four worlds is mapped.

Starting from the base of the tree of life, the four worlds are: physical, emotional (astral), mental, and spiritual.

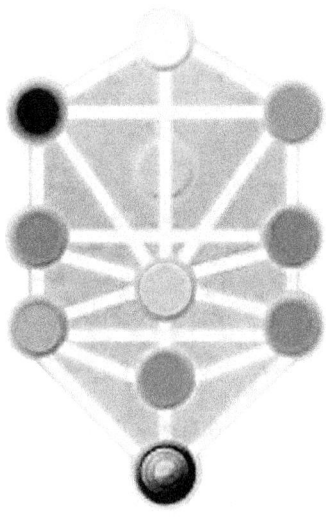

Spiritual level: World of *Atziluth* [archetypal, fire]
Kether–Crown
(WHITE BRILLIANCE)
(**BLACK**) *Binah*–Understanding; *Chokmah*–Wisdom (GRAY)

Mental level: World of *Briah* [creative, air]
(SCARLET) *Gevurah*–Might; *Chesed*–Mercy (BLUE);
Tiphareth–Beauty
(YELLOW)

Emotional (astral) level: World of *Yetzirah* [formative, water]
(ORANGE) *Hod*–Splendor; *Netzach*–Victory (EMERALD);
Yesod–Foundation
(VIOLET)

Physical level: World of *Assiah* [active, material]
Malkuth–Kingdom
(RUSSET + CITRINE + GOLD)

Color Rays and their Uses in Healing

The INFRARED Ray—Infrared is healing for skin infections, headaches, and indigestion.

The RED Ray—Red equals fire. Red stimulates and excites adrenalin, increases circulation, and revitalizes the physical body. (Powerful. Use red with caution, and always follow with green or blue.) Healing for heart disease, circulation, loss of vitality, eye diseases, and mental problems.
(Note: *Red is not for inflammation, paralysis, or emotional disturbance*).

The ORANGE Ray—Stimulating and warming, orange enlivens emotions and imparts a feeling of well-being. It strengthens the lungs, pancreas, and spleen, and is healing for spasms, cramps, asthma, bronchitis, epilepsy, constipation, diabetes, gallstones, diarrhea, and menopause.

The YELLOW Ray—A positive vibration for mental attitude and vitality, yellow assimilates and distributes energies to the other *chakras*. Yellow affects the solar plexus. It is an antidepressant and is healing for motor nerves, muscles, bile, skin, diabetes, liver diseases, impure blood, high blood pressure, skin, hemorrhoids, sexual diseases, flatulence, and constipation. (Note: *Yellow is not for fever, inflammation, or excitement.*)

The GREEN Ray—Nature's tonic, green promotes balance and harmony. It harmonizes an excitable nervous system and is good for the heart and blood. Green relieves tension, stimulates the pituitary gland, builds muscle and tissue, and is healing for headaches, weak digestion, colic, cancer, skin, hypertension, and ulcers.

The BLUE Ray—Cold and astringent, blue provides antiseptic healing for the throat, and calm and peaceful healing for a fever or inflammation. Blue is the antidote to red. It stops bleeding and is healing for hoarseness, biliousness, cuts, burns, the throat, asthma, laryngitis, childhood diseases, insomnia, and shock. (Note: *Blue is not for colds, paralysis, rheumatism, or high blood pressure.*)

The INDIGO Ray—Indigo works on emotional and spiritual levels and is cooling, astringent, and electric. Use it to get rid of obsessions. It works on the parathyroid gland, reduces bleeding, and is healing for pneumonia, lung, and stomach complaints, inflamed ears or eyes, cataracts, earache, deafness, nose problems, paralysis, spleen, epilepsy, and excitable nervous and mental disorders. (Note: *For depression and inertia, use the orange ray.*)

The VIOLET Ray—Violet calms the overstressed, creative, high-strung person. Violet depresses the motor nerves and the lymphatic and cardiac systems. It purifies the blood and stops tumor growth. It maintains potassium balance, heals eyes, and, along with blue, heals excitable mental disorders and insomnia. (Note: *Use yellow for depression.*)

The ULTRAVIOLET Ray—Ultraviolet is healing for viral or bacterial infections.

Unless you illuminate
the full spectrum of your potentials,
they will remain unavailable
to you.
—Abraham Maslow

Your attitude is a box of crayons that color your world. —Allen Klein

Why do two colors, put one next to the other, sing? —Pablo Picasso

I am learning to notice the different colors of the stars. —Maria Mitchell

We are a nation of immigrants, a quilt of many colors. —Jay Parini

Ask
yourself: What
is my favorite color?
Then ask yourself
why.

Who are those

you've loved and known

but opal shards of skyfire

flung across time's night

in a brightly-colored arc?

Ermanno
Borra, Ph.D,
interviewed by
Linda Moulton Howe
(EarthFiles.com, 1/29/17)
described seeing rapid sequences
of color bursts originating in the
vicinity of 234 sun-like stars in
the universe—bright blue, then
pale yellow, then bright red—
laser-like bursts he believes may be
made by intelligent extraterrestrial
life as a sign: "Hey, we're here."

Everybody on the planet
has all the colors of the rainbow inside. —Alexia Fast

A Classical Interpretation of Colors

RED

Red warms, takes action. Red indicates passion (*positive*) or conscious or subconscious anger (*negative*).

The meaning of the color red is energy, passion, and action. It is a warm and positive color associated with our most physical needs and our will to survive. Red exudes a strong and powerful masculine energy. Red is energizing. It excites the emotions and motivates us to take action.

The color meaning of red signifies a pioneering spirit and leadership qualities, promoting ambition and determination, indicating a strong-willed drive and persistence. Red can give confidence to shy persons or those who are lacking in will power.

Being the color of physical movement, the color red awakens our physical life force. It is the color of sexuality and can stimulate deeper and more intimate passions in us, such as love and sex (*on the positive side*) or revenge and anger (*on the negative side*).

It is often used to express love, as on Valentine's Day. However, it relates more to the passions of sexuality and lust than love. Love is expressed more fully with pink.

At its most positive, red can create life with its sexual energy or use its negative expression of anger and aggression to fuel war and destruction.

Red can stimulate the appetite. It increases the craving for food and other delights.

Being surrounded by too much red can cause us to become irritated, agitated, and angry. Too little red, and we can become cautious, manipulative, and fearful.

In Chinese culture, red is the color signifying good luck, and it is traditionally the color for weddings. In Asian Indian culture, red symbolizes purity and is used in wedding gowns.

ORANGE

Orange is the color of communication and optimism (*positive*) or pessimism and superficiality (*negative*).

The color orange radiates warmth and happiness, combining the physical energy and stimulation of red with the cheerful quality of yellow.

Orange relates to gut reaction or instincts, as differentiated from the physical reaction of red or the mental reaction of yellow. Orange offers emotional strength in difficult times. It helps us bounce back from disappointments and despair, assisting in our recovery from grief.

The color psychology of orange is optimistic and uplifting, rejuvenating our spirit. Orange brings spontaneity and a positive outlook on life, and is a great color to use during tough economic times, keeping us motivated and helping us to look on the bright side. With its enthusiasm for life, the color orange relates to adventure and risk-taking, inspiring physical confidence, competition, and independence.

Orange is extroverted and uninhibited, often encouraging exhibitionism, or showing-off. The color orange relates to social communication, stimulating two-way conversations.

A warm and inviting color, it is both physically and mentally stimulating, so it gets people thinking and talking.

Orange is stimulating to the appetite. It aids in the assimilation of new ideas and frees the spirit of its limitations, giving us the freedom to be ourselves. At the same time, it encourages self-respect and respecting others.

Orange is probably the most rejected and underutilized color of our time. Young people respond well to it, however, as it carries youthful impulsiveness.

Orange. Some Variations

Peach. Peach encourages great communication and cogent conversation. It inspires good manners and puts people at ease. It has all the attributes of orange, but in a much softer, gentler, and more cautious form.

Golden orange. This version of orange encourages vitality and self-control.

Amber. Amber helps to inspire confidence and self-esteem. It can promote a degree of arrogance.

Burnt orange. This color emits a negative vibration, indicating pride, tension, and aggressive self-assertion.

Dark orange. Dark orange indicates overconfidence and over-ambition. It tries too hard to prove its worth and to boost its self-esteem, but when it fails, it develops a chip on its shoulder. It is the color of the opportunist who takes selfish advantage of every situation.

YELLOW

Yellow stimulates. It is the color of the mind and intellect. The color yellow relates to acquired knowledge. It is the color which resonates with the left, or logical, side of the brain, stimulating our mental faculties and creating mental agility and perception. Being the lightest hue of the spectrum, the color psychology of yellow is uplifting and illuminating, offering hope, happiness, cheerfulness, and fun.

Yellow inspires original thought and inquisitiveness. Yellow is creative from a mental aspect—the color of new ideas, helping us to find new ways of doing things. It is the practical thinker, not the dreamer.

Yellow is the best color to create enthusiasm for life, and can awaken greater confidence and optimism. The color yellow loves a challenge, particularly a mental challenge

Within color meaning, yellow loves to talk and is the great communicator. Yellow is the color of the networker and journalist, working and communicating on a mental level. Yellow is the scientist, constantly analyzing—looking at both sides before making a decision, methodical and decisive. Yellow is the entertainer, the comic, or the clown.

Yellow helps with decision-making as it relates to clarity of thought and ideas, although it can often be impulsive. Yellow helps us focus, study, and recall information. The color yellow can be anxiety-producing, as it is fast-moving and can cause us to feel agitated. Yellow has a tendency to make you more mentally analytical and critical—this includes being self-critical as well as critical of others. Yellow is non-emotional, coming from the head rather than the heart. Yellow depends on itself, preferring not to get emotionally involved.

Yellow is related to the ego and our sense of self-worth, how we feel about ourselves and how we are perceived by others. Yellow is the most highly visible of all colors, which is why it is used for pedestrian crossings. If you are going through a lot of changes in your life, you may find that you cannot tolerate the color yellow very well. This will usually pass. It simply indicates that you are having trouble coping with all of the changes at the moment, and yellow vibrates too fast for you, making you feel stressed. Many older people don't respond well to large amounts of yellow because it vibrates too fast for them.

A suggestion: temporarily introduce either green or soft orange into your life to balance and restore your energies.

Yellow. Some Variations

Light clear yellow. This color helps to clear the mind, opening it and making it more alert.

Lemon yellow. This yellow promotes self-reliance and a need for an orderly life. Lemon yellow can increase our sensitivity to criticism.

Cream. Cream, tinted with a hint of yellow, encourages new ideas. However, this very pale color can also indicate a lack of confidence and a need for reassurance.

Citrine yellow. Citrine is a superficial and fickle color, encouraging the serial relationship-hopper or teaser with unstable emotions. Citrine yellow can be deceitful, retreating from responsibility.

Golden yellow. This yellow is the color of the loner with an intense curiosity and an interest in investigating the finer details of any interests. Golden yellow is sensitive to criticism.

Dark yellow. Darker shades of yellow indicate an inclination toward depression and melancholy, lack of love, and a sense of low self-worth. It is related to the complainer and cynic.

GREEN

Green harmonizes. It is the color of balance and growth. Green can mean self-reliance (*positive*) or possessiveness (*negative*).

The color green is the color of harmony. In the psychology of color, it is the great balancer of the heart and emotions, creating equilibrium between the head and the heart. Green is the heart center of the body, and is also the color of anticipation of things to come.

The meaning of green is growth. It is the color of spring, renewal, and rebirth. It renews and restores depleted energy. It is the sanctuary from the stresses of modern living, restoring us back to a sense of well-being. This is why there is so much of this relaxing color on the Earth, and why we need to keep it that way.

The color green is an emotionally positive color, giving us the ability to love and nurture ourselves and others unconditionally.

A natural peacemaker, green must avoid the tendency to become a martyr. Green loves to observe. It is related to the counselor, the good listener, and the good social worker.

It loves to contribute to society. It is the charity worker, the good parent, and the helpful neighbor.

Being a combination of yellow and blue, the color green combines the mental clarity and optimism of yellow with the emotional calm and insight of blue—inspiring hope and a generosity of spirit not available from other colors.

Green has a strong sense of right or wrong, inviting good judgment. It sees both sides of the equation, weighs them, and often takes a moral stand in making a good decision. Negatively, green can be judgmental and overly cautious.

Green promotes a love of nature and a love of family, friends, pets, and the home. It is the color of the gardener, the home-body, and the good host. Green is generous and loves to share, but it also looks for recognition. It is friendly and can keep confidences.

Green relates to stability and endurance, giving us persistence and the strength to cope with adversity. It is also the color of prosperity and abundance, of finance and material wealth. It is related to the business world and to real estate and property. Prosperity adds a feeling of safety to green. On the negative side, green can be possessive and materialistic, with a need to own people and things.

Green. Some Variations

Pale green. As the color of new plant growth, it indicates immaturity, youthfulness, and inexperience. It allows us to see things from a new perspective, to make a fresh start.

Emerald green. This is an uplifting color of abundance in all forms, from material/emotional well-being to creative ideas.

Jade green. The color of trust and confidentiality, tact and diplomacy, it indicates a generosity of spirit: giving without expecting anything in return. It increases worldly wisdom and understanding in the search for enlightenment.

Lime green. It inspires youthfulness, naiveté, and playfulness. It is liked by younger people. It helps to clear the mind of negativity and creates a feeling of anticipation.

Dark green. There is a degree of resentment here. Often used by wealthy businessmen, ambitious and always striving for more wealth, dark green signifies greed and selfish desire.

Olive green. Though sometimes used to signify peace—as in offering an olive branch—the color olive suggests deceit and treachery, blaming others for its problems. But there is also a strength of character that can overcome adversity and develop caring about the feelings of others.

AQUA

Aqua helps open lines of communication between the heart and the spoken word. Aqua calms the spirit, offering protection and healing for the emotions.

In color psychology, aqua controls and heals the emotions, creating emotional balance and stability. It can appear to be on an emotional roller-coaster until it balances itself.

A combination of blue and a small amount of yellow, aqua radiates the peace, calm, and tranquility of blue and the balance of green with the uplifting energy of yellow. This hue recharges our spirits during times of mental stress and over-tiredness, alleviating feelings of loneliness and invoking instant calm and gentle invigoration.

Aqua helps with clear thinking and decision-making, assisting in the development of organizational and management skills. It is a good color to aid concentration and clarity of thought for public speakers, as it calms the nervous system, gives control over speech and expression, and builds self-confidence.

Aqua heightens levels of creativity and sensitivity. Aqua encourages inner healing through its ability to enhance empathy and caring. It heightens our intuitive ability and opens the door to spiritual growth. It is the color of the evolved soul. Aqua can also be self-centered, tuning-in to its own needs above all others. At the same time, it can help us to build our self-esteem and to love ourselves, which in turn supports our ability to love others unconditionally. At its most extreme, it can be boastful and narcissistic. Although aqua is self-sufficient, it fears being alone and can become aloof and unapproachable when lonely.

Aqua has strong powers of observation and perception, and can be quite discriminating. It has the ability to identify the way forward to success, balancing the pros and cons, and the right and wrong, of any situation. Aqua can sometimes be impractical, idealistic, and remote from emotional reactions, appearing excessively cool, calm, and collected.

Too much aqua in your life may indicate an overactive mind and lead to emotional imbalance and either over- or non-emotionality, while too little aqua may lead to a withholding of emotions, resulting in secrecy or confusion about your direction in life.

From a negative perspective, the color aqua can point to a lack of communication skills or to being unreliable and deceptive.

Aqua. **Some Variations**

Turquoise. Closer to green than blue, turquoise is refreshing and uplifting. It is creative and light-hearted, yet strong and individualistic.

Aquamarine. Enhancing creativity and inspiration, the color aquamarine calms and balances the mind and the emotions.

Teal. A more sophisticated version of turquoise, teal signifies trustworthiness and reliability. It promotes both spiritual advancement and commitment.

BLUE

Blue soothes. The color of trust and peace, it can suggest integrity (*positive*) or coldness and conservatism (*negative*).

The color blue is the color of responsibility, honesty, and loyalty. It is sincere, reserved, and quiet, and doesn't like to make a fuss or draw attention. Blue hates confrontation and likes to do things in its own way.

From a color psychology perspective, blue is reliable and responsible. This color exhibits an inner security and confidence. You can rely on it to take control and do the right thing in difficult times.

Blue has a need for order and direction, particularly within its living and work spaces. Blue seeks peace and tranquility above everything else, promoting both physical and mental relaxation. The color blue reduces stress, creating calmness, relaxation, and order. It slows the metabolism. The paler the blue, the more freedom is felt.

In the meaning of colors, blue relates most to one-to-one communication, especially communication using the voice, speaking the truth through verbal self-expression. It is the teacher, the public speaker.

The color blue is idealistic, enhancing self-expression and our ability to communicate our needs and wants. It inspires higher ideals. Blue's wisdom comes from its higher level of intelligence and a spiritual perspective. Blue is the color of the spirit, of devotion, and of religious study. It enhances contemplation and prayer. Blue's devotion can be to any cause or concept it believes in, including devotion to family or work.

Blue is the helper, the rescuer, the friend in need. Blue's success is defined by the quality and quantity of its relationships. It is a giver, not a taker. It likes to build strong, trusting relationships, and is deeply hurt if that trust is betrayed.

Blue is conservative, predictable, and the most universally-liked color of all, probably because it is non-threatening and safe. At the same time, blue is persistent—determined to succeed in whatever endeavor it pursues.

Change is difficult for blue. It is inflexible and when faced with a new or different idea, it considers it, analyzes it, slowly thinks it over, and then tries to make it fit into its own acceptable version of reality. Blue is nostalgic, a color that lives in the past and relates everything in the present and the future to its past experiences.

Blue. Some Variations

Pale blue. Pale blue inspires creativity, and the freedom to break free.

Sky blue. One of the calmest colors, sky blue inspires selfless love and fidelity. It is non-threatening and promotes a helpful nature that can overcome all obstacles. It is the universal healer.

Azure blue. A color of true contentment, azure inspires determination, ambition to achieve great things, and a sense of purpose in striving for goals.

Dark blue. Dark blue is the color of conservatism and responsibility. Although it appears to be cool, calm, and collected, it is the color of the non-emotional worrier with repressed feelings, of the pessimist, and of the hypocrite. Dark blue can be compassionate but has trouble showing it, as its emotions are deeply buried. Dark blue is a serious, masculine color representing knowledge, power, and integrity, and is used quite often in the corporate world.

INDIGO

Indigo is the color of intuition. It can mean idealism and structure (*positive*) or ritualistic and addictive ways (*negative*).

The color indigo is the color of intuition, perception, and the higher mind. It is helpful in opening the third eye. It promotes deep concentration during times of introspection and meditation, helping achieve deeper levels of consciousness.

It is a color which relates to the New Age, having the ability to use the higher mind to see beyond the normal senses with great powers of perception. It relies on intuition rather than gut feeling.

Indigo is a deep, midnight blue. It is a combination of deep blue and violet, and holds the attributes of both these colors. Service to humanity is one of the strengths of the color indigo. Powerful and dignified, indigo conveys integrity and sincerity.

The color meaning of indigo reflects great devotion, wisdom, and justice, along with fairness and impartiality. It is a true defender of people's rights.

For indigo, it is structure that creates identity and meaning. Functioning without structure can throw an indigo person off-balance. Organization is very important to such people, and they can be quite inflexible when it comes to keeping order in their lives.

Indigo loves ritual, traditions, religion, and institutional systems, planning for the future while conforming to things that have worked in the past.

Indigo stimulates right brain, or creative, activity and helps with spatial skills. During times of stress, it can become the drama queen, making a mountain out of a molehill.

Indigo can be narrow-minded, intolerant, and prejudiced. The negative meaning of the color indigo is related to fanaticism and addiction. Addiction encompasses everything, from a need for recognition to a need for illegal drugs; from the workaholic to the religious fanatic.

VIOLET

Violet transforms. Violet is the color of the imagination. It can be creative and individual (*positive*) or immature and impractical (*negative*). Violet relates to the imagination and to spirituality. It stimulates the imagination and inspires high ideals. It is an introspective color, allowing us to get in touch with our deeper thoughts.

The difference between violet and purple is that, while violet appears in the visible light spectrum: the rainbow, purple is simply a mix of red and blue. Violet has the highest vibration in the visible spectrum. Violet combines the energy and strength of red with the spirituality and integrity of blue. This is the union of body and soul, creating a balance between physical and spiritual energies. Purple or violet assists those who seek the meaning of life and spiritual fulfillment. It expands our awareness, connecting us to a higher consciousness, and is associated with transformation of the soul. The philosophers of the world are often attracted to it.

Within the meaning of colors, purple and violet represent the future, the imagination, and dreams, while spiritually calming the emotions. They inspire and enhance psychic ability and spiritual enlightenment, and at the same time keep us grounded. The color violet relates to the fantasy world and a need to escape from the practicalities of life. It is the daydreamer escaping from reality.

Purple and violet promote harmony of the mind and emotions—mental balance, stability, and peace of mind. They are a link between the spiritual and physical worlds, between thought and activity. Violet and purple support the practice of meditation. They inspire unconditional, selfless love, and encourage sensitivity and compassion.

Violet can be sensitive to the different forms of pollution in the world. This sensitivity makes violet prone to illness and allergies and vulnerable to its everyday surroundings.

Violet seeks inspiration and originality through its creative endeavors. It likes to be unique, individual, and independent. Artists, musicians, writers, poets, and psychics are inspired by violet's magic and mystery. Violet is the color of the humanitarian, doing good for others.

Combining wisdom and power with sensitivity and humility, violet can achieve much for those less fortunate. Specifically associated with royalty and nobility, purple creates an impression of luxury, wealth, and extravagance.

Purple has power and quality, demanding respect. Purple is ambitious and self-assured, the leader. Too much of the color purple can promote or aggravate depression in some. It is one color that should be used in small amounts by those who are vulnerable to depressed states.

Violet. Some Variations

Mauve. Mauve helps us make the best choices and decisions. It is concerned that justice be done and always does the right thing. On the other hand, it can indicate a degree of commonness, the social climber aspiring to higher status.

Lavender. Lavender is attracted to beautiful things. It has a fragility, sensitivity, and vulnerability to it.

Lilac. Lilac implies immaturity, superficiality, youthfulness. It is extroverted and enthusiastic, inspiring glamour, vanity, and romance.

Amethyst. A mystical color, amethyst opens intuitive channels. It protects the vulnerable and assists the humanitarian. It is the color of the evolved soul.

Deep purple. Dark purple is related to higher spiritual attainment. A powerful color, it can also indicate arrogance and ruthlessness.

MAGENTA

Magenta is a color of universal harmony and emotional balance. It is spiritual yet practical, encouraging common sense and a balanced outlook on life. The color magenta helps to create harmony and balance in every aspect of life—physically, mentally, and emotionally, as well as spiritually. A combination of red and violet, magenta contains the passion, power, and energy of red, restrained by the introspection and quiet energy of violet.

Magenta influences your entire personal and spiritual development. It strengthens your intuition and psychic ability while assisting you to rise above the everyday dramas of your daily life, so you can experience a greater level of awareness and knowledge. The color magenta is an instrument of transformation and change. It helps release old emotional patterns preventing personal and spiritual development and aids you in moving forward. Magenta is uplifting to your spirit during times of unhappiness, anger, or frustration.

Within the meaning of colors, magenta represents universal love at its highest level. It promotes compassion, kindness, and cooperation, and encourages a sense of self-respect and contentment in those who use it.

Gentle and caring in its approach, it generates acceptance, tolerance, support, and patience. Magenta is a color of contentment and appreciation for what you have acquired and achieved.

Most people feel more optimistic when near magenta.

It is the color of the nonconformist and free spirit. It pushes you to take responsibility for creating your own path, and it increases dream activity while assisting in turning your ambitions and desires into reality.

A strong and inspiring color, magenta can appear somewhat outrageous and shocking on one hand and innovative and imaginative on the other. It is creativity inspired by beauty.

Magenta is spontaneous and impulsive, yet resourceful and organized. It is invaluable in negotiating peace and calm in those who are at odds with one another.

From a negative perspective, magenta can promote despair and depression in some and can prevent others from dealing with challenges. It may be too relaxing for introverts and the chronically depressed. Being surrounded by too much magenta energy can generate arrogance and bossiness, making you feel overwhelmed, irritated, anxious, or intolerant.

An excess of magenta energy can be balanced by making an effort to introduce green into your surroundings.

Explorations into Healing with Color

THE SUNBOW—RINGS OF INNER BALANCE

Lie down on your back. Envision a red wheel, like a bicycle wheel without the spokes, placed flat, centered on your body between your chest and the tops of your legs. Feel red's expressions.

Now imagine a wheel of orange fitting exactly inside that wheel. Feel orange's expressions.

Inside the orange wheel, fit an imagined wheel of yellow and feel yellow's expressions.

Next, envision a green wheel that fits exactly inside the yellow one. Feel the expressions of green.

Then insert a wheel of aqua, and experience the expressions of aqua.

A blue wheel now fits exactly inside the aqua wheel. Tune into the blue energies and feel them.

After that, fit an indigo wheel inside of the blue one, and study the feelings that indigo imparts.

Finally, put a violet wheel inside the indigo wheel, and suffuse your spirit with the energies of violet.

When you are ready, see the full sunbow lying centered upon your body, and experience all of the colors at once. Bask in the glow of the entire color spectrum for as long as you want to, until you feel completely at peace.

This is the sunbow.

The Sunbow

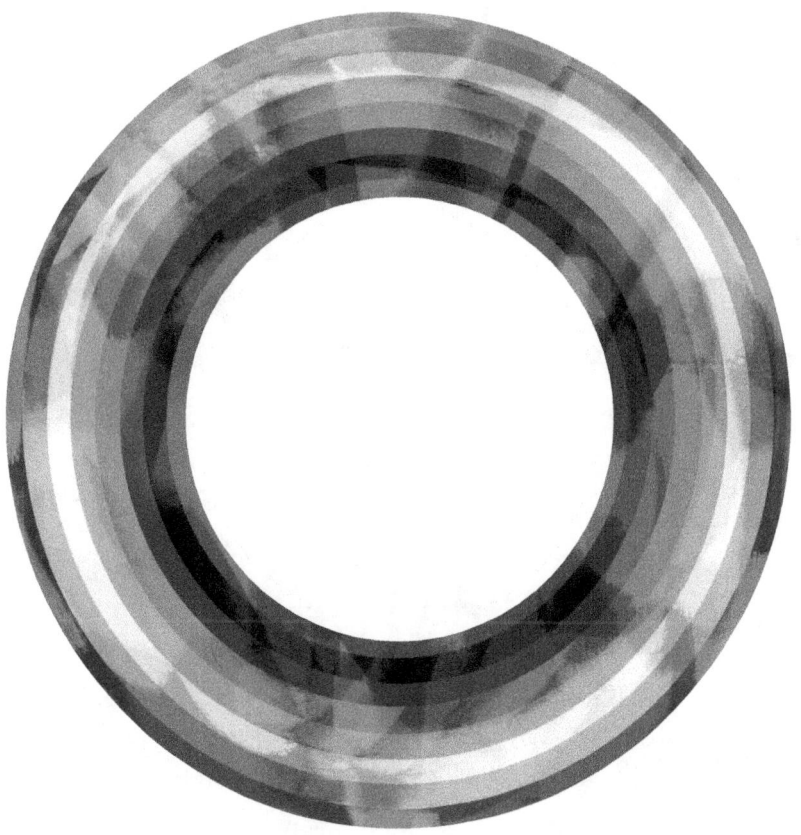

HUES, DISORDERS, AND COLOR HEALING

Hues and a few of their many color variations.	Types of disorders that may ...	link with excess of a color.	The opposite color heals.
INFRARED—dayglow	frustration with life/ deep hurt	infrared hue	ultraviolet hue
RED—cinnabar; crimson; rose	jealousy/ rage/ trauma/ anger/ obsession/ loss/ impulsiveness/ vengeance	red hue	green hue
ORANGE—flesh; apricot; coffee; peach	fear of the future/ foolhardiness	orange hue	aqua hue
YELLOW—lemon; ochre; cream	over-stimulation/ confusion/ emotional trauma	yellow hue	violet hue
GREEN—chartreuse; viridian	alienation/ dysfunctional script	green hue	red hue
AQUA—turquoise; teal	distancing/ lack of meaning	aqua hue	orange hue
BLUE—cobalt; cerulean	fear/ loneliness/ weight of the past/ negativity	blue hue	orange hue
INDIGO—denim; periwinkle	disappointment/ disconnectedness	indigo hue	yellow hue
VIOLET—purple; orchid; lilac	over-ambition/ fear of failure/ scheming	violet hue	yellow hue
ULTRAVIOLET—blacklight	lack of purpose/ bacterial, viral	ultraviolet hue	infrared hue

The Healing Quilt

IDENTIFYING A COLOR'S OPPOSITE HUE OR HUES IS USEFUL
WHETHER HEALING A DISORDER OR SEEKING EMOTIONAL BALANCE.

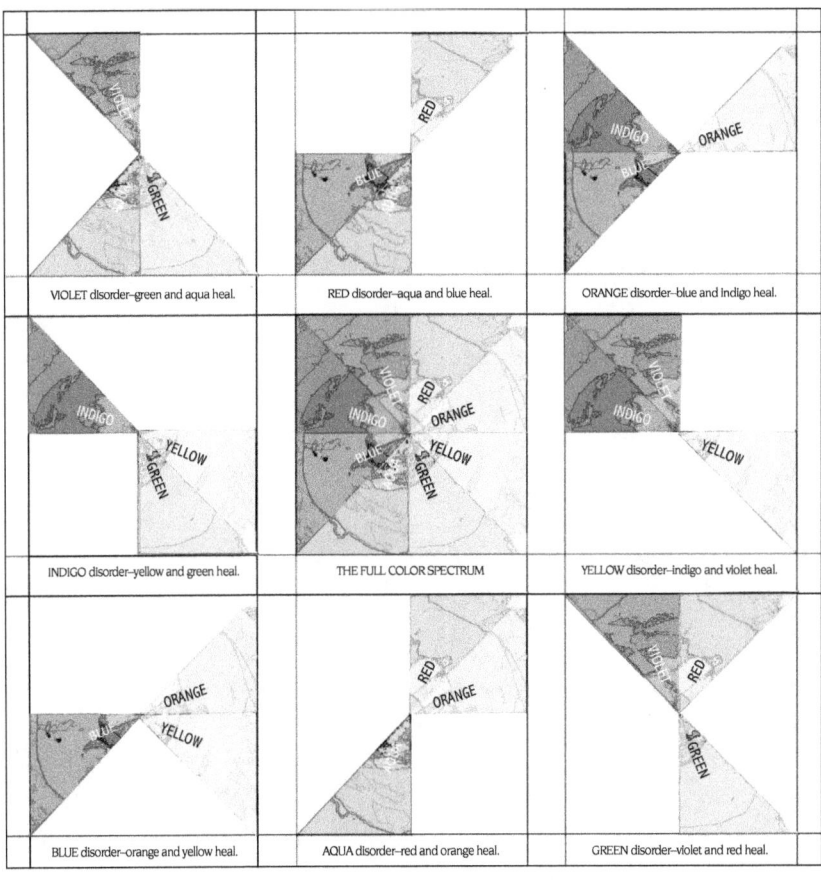

VIOLET disorder–green and aqua heal.	RED disorder–aqua and blue heal.	ORANGE disorder–blue and Indigo heal.
INDIGO disorder–yellow and green heal.	THE FULL COLOR SPECTRUM	YELLOW disorder–indigo and violet heal.
BLUE disorder–orange and yellow heal.	AQUA disorder–red and orange heal.	GREEN disorder–violet and red heal.